IN THE FOLD

Rachel Cusk was born in 1967 and is the author of *Saving Agnes*, which won the Whitbread First Novel Award, *The Temporary*, *The Country Life*, which won the Somerset Maughan Award and *The Lucky Ones*, shortlisted for the Whitbread Novel Award. *In The Fold* was longlisted for the Man Booker Prize. Her non-fiction book *A Life's Work* was published to huge acclaim in 2001. In 2003 she was chosen as one of Granta's Best of Young Novelists.

by the same author

Fiction
SAVING AGNES
THE TEMPORARY
THE COUNTRY LIFE
THE LUCKY ONES

Non-fiction
A LIFE'S WORK

Rachel Cusk

IN THE FOLD

faber and faber

First published in 2005
by Faber and Faber Limited
3 Queen Square London WC1N 3AU
This paperback edition published in 2006

Typeset by Faber and Faber Ltd
Printed in England by Mackays of Chatham, plc

A CIP record for this book
is available from the British Library

ISBN 978–0–571–22814–0
ISBN 0–571–22814–3

2 4 6 8 10 9 7 5

To Anna Clarke and Barry Clarke

LIUBOV ANDREYEVNA What truth? *You* can see where the truth is and where it isn't, but I seem to have lost my power of vision, I don't see anything. You're able to solve all your problems in a resolute way – but tell me, my dear boy, isn't that because you're young, because you're not old enough yet to have suffered on account of your problems? You look ahead so boldly – but isn't that because life is still hidden from your young eyes, so that you're not able to foresee anything dreadful, or expect it? You've a more courageous and honest and serious nature than we have, but do consider our position carefully, do be generous – even if only a little bit – and spare me.

Chekhov, *The Cherry Orchard*

ONE

I first met the Hanburys when Adam Hanbury's sister Caris invited me to her eighteenth birthday party. The invitation read as follows:

Caris Hanbury
invites you to celebrate her eighteenth birthday
at Egypt
on Saturday 21 July at 8pm
Carriages at Dawn
RSVP

'Where's that?' I asked Adam.

'What?'

'Where's "Egypt"?'

'It's where we live,' he said, after a pause.

'Why's it got that name?'

'I don't know. Everyone's always called it that.'

'Well, how are you meant to find it when it doesn't say where it is?'

There wasn't an address or a map or any directions. There wasn't even a telephone number.

'Everyone *knows* where it is,' said Adam.

Adam Hanbury and I occupied adjacent rooms in the university hall of residence: I had surmised, vaguely, that he was different from me, but such differences I regarded as somehow ornamental; as though, suspended between the involuntary world of childhood and the open road of adult life, our student characteristics were a temporary form of self-adornment. We were like a bank of flowers in their season, a waving mass of contemporaneous heads whose stalks and roots were for the time being obscured. The other two rooms on our floor were occupied by a pair of girls called Fiona and Juliet, who spoke in accents of biting gentility and were generally amiable, except in matters pertaining to the shared bathroom, where they exercised flaying powers of discrimination with which I now see they were biologically equipped and which, as they got older, no doubt unfolded into the visible characteristics of a social type. At the end of the year Fiona and Juliet wrote Adam and me a letter which they pinned to Adam's door:

Dear Boys, it read

Out of sympathy for your neighbours next year we thought it might interest you to hear some HOME TRUTHS about yourselves, as it is obvious no one ever loved you enough to tell you how not to disgust and revolt people, and there is obviously no chance of you getting girlfriends, who might have told you that if you want people to like you it's a good idea not to do your washing up in the bath, or at least to clean the bath out afterwards so that the next person doesn't think they've stumbled on a scene from the TEXAS CHAINSAW MASSACRE. Also not to leave pubic hairs in the sink, lest people wonder how they got there. We've counted at least ten – it's actually quite off-putting when you're trying to clean your teeth. On that subject . . .! Did your mothers abandon you at birth, or have they just forgotten to tell you that using other people's toothbrushes is unhygienic and rude, and in fact these days is tantamount to a criminal offence. Haven't you heard of AIDS?!!! Come to think of it, you always seemed suspiciously close. Though on second thoughts at least gays are meant to be TIDY. Is this some kind of double bluff we've uncovered here? I think we should be told.

Yours, Fifi and Jules

A few years later I met one of them at a party and she expressed a surprising depth of regret for this missive. I had forgotten it by then but she gave the impression of having thought of little else in the intervening period than how stupid, how pathetic she was to write it. I told her I didn't see why it worried her so much, when everything it said was basically correct. For some reason this observation actually intensified her remorse. I remembered once opening the door to her room to drop off her post in the mistaken belief that she was out, and finding her standing there naked except for high heels and some items of exotic underwear that she was in the process of fastening. I apologised and was shutting the door again, but she said hello and gave me a horsy, hostessy smile, so with a thudding heart I handed over her letters. The other one, her friend, was always talking about her mother, who was tyrannical and upset her strangely, and who reported her to the college dean for staying overnight with her boyfriend, even though there was no rule against doing this.

'Don't you think that's a bit pretentious?' I said to Adam.

'Not particularly,' he said.

'Well, what about people who don't know where it is? What are they supposed to do?'

'I think it's more the opposite. It suggests the only people she's inviting are friends of my parents.'

'She's never even met me,' I said, though at that time it was not in my constitution to refuse invitations. 'Why is she inviting someone she's never even met?'

We drove there in Adam's car, which was so decrepit that the doors were tied shut with string, so that the only way to get in and out was through the windows. When people saw you doing this they clearly thought something criminal was occurring, although they could never establish exactly what it was. Inside, the car was warm and rancid-smelling, and the compostable matter worked into its floor and upholstered surfaces gave off a rich atmosphere, generating heat as it lived out its cycle of maturity and decay. I often experienced feelings of comfort and security in Adam's car. Being driven in it was like being carried in the warm, smelly mouth of a kindly animal. We drove south and west from Bristol, and

3

then for more than an hour along a narrow road that dallied interminably down the coast, above intermittent glimpses of a marbled sea. The road was like a pointless, rambling sentence that never succeeds in conveying information or reaching any meaningful conclusion. Under a heavy, grey summer sky it passed by ragged farms and fields, by the static contemplation of cows and sheep, by yards strewn with the muddied metal skeletons of farm machinery, by more farms and fields and villages, neither diminishing nor increasing but always in more or less the same quantity, so that a feeling I often used to have in those days was gradually forced on me, the feeling that I had unintentionally left the proper path of my life and was now lost and far from home. At that time there seemed a constant risk of this occurring. It was as though my existence were a small room in a huge, complicated building, to which at the end of every day I was presented with the challenge of finding my way back. It began to oppress me that Adam kept his foot on the accelerator. I saw us worrying the seam of the meandering road with an inexplicable persistence. I began to look down every little lane we passed, glimpsing in the shady, silent tributaries a deep, expectant anonymity, like a dark body of water waiting at the bottom of an irresistible slope. I guessed that 'Egypt' was not going to be found down one of these lanes. We thundered by them without a backward glance. I received in that moment an intimation of the notion of privilege: of a world set apart from the world that was at hand.

After a while we came over a rise and the countryside opened out before us, sloping, green and wooded, with the flat, calm spread of the sea around it. The grey, wadded sky stayed behind us, stolid, diminishing, and ahead a great arc of blue stood over everything. A town was clustered around the small bay, and the sun cast shadows on its buildings so that it seemed highly contoured and quaint, like a toy town, with its little bright boats in the harbour and its houses splashed up the hill behind it.

'This is Doniford,' said Adam. He sat up straight and put his face close to the windscreen.

'Should I have heard of that too?'

'It's a hilarious place, actually.'

I was to hear this repeated often by the Hanburys, that Doniford was 'hilarious'. I still don't really know what they meant by it, which is a pity, because I'm sure they only said it for the benefit of visitors such as myself.

'Does that mean it doesn't have a pub?'

'Of course it has a pub.'

We went to a pub overlooking the little harbour, which Adam reached by driving the car right up on to the wooden esplanade and jettisoning it directly outside the entrance, a strategy which proved useful an hour later when we were forced to search the disgusting interior for money to pay for our drinks. Afterwards we climbed back in through the windows, in view of a small crowd of people that had gathered around the car on the esplanade. There was no communication between Adam and these people. The only thing that suggested his familiarity here was the confidence with which he ignored them. He careered off the esplanade and roared on through the town with his window rolled down and his open shirt flapping madly at his neck in the sun. A cavalier spirit seemed to have seized his body. He drove faster, until the houses looked askew, like great trees falling in our path, and the road undulated crazily in front of us.

'I've got to get up speed for the hill,' he shouted above the noise of the engine.

We rolled up and out of Doniford and shot into a narrow lane that steeply ascended the flank of green that lay massively behind the town. A feeling of weightlessness possessed the car, as though we had taken flight. I glanced at Adam and felt the first intrusion of a process with which I am by now familiar. It is the process by which whole-hearted acceptance becomes slowly interred in recrimination. With his hands gripping the wheel and the summer sun gilding him from the west, Adam Hanbury had the look of a demon. What gave him that look was the fact that he was going home: he was connected to the earth; suddenly he was subjective, malevolent, interested. I felt him peeling away from me, as though with the adhesive of prior experience. I saw that I would have to fend for myself. The car slowed almost to a halt as we approached the rise. It crawled over and then span away victoriously down a little slope before biting on a second incline. The green hill opened out in the sunshine. The muddle of the countryside along the coast had given way to a landscape of great, unfamiliar splendour. It was as though we had risen through the clouds up into the roots of another world. It looked bold and sombre even in summer. The grass was like felt and the shadows were dark blue and inky. On that golden day it looked like a painting, executed as though from memory: its sheep and horses, its fields and fences, looked recollected, dreamt-of, in their little auras of sunlight. Right in the lap of the hill, shimmering as though they were surrounded by water, were two smaller rises of a strange, distinctly pyramidal shape.

The road passed through a pair of broken stone pillars and became a track, studded with potholes and protruding bits of rock and brick. On one side were a pair of new, grey, industrial-looking structures. On the other the lush green flank of the hill rose further still. Distant clouds of sheep passed across it, parting and re-forming around the thick trunks of trees.

I said: 'What do you grow?'

'You can't grow anything up here,' scoffed Adam. 'It's too high. The time and money people waste trying to find a crop you can sustain on a hill farm,' he continued, as though I myself were responsible for this scandal. 'The only things that have any business on a hill farm are sheep. That's all there's ever been at Egypt and all there ever will be.'

We jolted along for about a quarter of a mile until we came to a pond that ruminated in a circle of trees and beyond that a range of old buildings – round, rectangular, barn-like, some decrepit – that culminated at the far end in a large house. The house was white and flat-fronted and exposed, and faced with a startled expression down the hill towards the sea. The outbuildings were made of a softer, golden-coloured stone and stemmed from the side of the house as though in mitigation, by a series of uneven steps and archways, until they subsided into a pretty conical ruin with a pointed, rotten roof. Chickens were roosting in the glassless windows. At the front of the house I saw a green table of lawn, pierced by croquet hoops. A warm wind blew in through the open window. When it passed through the trees outside it made a rushing sound like the sound of the sea.

Adam said:

'We're here.'

He said it sighingly, as though succumbing to the irresistible force of the *status quo*. The cooling engine made ticking noises. In the black window frames where the fat, rust-coloured chickens sat I suddenly saw a face. It was the white face of a boy.

'Who's that?' I said.

'Who?' said Adam.

'Up there with the chickens. I saw him looking at us.'

The face had gone; the dark void of the ruined interior replaced it.

'It was probably Brendon,' said Adam. 'He's always up there.'

'Who's Brendon?'

'My brother. Come on, let's go.'

We got our bags and went around the side of the house, through the succession of archways into a small courtyard, where a little pot-bellied dog hurtled around yapping over the cobblestones, and through a low door into the house itself. Another dog barked from somewhere inside. We entered a cool, gloomy tiled hall full of dark furniture. I could hear voices.

'– only six of white wine.'

7

'Six? There can't only be six – Paul, why didn't you get more wine?'

'I don't want them pissed. I don't want pissed teenagers on my property,' said a man's voice.

'– milk and country dancing.'

'The problem is that they vomit.'

'– thought they should have non-alcoholic drinks.'

'White wine *is* a non-alcoholic drink,' said the man's voice. It was a particularly carrying voice.

'I want to make *kir*.'

'Darling, she says she wants to make *kir*.'

'*Kir* is a woman's drink.'

'I told you. I told you that was what I wanted.'

'What about Jasper? Hasn't he got any? Darling, go and ask Jasper.'

'I don't want to ask Jasper!'

I followed Adam into a large, low-ceilinged room whose far wall was entirely occupied by a black hearth tall enough for an adult to stand in and twice as wide. In the centre of the room was a table like a big door plinthed on thick wooden legs. Its weathered surface was instantly mesmerising. It was scarred and polished like skin, and it seemed to undulate a little, as though it were a living medium, a living presence in the room. The walls were full of things, on shelves and racks and hooks, things stacked or hanging or made to stand in lines, all different and densely patterned with light and orderly, convened, so that the place had the atmosphere of an eccentric sort of museum. Two women and a man sat at the table. Another man was standing by the black maw of the fireplace with a grey, rough-haired dog prostrate at his feet. A girl was sitting by the open window, on top of a wooden sideboard. The warm, twittering day stood immured behind her, beyond the glass. In the instant before they registered our arrival I formed an impression of the drama, almost the theatricality, of their grouping. I was accustomed to the bright, depthless circle of people my own age, who spilled out into the world like some

8

fast-flowing liquid, spreading and spreading until we found something to block our path. The people in the kitchen were not like that: in their somatic presence I discerned wells of motivation, as though bored into the ground beneath them. It seemed that they might never move but might remain there, like musicians holding their bows, situated in a meaningful entanglement. The girl looked up.

'Look what's blown in,' she said.

The two women at the table were of a similar age, somewhere in their late forties I guessed. One was dark and the other fair. They were different and yet the same. They had an uncanny, conspiratorial look about them, like a pair of witches, or two characters from a fairy tale.

'Now the men arrive,' said the fair one. 'Now the party can begin. We just needed the men to arrive, as a catalyst. Now we can work up our enthusiasm.'

'He went and bought three kegs of bitter,' said the dark one. 'Isn't that the end? Don't you think that's the end?'

The dark one was big and thin and angular, with complicated, jointed parts like a mathematical instrument. She had closely cut hair and a dull, sallow complexion. Her narrow face had a downward aspect to it: her nose sloped and her mouth was downturned and her eyes drifted down at the corners too, which gave her a mournful expression, as though her hopes were gradually subsiding.

'Three kegs of bitter for a summer party,' she said gloomily, 'and six bottles of white wine.'

'That was not the plan,' said the fair one. She had a loud, distinct, drawling way of speaking. She seemed perpetually to be smiling and speaking out of the side of her mouth. 'That was not the idea at all.'

'This is Michael,' said Adam.

They all looked at me while Adam spoke their names. I couldn't catch them: they passed over me quickly, like the shadows of birds. Only the name of the man by the fireplace, Paul, snagged in my ears. There was another man at the table, but I wasn't sure which of them was Adam's father.

'Would *you* have bought three kegs of bitter for a summer party?' said the dark woman, to me. 'Perhaps you would, being male. The women won't drink it, though. That's the problem with letting the men organise the drink. They only think about themselves, don't they?'

'We've got the wine,' said the fair one. 'Don't forget the wine, Vivian. We'll measure it out. We'll sit on the grass and drink it out of buttercups.'

'I wanted to make *kir*,' said the girl in the window.

'We're having dew,' said the fair one, 'and we're drinking it out of buttercups.'

'Can you drive?' demanded the man by the fireplace. He was speaking to me. He took something out of his pocket and lobbed it across the room towards me. I caught it shakily. It was a set of car keys. 'Take my car, would you, and go down to Doniford for some wine? We've got to shut these women up. We've got to silence the harpies.'

'And some *cassis*,' said the girl. 'We have to have *cassis*.'

'Try the Spar on the high street,' said the fair woman, with what I later understood to be sarcasm. 'They're bound to have it.'

'Well, give him some money!' said the man impatiently. 'What's he supposed to do, steal the stuff?'

It was the dark-haired woman who responded to this command. She opened a battered leather handbag and took out her purse.

'Do you know where to go?' she asked concernedly, putting some notes into my hand. Her drooping face was close to mine. Her skin was dry and soft, like dust.

'Come here,' said the man by the fireplace, holding out his arms to Adam. 'Come and kiss your father. Let me get the feel of you.'

'I'll work it out,' I said.

Adam's father's car was an old green Jaguar with cracked, cream-leather seats. It breasted the road like a ponderous

10

boat. From the driver's seat the world seemed to swing alarmingly from left to right. I was not a very practised driver. In fact, I had only driven a car on my own two or three times before. I sailed down to Doniford on a wave of risk, concerned only with the amount of time I would be seen to have taken. At one point the brown, feathered body of a little bird thumped against the windscreen and fell away – I grimaced but did not stop. When I found myself back at the house at the top of the hill, in the sun and the wind, with three cases of wine and two bottles of cassis, I had almost no recollection at all of the journey. In the hot little town, wandering distraught and excited amongst the summer crowds, I had glimpsed myself repeatedly in the dusty glass shopfronts, and only these pieces of glass bearing my reflection remained lodged in my memory. Again and again I had seen myself and been amazed by how limited and strange the image was, how little it expressed of what I felt.

'You're a young buck, aren't you?' said Paul admiringly, when I entered the courtyard carrying a box of wine under each arm. 'You're a good-looking boy. I'd give anything for a day in that body of yours, just a day.'

He took the boxes from me and ripped them open. Adam was standing a few feet away in the sun, emptying ice from big bumpy bags into an old metal bathtub with clawed feet. Paul had taken his shirt off. I saw his gnarled, ruddy chest and his wiry arms. He was surprisingly small in stature and his legs were short and thin and rather bowed, but his head was very large and his features prominent, and a plume of bushy grey hair rose grandly up and back from his forehead. He had something of a goat about him, or a satyr.

'D'you look after yourself?' he said, scrutinising me. 'Lift weights and whatnot? I never needed that, but then I had the work on the farm. You don't always get the right shape that way, though. I'm in two pieces – the top part's the farm, the bottom's the horses.'

The other man had emerged from the kitchen and was

leaning against the frame of the door to the courtyard watching us. He was around the same age as Paul and resembled him sketchily in the face, but he was tall and slender and wore slightly effeminate clothes, a primrose-yellow shirt tucked into his trousers and a silk handkerchief tied around his neck. He had a full, neat moustache that nested on his upper lip like a little animal.

'Most of the farmers around here look like pregnant women to me,' he said disdainfully.

'Take David,' said Paul, pointing at him. 'He looks all right with his clothes on, but underneath he's like a rag doll. He and Audrey eat rabbit food – they nibble away like a pair of bunnies. Some women can manage on that but others get a bad smell when they're underfed. You can smell it on their breath, the stomach acids. Audrey never suffered from it, but others do.'

'Apparently they do no physical exercise at all,' said David. 'They ride around on those little tractor bikes and never use their legs. Don Brice got gangrene that way, you know. Disgusting, isn't it? It's one thing if you have intellectual pursuits,' he said, to me. 'I've always thought you had to be one thing or the other, intellectual or physical. I'm an intellectual myself. You'll perceive that I'm in a minority around here. What are you reading, Michael?'

'Excuse me?'

'At university.' He smiled patiently.

'Oh. The same as Adam. History.'

'Ah.' He folded his arms with apparent satisfaction. 'What do they call it? The story not of great deeds but of great men. Actually, I myself am something of an historian.'

'Really?'

'Yes, I'm writing a book.'

'Don't get him on his book,' said Paul grimly. He was plunging the wine bottles by their necks into the bath of ice.

'It's just a little local history,' said David deprecatingly, making a swatting motion with his hand. 'A mere nothing.'

'Go on then, ask him what it's about,' said Paul. 'Go on, be quick.'

'What's it about?'

'Since you ask,' said David, 'it's about a murder.'

'Oh,' I said.

'A murder that was never solved.' He paused dramatically. 'Eleventh of March 1883 – beware the Ides of March, eh? A woman killed, brutally, with an axe, while her small son looked on, and no one ever able to say who did it, or why.' He paused again. His blue eyes were very wide open. 'Annie Askey. A harmless woman killed with an axe one night as she sat sewing at her kitchen table.'

'Where did it happen?' I asked.

'Right here,' he said brightly. 'In this house! The man of the family, Martin Askey, sold it to our great-grandfather. I think it's still the same table, isn't it?'

'Of course it's bloody not,' said Paul crossly.

'For an area with such a low population density, Doniford and its surrounds can lay claim to a remarkable catalogue of the most gruesome murders,' said David. 'This is by no means an untypical example.'

'He didn't sell it,' said Paul. 'He exchanged it for a fishing rod. They were pissed at the pub one night and he swapped the house for a fishing rod. Personally I always thought that was suspicious, don't you think? I think the rum bugger killed her himself.'

'Why on earth would he have done that?' said David. 'What possible motivation could he have had to kill his own wife?'

'He probably couldn't stand the bloody sight of her.'

'He's the prime suspect, Uncle David,' said Adam. 'The family are always the prime suspects.'

'You wouldn't kill your wife in front of your own son,' said David reproachfully.

'I imagine he couldn't help himself,' said Paul.

'You make it sound as if there were no principle of honour

13

between men and women,' said David, his moustache quivering. 'No integrity! No sacred bond! Don't listen to these relativists,' he said to me, distressed. 'My own theory is that it was a vendetta of some sort, against Martin Askey himself. Perhaps he'd mistreated one of his labourers. That's the theory I advance in my book, incidentally. That the quasi-feudal way of life in a farming community such as this provoked high levels of violence. It's quite an unconventional theory in its way – people tend to idealise life in the highly systematised societies of the past. They prefer the passion motive. But I believe human beings are quite capable of suppressing their passions. It's power they can't resist!'

'Do you know what happened to the boy?' I asked.

David put his face close to mine. His eyes bulged out from their sockets. I could see the numberless, coarse filaments of his moustache.

'He never spoke again,' he said, triumphantly. 'He grew up mute – silenced by what he had seen. Hence unable to bring the perpetrator to justice!'

Presently Paul sent us inside to fetch the glasses. In the kitchen the women were sitting at the table. The dark-haired woman was frantically chopping cucumber and flinging it into a large glass bowl. Her big, bony hands were white with stress around the knuckles. The girl, Caris, was drawing ringlets of ivy from a pile in front of her and twining them around glass jars with candles in. Next to her sat the other woman, who was turned sideways in her chair and was examining the girl's profile raptly, occasionally lifting a hand to tuck strands of hair behind her ear. I saw that Caris was both irritated by the attention and transfixed by the warmth of it.

'Mum, could you pass me the scissors?' she said.

'What's that, darling?'

Caris leaned over to get the scissors herself, thus causing her mother to remove her hand. When Caris returned to her chair, her mother presently resumed caressing her hair.

14

'Do you like them?' said Caris. She held up one of the little jars and smiled.

'They're sweet,' said her mother vaguely. She turned her face away. I noticed her withdrawing her hand. 'Vivian, how are we going to feed all these children? I suppose at least half of them will be anorexics, but still, one salad and a few things on crackers is on the frugal side, don't you think?'

'There's meat,' said Vivian severely, who was making the table shake with her chopping.

'There's meat,' repeated Caris's mother generally, as though to an invisible audience. 'What meat is there?'

'Paul's doing it outside. I think it's sausages.'

'The sausages are vegetarian,' said Caris.

'The sausages are ethical,' said Caris's mother. 'Vivian, do you hear that? They may not be edible but at least the sausages are ethical.'

It had taken me time to get used to the older women's faces, rather as eyes take time to adjust to darkness, but now I could see that Caris's mother was very good-looking. She was slim and slight, with daintily rounded limbs like the limbs of a child. She had streaked dark-blonde hair cut in a messy, youthful style, and a wide, laughing mouth. A gorge of brown, freckled breastbone, roped by jewellery, was disclosed by her close-fitting dark blue shirt. She drummed her long, rounded, coral-plated fingernails on the tabletop. Her little face was spiteful and merry.

'Paul offered her a suckling pig but she didn't want it,' said Vivian. 'He did offer it, though. The thing was that she didn't want it.'

'I'll say she didn't. Poor little pigling. Ethical sausages much nicer.'

'The problem is that it's impossible to please everybody,' said Vivian. 'You offer to throw a party and then you find that people start wanting different things.'

'I don't want different things,' said Caris. 'I want it to be just like all the other parties.'

'Where are the glasses?' said Adam.

'I want it to be like the parties you had when we were little,' said Caris.

'Those were not vegetarian parties, darling,' said her mother. 'They weren't vegetarian, were they, Vivian? They were distinctly unprincipled.'

'I remember you used to stay up all night,' said Caris. 'And when I got up in the morning and came out you were all still there.'

'Yes, it was a bit much, I suppose,' said Vivian. 'I remember the men used to go off to bed while we had to do the washing up and make breakfast for the children. It was a bit much, really, when you think about it.'

'We need the glasses,' said Adam.

Caris rose from her chair. 'I'm going upstairs to get dressed,' she said.

'Shall I come?' her mother called after her. 'We can beautify ourselves together like little Cinderellas for the ball. Darling, shall I come?'

Silence emanated from the stairwell.

We took the glasses outside, where Paul was putting tables on a sloping stretch of lawn in the wind. We pegged white sheets over the tops. Then we carried out wooden benches, one after the other. I didn't know where they had got so many benches, but the ease with which they produced them suggested that this was a well-worked routine. We arranged the glasses in rows under a green and white striped canopy that flapped crazily in the wind. The lawn and the hill were bright in the sun. People began to arrive. The two women came out.

'I thought that was your mother,' I said to Adam.

'Vivian?'

'The dark-haired one.'

Vivian was wearing a complicated selection of draperies that I imagined did not show her to her best advantage, but rather emphasised the dispirited quality of her physiognomy.

The draperies were white. From a certain angle they looked like a series of bandages that had come loose. Adam's mother was standing next to her in her tight-fitting blue silk ensemble and shoes with very high heels. She was looking about with the bright, abrupt movements of a bird. She looked contrastingly compact: her containment in her small, firm body was strangely threatening, as though she might at any moment explode.

'Audrey's my mother,' said Adam. 'Vivian's married to dad. She married him when I was twelve.'

'Do you like her?'

'Of course.' He affected surprise.

'Don't you resent her?'

'Not really.'

'How come all of you live with your father and not your mother?'

'This is our home. It's the place that matters, not the people in it,' said Adam, which I thought was a strange thing to say.

'What about your mother?'

'She has a house in Doniford. She lives with Uncle David. I don't think they're lovers or anything. I think he just lives there. He hasn't got any money. He's pretty hopeless. Mum's here a lot. She comes up nearly every day.'

'I can't believe they all sit around the table together.'

'Why not?' said Adam, with the patrician air he occasionally assumed and which I found quite irritating.

'People's feelings usually prevent it,' I said.

'Do they? How boring.'

He produced a packet of cigarettes and we each lit one. The smoke was quickly scooped up off the green hill by the wind.

'This is a fantastic place,' I said.

Two girls with yellow hair came out of the house and walked towards us across the lawn. They looked slightly discomfited as the wind blew their clothes against their bodies. One of them was about my age. The other one was younger and had a red rash on her face.

'You're back!' cried the older one. 'When did you get back?'

'This is Michael,' said Adam. 'This is Laura, and that's Jilly. My stepsisters.'

'Don't call us that!' shrieked the older one. 'I think it sounds so awful!'

She was solidly built, with thick, white arms and skin that was so even-toned it seemed not to be skin at all but a sort of casing, like that of a doll. She looked as though she could never be troubled by anything. Her sister was the opposite: she was thin and jointed and awkward-looking, and her rash, which I now saw spread over her neck and down her arms as well as her face, gave her a look of public suffering, almost of election. Their yellow hair had a synthetic appearance. If these were Vivian's daughters they were nothing like her. They were like things that had accrued to her by accident.

'Mummy's in a complete state,' said the older one.

'She didn't want the party,' said the younger one.

'It's just that Caris has been so demanding,' said the older one, rolling her eyes cheerfully.

'She likes to be the centre of attention,' said the younger one.

'What's it like, getting away from this place?' said the older one. 'Is it really great?'

'I can't wait to get away,' said the younger one. 'I can't wait to have a house of my own. I'm going to have horses. I'm not going to have sheep. I hate sheep. At our old house we didn't have sheep.'

'It's not too bad,' said Adam.

The older one turned to me. 'Is it really great?' she asked.

'At our old house we had a swing made out of a car tyre,' said the younger one, also to me. Her red, distressed face was pinched. 'It used to swing you out over the pond and if you fell off you went into the water. Daddy used to make us go really high.'

'Have you made lots of friends and gone to lots of parties and things?' said the older one.

At that moment Caris emerged from the house. She came out of a door at the back and stood alone. She looked more extraordinary than any person I had seen before, although it is hard to say exactly why she gave this impression. She was wearing a simple white dress that left her arms and shoulders bare and she had her brown hair loose. A wreath of ivy sat on the top of her head. She wore no shoes or jewellery. Her pale face was very beautiful. She looked like a goddess. Everyone turned and when they saw her they applauded riotously. I happened to catch Audrey's eye and she gave me an inscrutable, imploring look. A stocky, dishevelled man in a pale suit approached Caris over the lawn and when he reached her he took her in his arms and kissed her in front of everybody. I was surprised by this because he was much older than her. Her face when he let her go was like the open face of a flower.

'Who's that?' I asked Adam.

'That's Jasper. He's an artist. He lives in the lodge down by the gates. He rents it from dad. He's staying for a year because he's got some grant from Doniford council. He's pretty good, actually. Caris is his muse.'

'Does he paint her?'

'Absolutely. Even in the buff.'

'Doesn't your father mind?'

'I don't think so,' Adam shrugged. 'Jasper's sort of an abstract expressionist anyway. It doesn't look that much like her. There's one hanging in the window of the gallery on the high street and you'd never know.'

I laughed. The evening softened and lengthened out towards the sea, which lay pacific and opaque far below. The lawn was crowded with people in the dusk, shouting and laughing noisily. Their noise in this empty, elevated place flew wildly up into the air like a river of sparks from a beacon; the party was like a big fire laid out on the hill, generating heat and light in the falling darkness, growing molten and indistinct at its core. Someone lit Caris's candles.

19

Someone else put on some music. I saw Paul Hanbury roaming the lawn with his shirt unbuttoned and a bottle of wine dangling from his fingers. I saw Caris standing near me in her luminous dress and I said:

'Happy birthday.'

'Thank you,' she said, smiling brilliantly, as though I had paid her a compliment.

'It's a good party. It was nice of you to invite me. Especially since you'd never even met me.'

'I feel as though I *had* met you,' said she earnestly. 'Adam talks about you a lot. I feel you were meant to be here.'

I was surprised to hear that Adam talked about me. I couldn't imagine what he would say. It caused me to feel an inextricable mixture of pleasure and affront, though I liked the feeling of being possessed. I liked to be compelled through my own resistance. I liked too the fact that the Hanburys' privileged circumstances left me with the illusion that I was indifferent to them.

'Are these your friends?' I asked, because I had noticed that most of the guests on the lawn were far older than Caris.

'Of course they are,' she said, smiling incredulously at me in a way that nonetheless managed to suggest that they might not have been.

'Even him?' I asked.

There was a corpulent old man with a walking stick standing entrenched in the middle of the dancing. He wore knee-length breeches and a tweed jacket.

'That's Barnsie,' protested Caris, laughing. I was gratified to see her face turn red. 'He always comes to our parties. Mum and dad used to have the most amazing parties,' she added. 'I seem to remember even Barnsie getting pretty wild. They could last for *days*. I remember when I was little going to bed and then getting up in the morning and finding them still at it. They'd carry all the furniture out on to the lawn. I used to come out here and find dad sitting on the sofa on the grass at breakfast time, smoking a cigar.'

It irritated me that she kept talking about the past, as though the superiority of that era were a matter of agreement between us; as though we were two diminutive people whose stature had relegated them to a life on the sidelines.

'Your family are very unusual,' I said.

'I know,' she said quickly. 'I keep having to remind myself that one day soon I should leave Egypt and go and see some other part of the world. I don't want to. I want to stay here. I think I'd be quite happy, wandering in the fields, painting pictures of flowers.'

'What are you going to do?'

She sighed in the dusk.

'Paint,' she said. 'Not flowers, though. I don't know what. That's what I have to work out.'

'Shouldn't you have worked it out already?' I said. 'I mean, shouldn't you have at least some idea what you want to paint before deciding to become an artist? I mean, what's the point of just *painting* for the sake of it? What's the point?'

She folded her arms and looked at me sideways.

'Oh, I see,' she said finally, with a smile. 'You're one of those, are you? The sort of person who thinks everyone should be in a *category*.'

'I was only questioning the idea that an artistic impulse could exist separately from what it wanted to express.'

'Of course it can,' she said. 'An artist doesn't emerge fully formed. He has to evolve.'

'But you're talking about *wanting* to be an artist. I'm talking about being one.'

'What's the difference? You make it sound like there's some huge, important difference.'

'Of course there is! You can't just wander around saying you want to paint. Either you paint, or you don't. I just think that if you were meant to paint you would know what your subject was. You wouldn't need to look for it.'

'You only say this because I'm a girl,' said Caris presently. Her brows were furrowed above her glittering brown eyes.

I saw that I had offended her. 'If I was a man you wouldn't say it – you'd be egging me on, giving me money and grants and trumpeting the fact that you'd discovered me. Whereas in fact what you want to do is crush me, isn't it?'

She looked at me with her delicate face. I had to concede that there was some truth in what she had said.

'Why do you want to crush me?' she asked, wonderingly, with a little smile.

'I want you to stay as you are,' I said. 'As you are right now.'

'Do you know where we're standing?' she said.

I looked around me. We had wandered away a little from the party. We were in a place of foliage and moonlight where things snapped beneath our feet. The big, black presences of trees were around us.

'We're in a ring of oaks,' she said. 'It's magic here, you know.'

I bent forward and kissed her. The distant commotion of the party was in my ears. Some seconds passed. Kissing Caris was like kissing a child. She was warm and sweet and she gave the impression of being entirely indifferent to what I was doing. She did not look as she had looked when Jasper the artist kissed her. I decided I would have to marry her. I would marry her and live with her at Egypt, along with all her family and perhaps even Jasper himself.

'Happy birthday,' I said again, stupidly.

Everyone was dancing on the lawn. The music and the shouting echoed down the hill in long chimes into the valley. I saw Paul Hanbury dancing with a very tall young woman, who swayed before him like a stalk of wheat while he scurried around her, crab-like, casting her salacious looks. When he saw me he grasped my hand and we all danced around together, me, him and the swaying girl. I couldn't see Adam anywhere. I saw Vivian, standing by the drinks table with her arms crossed awkwardly over her stomach, talking to an elderly lady. Numerous children were dancing amongst the adults. Sometimes they danced with each other. More often their mothers danced with them, kind and weary-faced, stooped over. I noticed a fair-haired boy of eleven or so standing beside Vivian, gulping unnoticed from the wineglasses on the table. After each gulp he would look around him with a startled expression on his face. I guessed he was Adam's brother Brendon, the boy I had seen in the chicken house.

When I turned back to the dancing, Audrey had manifested herself in front of me. She stood in her tight-fitting blue costume and high heels, one arm flung into the air and a bare leg planted dramatically out in front of her. She presented herself to me, glaring at me with the fiery, warlike countenance of an exotic bird embarking on its mating ritual. I saw that she was extremely drunk: she was incandescent; she was on fire. She began to dance around me in a strutting fashion, pausing occasionally to assume her dramatic pose, eyes blazing, arm aloft, as though offering me a challenge. Round and round me she went: I shadowed her uncertainly. In her exertion her face had grown warm beneath its make-up; the different colours shimmered greasily as though they had come alive, as though she were a living image of herself. Audrey clapped her hands on my shoulders. As she circled me she moved her hands over my shirt and said something with her painted mouth that I didn't hear over the music. She bared her even, slightly yellowed teeth in a smile. A feeling of apprehension stirred in my stomach. She gave me an impatient look.

'Do you like me?' she said hotly into my ear, before circling me once more.

I smiled urbanely, or so I thought, and did not reply.

'You can have me, darling,' she said, into my ear. 'You can take me now.'

'I don't think that would be a very good idea, Mrs Hanbury,' I said quaveringly.

'I need somebody to fuck me,' she said. 'I need somebody to fucking fuck me!'

She sounded quite annoyed about it.

23

'I'm sorry I can't help,' I said.

'I gave away my man and now I'm lonely,' she said in my ear, in a little-girl voice. 'Audrey gets very, very lonely on her own.'

'I'm sorry to hear that,' I said.

I felt a firm, male grip on my arm.

'Now, now, Audrey,' said Paul. 'Don't get randy with Michael. Was she getting randy with you, Michael?'

'Where's Brendon?' said Audrey vaguely.

'Darling, I haven't a bloody clue,' said Paul. 'What are you worrying about Brendon for?'

'Someone should really put him to bed. All these children!' She made an irritated gesture with her hand that clearly incorporated me. 'They should all be put to bed.'

'Is it good for you up here?' said Paul. 'Do you like it? Not everybody does.'

'I like it very much,' I said.

'That's because you've got manners,' said Paul. 'Tell Audrey to keep her hands off you – you're a good boy. She gets a little heated sometimes, that's all. It might be the menopause coming early. Her mother was the same.'

'Oh, it's fine,' I said.

'The people with manners like Egypt,' said Paul. 'It's the ones that think too much that don't. They find something false in it, you see, and they start to get ironic. I don't like people being ironic – to me it means they've forgotten how to be natural. What are your people like, your family? Are they good-looking too, or are you the black sheep? Would they like it here, do you think?'

'I'm sure they would,' I said.

I realised as I said it that this was not true – they would hate it, but I wasn't sure why. I wondered if this meant that they were ironic, and if the presence I sometimes felt in myself of something caustic was an inherited characteristic, like eye colour. I felt an urgent desire to slip free of that tendency. Someone had set up some fireworks in the field below the lawn and we went down to watch them. They banged like pistol shots in the darkness. Everyone whooped and clapped as they streaked up howling and burst into fountains of light. After a while the grey light of dawn slowly filled the valley. It was almost opaque: from where I stood on the hill it looked as though we were surrounded by sea. I stood on my own and watched it. I watched it and waited, as though I were a stow-away on a big, creaking ship making its way through the indifferent waters, watching the diminishing mainland, wait-ing for it to vanish and for my place on this laughing, unknown enterprise to be secured.

TWO

Recently a series of events caused me unexpectedly to meet the Hanburys again.

I mentioned once to my wife Rebecca the fact that Adam Hanbury still lived in Doniford, no more than sixty miles away. At one time we had been inseparable: now we could see each other any day we chose, yet we had not met for five or six years.

'He'll come around,' said Rebecca, sagaciously.

I guessed she was referring to the 'big wheel', a theory of events she had lately taken to propounding. Its basis was that existence is not linear but circular and repetitive. The idea was that you didn't have to go out and get anything – you just sat and waited for it to come to you, and if it was meant to, it would.

'He might just keep going the way he's going,' I said. 'We all might.'

'It'll turn,' said Rebecca.

She revolved something invisible on the axis of her hand to illustrate her point. I was surprised to see how slow and grinding the revolution was, as she conceived it. Her hand only moved an inch or two. She spoke quite blithely, though. It was not a chore to her, this turning. It was a spectacle from which evidently she derived a certain joy. I wondered whether the fact of our estrangement altered what I knew of the three years during which Adam and I were friends. It made me feel uneasy suddenly to think of it, as though everything that had happened since rested structurally and irremediably on that intensity that had given way so silently to indifference. Or, as though I had failed at numerous points in my life to establish whether it was for their lasting signifi-

26

cance or their transitory attractiveness that I had chosen my circumstances, with the strange result that in the light of my friendship with Adam Hanbury, the existence I had constructed without him appeared to me momentarily as both insignificant and totally binding.

'I heard he got married,' I said. 'I think they have some children.'

My wife shrugged and smiled a mysterious smile. It was unclear whether she was acknowledging she could provide no proof of this, or indicating that the subject of marriage and children was beneath her commentary. I wanted to take issue with the big wheel and the idea that we were all stuck on it going round and round, endlessly held at a remove from the things we wanted. I suspected Rebecca only liked it because it proved that nothing was your fault.

'I don't understand,' I persisted, 'why we don't see each other. We used to see each other every day.'

'I don't know,' said Rebecca, who was apparently becoming irritated. 'It obviously wasn't your time.'

She meant, in terms of predestination.

'Was it all a waste, then?'

'How should I know?'

'You're always telling me I should ask more questions.'

'Some questions don't have answers,' said Rebecca. She looked fatigued. She fanned her face with her hand.

She had complained several times about the fact that I never asked her anything. What should I ask her? She didn't know – that was one of the questions that didn't have an answer. Sometimes I saw in her a yearning for a time of reckoning that I felt she didn't fully understand. She seemed to think that a move into an era of analysis and interrogation would constitute a new, living chapter in our relationship, or a new source of nourishment, as though after a famine; where to me it was clear that it would signify only that our relationship was over, that the disaster had occurred and that neutral forces of rationality, of law and order and civilisation, were now washing over the wound. Marriage seemed to me to depend on two people staying together in time. It was like a race you ran together, a marathon. You kept your eyes ahead and you tried to surmount your weariness, and you reconciled yourself to the fact that while it may not be strictly enjoyable, at least running this race was healthy and strenuous and relieved you of the burden of thinking what else you might do with your time. I remembered a period of weeks or months when waking to the fact of my life with Rebecca was like waking to find an intricate, moving pattern of sunlight on my body.

She was wearing a garment that resembled a complicated piece of Victorian underwear. It was cross-hatched with ribbons and little buttons and straps and it was edged with gathered lace all around the neck, so that in its painstaking envelopment of her form it seemed almost to be expressing love for her. Her face was mournful. I had the feeling I had begun occasionally to have, as though I were reaching the bottom of a long fall into water and were experiencing the change in pressure as I hollowed out the end of my trajectory and began to rise again. All the things I had gone streaking past on the way down now hovered around and above me, immanent, patient.

'Given that you always claim to feel so powerless,' I said, 'I don't see why you cleave to theories that make a virtue out of passivity.'

'What are you talking about?' she said.

Her pale-blue eyes flashed past mine, little rents in her countenance. She looked momentarily lively. I had come to view Rebecca's demeanour as involuntarily symptomatic of her consciousness, as though it were a drug she had taken whose crests and falls I had learned to read.

'If I haven't seen Adam Hanbury it's because I haven't bothered to pick up the telephone and talk to him. It isn't because of any wheel, or because it wasn't our "time".'

In fact, as I spoke I realised that, as was often the case with Rebecca and me, the truth lay somewhere between us, lost.

'Call him, then,' shrugged Rebecca, with the clear suggestion that she regarded this as a typically dull, even a craven way to proceed, compared with waiting for Adam to 'come around'.

That conversation was the first sign of the Hanburys, as a green spear poking through the brown earth might be the first sign of spring. Rebecca and I lived in Bath, in the middle of a Georgian terrace on Nimrod Street, in a house that belonged to Rebecca's parents but which they were continually conferring on us, in one of the long, complicated strands of human intercourse of which their life was woven. The Alexanders liked to exist in a condition of sustained embroilment. Emotion by itself was a poor dish to serve up, without the accompaniment of a decent helping of practical, financial and social entanglement. It was this quality that attracted me to them, as it had attracted me to the Hanburys. Rebecca's family never seemed to feel the need to bring anything to a conclusion. Whenever life retreated from them a step or two their response was always to pursue it and offer more, to attain new heights of risk and ridiculousness. They lived in a big house up the hill in Lansdown, which gave out views of the city that appeared to have been expropriated by conquest, and which was so beautiful and original inside that from the first minute I saw it, it could not help but become a factor in my feelings for the Alexanders. Every time I went there it aroused a strange need in me, as though for consummation; yet it made me anxious, too, with intimations of loss. The most striking feature of the house was at the back, where they had demolished a whole section of infrastructure to create one vast room. Entering this room was like rounding a bend to a view of the sea and feeling the burden of proportionality lift from your chest. It was the height and width of the whole house, and at the far end the outside wall had been replaced with enormous panes of glass, so that it shimmered and moved like water when the light came through. Up this wall of glass the Alexanders had trained three dark-green, tropical-looking cheese plants which stood in three big tubs on the floor. Over time they had climbed and extended themselves and met one another to form a great green web over the giant window. Some of their thick, rubbery leaves were two feet or more across and they curled out into the room from the dark, vigorous tangle of stems. The effect was slightly grotesque: the presence of this dark, creeping, living thing in the atrium of light was somehow monstrous. When I first saw it, it reached to about two-thirds the height of the room, but over time it found the ceiling and began to move inexorably outwards, horizontally over our heads. It both irritated and charmed me that the Alexanders had arranged something about which it was impossible to feel neutral at the very centre of their domestic habitat. Sometimes I found the presence of the plant almost intolerable, and sometimes it appeared to me as a stroke of genius, without which the room would lie naked and victimised in its bath of light. The sun came in as though through a pattern of lace. In summer, when the windows were open, the big, stiff, curled leaves slowly nodded and made the light wink and dance.

The house was full of paintings: they hung around the walls like witnesses to the proceedings, though none of them represented anything recognisable, and often I would glimpse up to see one of these confusions of paint and feel startled by the way it seemed to replicate something about myself, some interior chaos that was always silently revolving at the borders of the life I was establishing for myself. Rebecca's father Rick owned an art gallery in the town. He liked to give the impression that a sort of precariousness was conferred on this enterprise, by a force that was conflated with creativity itself, but I never saw any sign of it. On the contrary, Rick's gallery was constantly awash in an apparently inexhaustible fund of notoriety and success, and the more these two commodities could be observed in the infallible business of their synthesis, the clearer an impression of its elemental steadiness could be obtained. The first time Rebecca took me there Rick was in the act of hanging a painting on a wall. His sleeves were rolled up and lengths of his wiry black and grey hair kept flopping in his face as he paced repeatedly away and back again, looking at it. When he saw me he cried out, and flagged me over in the sort of masculine summons that usually precedes a request for physical assistance.

'Just the man I need!' he shouted.

I went and stood beside him. In front of us was a painting about which I could tell nothing but that it reminded me of myself, though not in the usual way. I recognised in it a quality of self-consciousness, as though it were not entirely immersed in what it was.

'What do you think?' said Rick.

He moved closer to me and folded his thick, white, hairy arms. I folded my arms too. We stood there in a kind of spectatorial intimacy.

'What's the title?' I said.

'Oh, fuck, I dunno,' said Rick, darting heavily forward and looking at something on the frame. 'It's *Panic II*,' he declared over his shoulder. 'I don't know what happened to *Panic I*. Maybe it saw *Panic II* and, you know –' he guffawed '– panicked.'

Silence fell. We looked at the painting. Rebecca had disappeared. I wished Rick hadn't asked me what I thought, but at the same time I construed it as a test, something unavoidable that would have found me out one way or another.

'Go on,' said Rick softly. 'What do you think?'

'I'm not really the person to ask,' I said.

'Go on,' he said, softer still.

'I think it's slightly – derivative?' I said finally.

'That does it!' yelled Rick. 'I'm not taking it! Three bloody thousand pounds my arse!'

My heart jolted in my chest, as it had when Paul Hanbury threw me the keys to his car that day on Egypt Hill. On both occasions, for reasons of unintelligible benevolence, I was incorporated into the world of another man's masculinity.

Rebecca's mother Ali had pale green eyes that never seemed to blink. She was small and slight and olive-skinned, and she did everything slowly and with an air of deliberation, keeping herself in the light, holding herself still, as though she lived in a frame and were perpetually making pictures there. She had delicate, unblemished hands with which she touched you frequently and confidentially, and her voice was delicate too, so that her talk, which issued from a single, arterial vein of frankness, was somewhat intoxicating. After an evening spent talking to Ali I would often suffer the next day from feelings of shame and contamination. I interpreted these feelings as proof of a constitutional weakness. They were a sort of allergic reaction, to the moral ambivalence that prevailed amongst the Alexanders, although none of them had ever done anything wrong as far as I knew. It was rather that they had no interest in seeming to be virtuous – they may even have been afraid of it. Instead, they concerned themselves with domineering feats of patronage and ostentatious magnanimity. What impressed me as I came to know them was that, unlike most people, the Alexanders actually invested their integrity entirely in their ostentation. The house in Nimrod Street was a good example of this. For six years we lived there free of charge on the basis of a single conversation, in which Rebecca mentioned that we were thinking of finding a place outside Bath, in the countryside.

'Why the fuck do you want to do that?' said Rick.

In spite of the fact that Rebecca was its advocate, this idea had originated with me. Rebecca was pregnant at the time and was peculiarly malleable and open to the wildest suggestions.

'I don't want to live in a flat,' said Rebecca. 'In Michael's flat people walk all over the ceiling. At night it's like sleeping in a grave with people walking all over it.'

'Tell them to fucking shut up then,' said Rick. 'Tell them to take their fucking shoes off or you'll call the police.'

'I think they're doctors or something,' said Rebecca. 'They have these alarms that go off all night.'

'They're doctors,' I confirmed.

'Why don't you do what anyone normal would do,' said Rick, 'and move house? Move around the corner. Move out of earshot. Give the doctors some elbow room. Don't move to a fucking village.'

'I want a garden,' said Rebecca.

'Why do you want a garden? So you can grow a fucking carrot? So you can sit there and eat carrot stew in some Jew-hating village –'

'Oh, come on,' said Rebecca.

'He's not exaggerating, you guys,' said Ali over the noise, in her empty, pacific voice that always seemed to float like a lifeboat on the surface of a conversational tumult. 'People in the countryside are actually really racist. Especially against Jews.'

'I'm not Jewish,' said Rebecca. 'I'm not anything.'

I started to tell them about Doniford and the Hanburys, which was the blueprint I had in mind for our move to the countryside, but unfortunately they were now locked in debate about whether Rebecca was Jewish or not.

'I think you're really uptight,' said Ali. 'It really worries me that you're so uptight.'

'I don't have to be something just because you say I am,' said Rebecca.

'What about your grandmother?' said Rick. 'What about what she went through? Did she go through that for you to go and live in some village with Miss Marple?'

'She was Catholic,' said Rebecca. 'She was baptised. At least I'm not talking about living a lie.'

'That's not fair,' said Ali, shaking her head.

'Anyway,' said Rebecca, 'Michael isn't Jewish. Our children won't be Jewish.'

'Did we ever say anything about that?' demanded Rick, holding up his large white hands. 'Tell me, did we ever say one thing about that?'

'What's so great about this big bourgeois dolls' house anyway?' exploded Rebecca, finally returning to the point. 'All people do here is go shopping! All they care about is renovating their houses so they can pretend they live in the past! If you took their little museums away from them they'd be as racist as anyone else –'

'Look,' said Ali, laying one hand on my arm and the other on Rebecca's. 'Look, what you two need is a gorgeous little Georgian terrace with lots of light and some original features, and I promise you you'll feel *completely* different.'

Ali often took this route in conversation, of recommending as a panacea the very thing by which you claimed to be being tormented.

'We can't afford that,' said Rebecca sullenly.

'Have Nimrod Street,' shrugged Ali.

'You've got tenants in there.'

'Have it.'

'In fact, darling, they're leaving anyway,' said Rick agreeably, with the distinctive accord the Alexanders always found in such moments.

'Have it,' said Ali again, dramatically, as though this were grist to her mill.

'Hey!' wailed Rebecca's brother Marco, who was listening. 'That's not fair!'

Marco was in his last year of the sixth form at a boys' school in the city. He was a big, thick-fleshed boy with black hair that stood out in wild curls all over his head, and a sallow, pitted face on which he perpetually wore an expression of soporific surprise. Whenever I saw him I was reminded not of myself at his age, but of other people at that time who I'd seen but one way and another never got to know.

'Look,' said Ali, 'just shut up, all right?'

'Yeah, just fucking shut up,' added Rick.

Rick and Ali often spoke like this to their children. With the exception of Rebecca, they all recognised verbal abuse as a form of good manners. For the Alexanders, conventionality in matters of domestic conduct was the ultimate humiliation. For example, I remember around this time an evening during which Rick repeatedly accused Marco of being cold to Ali, because he wouldn't let her drop him off at school on her way to work, but insisted on walking there himself.

'Why don't you want her to take you?'

'I just thought she might want to steer clear of school for a while,' Marco finally disclosed.

'Why?'

There was a pause.

'She didn't make the list,' said Marco heavily.

'What list?'

'The *list*.'

'Oh,' said Rick.

'What list?' I asked.

'I don't believe it,' said Rick. 'Well, that's a fucking disaster.'

'There was nothing I could do,' said Marco, holding out his hands helplessly.

'You've got to get her on the list,' said Rick.

'Believe me, I tried. No can do. It's a democratic process.'

'What list?' I asked again.

'Go on, tell him,' said Rebecca loudly to her father and brother. 'Tell Michael exactly what you're talking about! God, I don't believe it,' she added, putting her head in her hands.

'What's the list?' I said.

'Every year,' said Rebecca, with disgust, 'the pupils at Marco's school make a list.'

'Of what?'

'Mothers.'

'You know, the fit ones,' said Marco.

'They make a list of the mothers they'd most like to sleep with,' said Rebecca in a sing-song voice. 'They vote on it.'

'This is the first time she hasn't made it,' Marco said.

'It's so *embarrassing* for her,' said Rick.

'I know, I know,' said Marco. 'I told them, I really did. Apparently it happens all the time with the top year, because so many younger mothers are coming up the school. Believe me, I tried, but Alex is a real stiff. He hates my guts.'

'So make friends with him,' said Rick. 'Kiss his arse. Just get her on.'

'I can't!'

'Why not?'

'I'd have to nominate her myself,' said Marco sheepishly. 'That's the only way. I just thought, you know, there has to be a limit.'

The day our son Hamish was born I woke in the early hours of the morning when it was still dark. The night seemed to have been full of shadows and motion, like a night spent on a train. Rebecca was sitting on the edge of the bed. Her great body made a depression in the mattress that seemed infinite.

'What's the matter?' I said.

She sighed.

'I'm so tired,' she said indistinctly.

'Can't you sleep?'

'I've been up for hours. I've been pacing the room, like mum said to do.'

Her voice palpitated dramatically between self-pity and common sense.

'Does that mean it's started?' I said.

'I can't believe you didn't wake up,' she said.

I considered this, there in the thick, crumpled dark.

'Well, one of us might as well get some sleep,' I said.

'How could you sleep with me walking around your bed? What did you think I was doing?'

'I didn't realise you were walking around.'

'How could you lie there asleep while I was in pain?' she shrieked.

I had to remind myself that what I had or hadn't done was now irrelevant. Events were overtaking us. In the taxi Rebecca sprawled, affronted, on the back seat, while I sat next to the driver. Every time I glanced back at her, her belly seemed to rise and impose itself between us. It seemed to erupt through the surface of the life on which we had agreed, and I saw everything cascading down its numinous sides. I felt a part of that landslide: I felt myself plummeting down to a region of irreparable disorder. Occasionally Rebecca would groan, a melancholic, interior sound. I tried to hold on to her in the jolting car when she made this noise, but it was as though it were a strong current bearing her away on the waters of her own experience. I watched her recede into the darkness of herself and then return, thrown back into the yellow light of the car, each time more dishevelled and wretched; and I waited for her to retaliate with the sense of her own autonomy, to locate in herself the primitive instinct that would tell her how to negotiate this storm of her body, but she didn't. She cried and groaned with what appeared to me to be more than pain, to be an actual constitutional flaw. I understood that I was witnessing her in the last minutes of her wholeness, as I might have watched a fragile, falling object in the seconds before it hit the floor. It was around that time that Rebecca vacated one part of my consciousness and took up residence in another. Her new home was far more crowded: it housed everyone, more or less, whom I loved under obligation. As I pretended that this change had not occurred, I felt it didn't really matter that it had. All that had happened was that I was, at my centre, alone again.

Hamish was a big, peculiar baby with flowing blond hair and the prominent features of a general or a politician. He seemed to relish pointing out the obvious, and treated everything as a joke: in this way he was identifiably male, though in spite of his size and virile countenance there was something effeminate about him. He was like a big, exuberant, bad-mannered amphibian, or a laughing, androgynous cleric. The spectacle of Rebecca looking after him suggested that of a teenaged girl entertaining her first, unruly boyfriend in the family home. She giggled, or reddened with shame; she was by turns prim and infantile, and then, as time went on, intermittently burdened, disgusted, recondite, submissive. It was Rebecca who had wanted the baby, but from the start I had

37

the subdued sense that Hamish would ultimately be transferred to my sphere of responsibility, like the pets people buy their tender, clamorous children; children who then harden, as though the giving, the giving in, were proof in itself that in order to survive and succeed in the world you must be more callous and changeable than those who were so easily talked into acceding to your desires. I knew Hamish and I were in it together. I knew it even as Rebecca put him in the pouch she wore on her front and picked her way, moon-faced, farouche, through the streets accepting the compliments of strangers.

Rick and Ali treated Hamish as they treated everything, with an instant familiarity that nevertheless appeared to recognise no precedent, nor any attendant codes of conduct. Ali said that Hamish reminded her of her brother Chris. She said it no matter what he did, so that over time she created the strange impression that Chris was a fiction being manifested by Hamish in instalments. When she said to Rebecca, 'That's just what Chris used to do,' or, 'When he laughs he sounds *exactly* like Chris,' Rebecca would say 'Really?' as though she had never met Chris in her life, and had perhaps not even heard of him until that moment. Rick liked Hamish the most. He took him out for solitary walks, as though to visit some distant shrine of male heredity. He would say to Ali, 'Shut up about your fucking brother the jailbird. What's he got to do with anything?' Chris was a tax exile. I don't think he actually went to prison, but apparently he borrowed some of Ali's money years before, and never paid it back.

When Hamish was two Rebecca was offered a part-time job at the gallery. At first I was relieved by this development, since it represented, obliquely, a slackening of the hold the concept of 'art' had on her. For as long as I had known her Rebecca had claimed to be an artist, while never to my knowledge producing an item made by her own hand. A few times she got close to attempting it, a proximity which expressed itself in the immediate onset of illness and depression, accompanied by unexplained pains down the left side of her rib cage. I could not understand her insistence on giving a harbour to the tyrannical expectation that she create. This expectation came from herself, but it had its roots, I thought, in her parents and her need to surmount their capriciousness while remaining within the circle of their concerns. At university, where we met, Rebecca studied law, and though in the end she struggled to get her degree, I could see in her decision to take it something I had not seen since, namely a determination to forge for herself a more normative, classical, even useful existence than that to which she had been born. I could see in it a slightly punitive urge to stick to the facts. I wished sometimes that I had known the girl who had felt that urge. It had already begun to lose its momentum, to give way to doubt and self-consciousness, by the time we met. The law had become a source of oppression from which she wanted only to free herself; and art, whose peculiar strictures I suspected of having driven her to law in the first place, now reappeared in the guise of her liberator. What had she been thinking of, surrendering herself to a life of confinement and responsibility, of adherence to the letter of things? It was freedom that she wanted, most particularly the freedom to express herself. So requisite was this freedom that even the impingement on it of self-expression became intolerable. Yet she sought release: when she didn't get it her freedom was tainted; it became a drag on her, a burden. She longed to give voice to something, but what? Sometimes, with an air of urgency, she would take her pad and pencils and establish herself somewhere with the intention of drawing. It was always drawing she seized upon to guide her out of this conflict, as though it were a first principle she had forgotten and to which she was now going to make her obeisance. The problem was that as far as I could see what Rebecca wanted was not to create but to discharge, to rid herself of a blackness, a pollution, that mounted inexorably in her system. The discipline of drawing was obstructive to this process: it was far too narrow a channel for her tumultuous feelings. After an

39

hour or so of frantic marking and rubbing out on the paper she would throw her pencils on the floor as though she were throwing off her manacles or descending from a tightrope. She always looked more fleshly somehow, more earthbound, in the wake of an unsuccessful approach to the shrine of creativity, as though for an instant she gloried in the mere fact of being human. As far as I could see, all Rebecca's masochistic female tendencies went into this abusive relationship she had with art, leaving her overly assertive and somewhat self-centred and preoccupied in her dealings with me.

Rick's gallery was riding the wave of a middle-class spending boom. He changed the name, from *Rick Alexander* to *discriminate*. At that time he was setting up another, smaller gallery on the Dorset coast, where many of what he referred to as his artists lived, and so increasingly Rebecca was left to run things in the city on her own. I was surprised by her aptitude for it. Sitting at her father's perspex desk in the big white space she was a creature in its natural habitat. It was as though her life had come in only two sizes: she had outgrown the first, and now the second fitted her perfectly. It was in this period that Rebecca first complained that I never asked her questions. One evening she said:

'Why have you never asked me how it felt having Hamish?'

I considered the question. My memory of Hamish's birth remained also the memory of the first failure of authenticity in my feelings for Rebecca. For some reason it had never occurred to me that she might have undergone the same change.

'I don't know.'

'If you were hit by a car and were injured and in terrible pain, wouldn't you think it was strange if I never asked you how you felt? Wouldn't you think it was strange if I just *never mentioned it again*?'

'That's not a fair comparison,' I said. 'You don't get any reward for being hit by a car.'

'You might get compensation. You might get insurance money. Wouldn't it be strange if you were suddenly very rich and in a wheelchair and I never mentioned it, or asked you how you felt?'

'I don't know why I didn't ask,' I said. 'I wasn't sure you'd want to talk about it.'

'Correction,' she said, erecting a white, forbidding finger in the air. 'You mean *you* didn't want me to talk about it. You couldn't stand the idea of me talking about it. That's because the idea of *me*, of my subjectivity, is disgusting to you.'

'Have you ironed your hair?' I asked.

There was a pause.

'What?'

'Your hair looks different. It looks as though you've ironed it.'

I had seen Rebecca's new hairstyle everywhere lately. On the crowded pavements of Bath, which appeared to move, as though with infestation, in a single, avaricious body, I had seen it one day on nearly every female head and had concluded vaguely but regretfully that the hair with which I was familiar had become a thing of the past. I had had this feeling several times, the feeling that I had missed an episode in an important series; that, like someone rising from a coma, I had been made mysteriously destitute by the mere continuation of things. Women's hair, as I remembered it, was remarkable for its diversity, and for the appearance it had of being a living thing, like a pet, that accompanied its owner with any and every degree of refinement, misbehaviour or submissiveness. Rebecca's hair was light red and coarse and tangled and sometimes, when I was close to it, reminded me of the red rag rug I used to have in my student room. The 'new' hair hung like a pair of curtains on either side of the face, or like a pair of dismembered, glossy wings. It looked synthetic and slightly ghoulish. The style had spread almost overnight, like a virus that had struck within my own four walls before I had had time even to absorb the fact of its existence. Or rather, it was as

41

though my seeing this fashion but failing properly to notice it had culminated in it taking possession of Rebecca's head, much as her neglected feelings had. She had to constantly hold her head up to keep it in place, as though she were swimming and trying to keep her face out of the water. What irritated me, I realised, was not the prospect of Rebecca's subjectivity, but her expectation that I myself should have emerged from Hamish's birth completely unaltered.

'Actually,' I said, 'you've never –'

I was about to observe that Rebecca had never asked me how I felt about having Hamish either, but by this time she had risen and was towering unexpectedly over me where I sat on the sofa. In her hand she held my large black-leather ring binder, into which I had the habit of writing every necessary or important piece of information that came my way, and which over a period of years had therefore come more or less to represent my brain. She raised her arm and dashed it violently to the floor. The binding snapped open and a blizzard of paper bloomed out into the air. For some seconds the dry, densely written pages snowed softly and heavily over every available surface.

'I can't believe you did that,' I said.

Two or three weeks later she threw a heavy crystal fruit bowl at me, which hit the wall behind my head and separated instantly into a million little diamonds that sped purposefully away across the floor in different directions. We had to get Ali to come and take Hamish for a couple of hours while we found them all.

'Come on, you guys,' she said, on the doorstep. 'You're being really stupid. You've got to sort this out.'

'No one else knows how despicable you are,' said Rebecca, to me.

'*Everyone* goes through these patches,' said Ali. 'Honestly, everyone does.'

'You're worse than the worst Nazi,' said Rebecca, to me. 'Hitler was better than you.'

42

'What you guys really need,' said Ali, 'is to spend some more time together.'

'If they knew what you were like they'd take me away from you,' said Rebecca, to me.

'Rick knows this sweet little hotel in Cornwall,' said Ali, grabbing both our arms and squeezing them desperately. She put her face close to ours and spoke in an urgent voice. 'Look, you just need to go to bed. You need to spend *all day* in bed. You need to work it out. All right? All right?' she reiterated, squeezing harder.

'All right,' I said evenly. I was holding my breath. I felt that if Ali didn't go soon my lungs would explode.

Rebecca bought a pair of boots that looked as though they had been commissioned to effect my particularly horrible murder. They were black and went up to her knees, and had heels like knitting needles. The toes were sharpened to a point that extended two or three inches out at the front. For a year she wore these boots nearly every day. She clicked menacingly off to the gallery, with her hair in curtains and a devious expression on her face. She mentioned a whole galaxy of men she met there; she charted for me, at length, their ever-changing positions in the heavens of her favour, where they stood governed by the sun of emotion and the moon of art. At length these stars receded back into their darkness, leaving Rebecca to the contemplation of a new artist Rick was selling, a man called Niven. He had only a single name, like a planet. It was Niven, I think, who introduced Rebecca to the concept of the big wheel. I believe I also have him to thank for the discreet retirement of the black boots. Niven admired only what was natural. He was often to be found in Rick and Ali's kitchen, his long, attenuated body, from which a voice of unexpected power and solidity issued like the proboscis of a predatory insect, draped over two or more chairs, pouring wine down his tanned and prominent gullet. Niven had a large, roughly made head and a massive, meaty chin and a nimbus of thin, curly, brown hair. His eyes were like a pair of small shallow puddles. Ali claimed to find him irresistibly attractive.

'He's such a shit,' she said. 'I always go for the shits, don't I, darling?'

'You're too much like hard work for Niven, darling,' said Rick. 'He says he wants a handmaiden.'

'A handmaiden?' said Rebecca. Her tone was very sour. 'What does that mean?'

'A helpmeet,' said Rick. 'A slave to his talent.'

'He'd be better off finding someone with some money,' said Rebecca. 'Or some connections.'

I rolled my eyes. This sort of comment had, apparently overnight, become Rebecca's speciality.

'Now how did he express it?' said Rick. 'I think he said, "I put in the fuel, I get to drive the car."'

'God, I bet he's a fantastic lay,' said Ali dramatically. 'Don't you think, Becca?'

'For Christ's sake, listen to you,' said Rebecca. 'You're such a fake. You're such a sad old woman.'

'That's really unfair,' wailed Ali. 'You don't know what it's like being married to Rick! He's got all these gorgeous young female artists just throwing themselves at him to get space in the gallery.' She leaned forward confidentially, though Rick had wandered upstairs by now. 'He told me that the other day this really beautiful girl came in and sat on his desk and said, you know, *what do I have to do*? What do I have to do to get in here?'

I snorted with laughter. Ali and Rick always tried each to promote the attractiveness of the other, as though it were a consignment of something they needed to get off their hands before the market crashed. In fact Ali was by far the better looking of the two. Rick was perfectly charismatic, but it was hard to imagine anyone flinging themselves at him, even for the sake of career advancement.

'It's not funny,' said Ali mildly. 'It's really difficult for him to resist.'

'What Niven needs is someone who can structure his creative life,' said Rebecca. 'That's very different from being a doormat. He needs someone who understands what an artist is, who can stop him consuming himself.'

I lifted my eyes to my wife's face and wondered whether she was considering offering herself for the position. A few weeks later, sitting in the pub one evening with some people we knew, I became aware again of the way Rebecca was talking. This time she was pouring her heart out to someone called Mike, the boyfriend of a friend of ours. We'd met him for the first time that evening. He had a white, startled face, and round, wire-framed glasses that may have contributed to his look of alarm as Rebecca bared herself to him. She said things I had never heard her say before. She appeared to believe herself to be visibly involved in some disaster or emergency, as though it were plain to everyone that she had come to the table buried in rubble or trapped in wreckage, and could be expected to be candid about it. On the way home I said to her:

'You can't talk like that to other people.'

'Like what?'

'You make yourself look ridiculous. You make me look ridiculous.'

There in the street Rebecca swung at me with her handbag. I hadn't noticed the handbag until that moment; it was new. It was a little pink leather thing on a long strap. On the front it was decorated with a pattern of raised metal studs in the shape of a pair of lips. These lips met my cheek in a hard and painful sort of kiss.

'I don't know what's wrong with you!' I shouted, with my hand to my face. 'But you're upsetting me and you're upsetting our son! He can't even speak any more!'

It was true: Hamish was nearly four and made virtually no sound except a loud ringing noise like that of a bicycle bell. It was extremely startling when he did it. The teachers at his nursery school frequently expressed their concern, though I myself wasn't entirely mystified by it. In fact, sometimes I wanted to make the same noise.

'I feel erased,' said Rebecca. She began to weep.

'I don't want to hear any more about your problems,' I said. 'It's nothing to do with me. It's up to you to make your life how you want it.'

'You're so cold. You're like a room I'm trapped in that just gets colder and colder. You don't touch me or hurt me – no one could ever say you've done anything wrong. That's what matters, doesn't it? It's really very clever, Michael. No one can connect you with the crime!'

'I haven't committed any crime.'

'You see!' she shrieked triumphantly. 'Do you see how you move to protect your reputation? You want to come out of this with exactly what you had when you went in. You don't want to pay the price. But that isn't living, Michael. You can't live without getting your hands dirty.'

'You seem very confident that you know what living is.'

'Everything has to furnish your sense of reality. Yours is the only consciousness. Your morality is the only morality.'

'I think you only feel alive when you're destroying something.'

Rebecca laughed.

'That's an old tactic, Michael. I'm not going to fall for that one.'

'I think it has something to do with your unsatisfied need to free yourself from your parents.'

At this she looked virtually ecstatic.

'That's right! That explains it! It isn't *your* fault – it isn't your fault you've messed up your life!'

'I haven't messed up my life.'

'Look at your violin!' she cried. We were inside the house by now and Rebecca was walking up and down in front of me with her arms folded. 'Look at it sitting there in its little case!'

I learned to play classical violin when I was younger, but

for years I had played folk and Irish music and every other Friday I spent the evening at a pub in Bath where a group of us played together. Sometimes a tiny freckled girl called Dolores sang with us, when the strange scribble of her life happened to cross our more linear arrangements. We were paid in beer from the bar. I had an old leather jacket and a red scarf and cap I kept for these occasions. It might have seemed that my Friday evenings were a hobby but I had a sense of them that was disproportionate to their frequency, a feeling that when I addressed myself in the privacy of my own consciousness it was to the figure in the jacket, scarf and cap that I spoke. I attributed to that figure particularly sustaining qualities of loyalty. Playing the violin was the only real skill that I possessed. I often thought that if my life ever became intolerable I could always put on my cap, sling my violin case over my shoulder and wander out into the world to make my way. Rebecca herself played the piano, quite soulfully: at least, she started well, but before long the music would begin to unravel in her fingers, and the image I had of us playing together would come apart in separate pieces. When this happened I felt that I partook momentarily of her artistic frustrations: I felt that I understood what it was to hold something in the mind that I was unable to bring to life.

'Sometimes I want to take that violin and break it over the table,' said Rebecca. 'Do you want to know why? Because it represents control. It represents perfectionism. It represents the selfish way you possess things.'

The case was lying open. Rebecca was standing right next to it. It did not strike me as being out of the question that she actually would take out my violin and break it over the table.

'When I hear you playing scales on that violin I want to weep. A grown man, practising his scales!'

'If you'd kept up your piano you could accompany me,' I said.

Rebecca shrieked and clawed the air with her fingers.

'The arrogance!' she said. 'The presumption!'

'I thought you were the one who cared about art.'

'You think I'm the enemy of self-expression?' she cried. 'You think I'm the enemy of art? That isn't art! That's the triumph of methodology! The only thing you can do on that violin is play tunes that have been played a thousand times before. It *should* be smashed – it should be broken! Better to be broken than to be the slave of method!'

'You're not actually that original, you know. That's what everybody wants. Everybody wants to destroy things! You think destruction is an honourable response to your feelings of containment but it isn't. What you're destroying is the chance to understand yourself.'

Rebecca appeared to give this idea momentary, involuntary consideration, as though it were something I had thrown towards her which she was unable to prevent herself catching.

'I'll say one thing for you, Michael,' she said finally, as though regretfully. 'You're consistent. You always have been.'

The houses in Nimrod Street had balconies on the first floor at the front. They were large, ornamental Georgian things: each one was made of a single slab of limestone fifteen feet long and four feet wide that extended across nearly the entire width of the house. They had cast-iron railings around them that bowed slightly outwards and then curled around delicately at the top in the shape of a stave. They gave the houses a privileged, slightly exotic appearance, extending out into the air with a little clean wedge of shadow underneath. I never looked at our house without this lofty shape imprinting its stony grace on me. It registered itself silently, repeatedly, as the symbol of some aspect of miracle, some necessary excess that embellished my existence yet could never entirely be within my possession; so that my comings and goings at Nimrod Street were always accompanied by the vague sense that my life was both more beautiful and more difficult than it needed to be. Often, when it rained, Rebecca and I had sat on our doorstep in the evenings with the stone roof overhead, but increasingly I stood under it alone, shutting myself out of the house in order to consider the possibility that my life with Rebecca was unsustainable, a thought that was like a small, panicked pet I wasn't allowed to keep indoors, and hence was forced to exercise outside, where it ran crazily up and down the front steps in the dark, occasionally venturing a few feet out into the street.

One morning, when I left to go to work, I closed the front door and was on the second or third step down to the pavement when the balcony dropped off the front of the building just behind me. The impact was so great that it was virtually soundless. It made a sort of void or vacancy in time. A tremor rose from the earth beneath my feet and passed through me like a momentary torrent of electricity, exiting with a burning sensation from the top of my head. I didn't turn around, or run: it was too late to move. Presently I noticed that the street was utterly deserted. For some reason I found this disconcerting, that there were no witnesses to this strange event. I looked behind me and saw the giant slab lying broken on the steps. It had broken into no more than three or four pieces. It broke like a heart, I thought. After a while I climbed over the pieces and with a shaking hand rang the doorbell. I could hear Hamish crying inside. Rebecca took a long time to answer.

It was only because I happened to be at home when the surveyor came that I was the one to whom the explanation for the falling balcony was given. The surveyor was a slim, clean-smelling man of about my own age. His name was Ed Reynolds. When I saw him standing on the doorstep amidst the rubble and the broken railings I understood how dangerous my life had become. Crystal fruit bowls did not come flying through the air at Ed Reynolds. Balconies did not fall on him from above. Standing there he explained to me how a small crack in the limestone had gone for several years unfilled, allowing a plant to grow up through the slab. I knew that plant: it used to put out purple flowers that waved outside our bedroom window in summer. In fact I had noticed before how it seemed to be growing out of the wall. It had a thick, twisted brown stem. At the time I found it quaintly characteristic of the Alexanders that flowers should be allowed to grow out of their walls: it seemed to add to the impression I had formed of them, that they acknowledged few rules and yet went joyously unpunished. In conditions of frost, the surveyor continued, the plant had expanded and contracted. This caused the crack to become unstable. A simple programme of repairs and maintenance over time would have prevented the accident. For these reasons it was excluded from the terms of most insurance policies. When I relayed this information to Rick and Ali they acted as though some personal stupidity in my dealings with Ed Reynolds had resulted in his presenting us with this verdict. For the first time I felt a coldness, an insubstantiality in their attitude to me. They didn't seem to understand how many times fate had loomed over Rebecca and Hamish and me in the form of the limestone slab, how nearly it had caught us. I had showed Ed Reynolds a photograph I had found of Hamish, aged two, sitting on the doorstep, under the balcony, in the sun. I had thrust it before his eyes repeatedly, as though I were possessed. I couldn't stop looking at this photograph. I couldn't separate myself from it. For a time it seemed almost to replace Hamish himself.

Adam Hanbury had become a surveyor. He had a practice in Doniford. Seeing Ed Reynolds had put me in mind of him, and so without much thinking of what I was doing I found his number and sat one day at the window dialling it, while I looked through the glass at the catastrophe which still lay strewn, untouched, over the front steps. A little bird alighted for an instant on one of the giant broken pieces of stone and flew away again.

'We were talking about you the other day,' said Adam, as

though it were a matter of months rather than years since we last spoke. I could hear a baby wailing in the background. 'Dad's got a boundary dispute going with the council. He's been driving us all mad with it so in the end I said, "Look, Michael's a lawyer, let's just ring him up and ask him." We had the wrong number, though. We rang this woman and dad kept telling her she was your wife and she kept saying she wasn't. They talked for about an hour in the end. When dad rings off he says –' Adam put on a low, comical, inebriated voice '– he says, "She wasn't a bad old thing in the end, Michael's other half."'

'Boundary disputes aren't really my line.'

'Oh no?'

'I gave all that up.'

'I didn't know that. What do you do now?'

I laughed. 'Let's just say I get paid a lot less for it.'

'And there was I,' said Adam, 'imagining you as an equity partner somewhere.'

He'd taken his mouth away from the receiver and his voice was indistinct.

'What?'

'I was asking was it a penance for something. It sounds very virtuous.' He sounded perplexed. 'Though I can't say I've never wanted to get off the treadmill. Only I'd have to get paid for doing it.' He paused. 'To be honest, I never thought I'd be where I am now. Doing the nine to five in Doniford.'

'I don't think anybody does,' I said.

'Don't they? I think that's what dad would call old bunkam. Not that he'd know what it's like. He's never had to sit behind a desk wondering how early he can leave without anybody noticing. What's annoying is that he appears to think this is the result of his own ingenuity.' He laughed mirthlessly. 'He's ill,' he added.

'What's wrong with him?'

'Prostate cancer. It's all right – it's a straightforward operation. But it couldn't have happened at a worse time of year.'

It was mid-March. Through the window the trees were still bare, except for the branches of the laurel that grew at the bottom of our steps. Its rubbery, imperishable leaves were thickly coated in white dust.

'Why's that?' I said.

'He's in hospital all week, and there are a hundred pregnant ewes at Egypt.'

'My God.'

'The first ones are due on Friday.'

'What are you going to do?'

'It's funny,' remarked Adam. 'That's just what dad wanted to know. I'm having to take half my summer holiday now. Lisa is not pleased,' he said in a low voice. There was a pause, then he added, more loudly: 'You don't feel like doing some lambing, do you?'

I laughed.

'Are you serious?'

'Of course,' said Adam, with the vague suggestion that he was not asking a favour but conferring a privilege.

His tone sent a strange thrill through me: an impulse, like a light, that travelled all around my limbs, illuminating great tracts of weariness. I felt as though I had been rowing against a hard wind and had just lifted my oars out of the resisting water, in order to succumb with mild terror to the pleasure of being blown wherever it was easiest for me to go.

I said: 'I'm not sure I can.'

'Oh, dad's hired someone to do the really nasty stuff,' he said, misunderstanding me. 'It would just be, you know, shepherding. We could put you up here.'

The baby wailed faintly in the background. I heard a woman talking: her voice rose and fell, rose and fell. There was the sound of dishes being scraped against one another.

'All right,' I said.

'Can you make it by Wednesday?'

'I don't see why not. I'll have to make some arrangements.'

'You're probably owed some holiday,' he said meaningful-ly, as though he had been told that I was. As it happened, it was true.

'A bit,' I said.

'You'd be doing me a real favour,' he conceded.

I said: 'Can I bring my son?'

'Of course,' Adam replied, after a brief hesitation which suggested that in fact he found the request slightly out-landish. 'How old is he?'

'Three. I thought he'd enjoy it, that's all.'

'Of course, of course. We're all, um, equipped. For chil-dren.'

'Thanks.'

'We live in Doniford now. In a sort of executive suburb. Our house is hilarious.'

I looked through the window at the spectacle of the front steps in the grey afternoon.

'Not as hilarious as mine,' I said.

'The girls will be pleased to see you,' he said.

I had no idea to which girls he was referring. Did he mean Vivian, or perhaps his strange, intimidating mother? Was Caris still there, after all these years? I wondered then whether farmers called their pregnant ewes 'girls'.

'And I them,' I said.

Rebecca responded to the proposal in a manner that defied my expectations. Yet I did not know what to expect; I was open to innumerable possibilities, all of them, however, dis-tinguished by the clarity and drama that were the signature even of Rebecca's misapprehensions, and that either caused or intensified an answering muteness in myself, so that in the very act of escaping her I found it so difficult to ascribe moti-vations to my own behaviour that I preferred to believe it was she who was escaping me.

She was clearing out the closet in our bedroom and did not desist from this activity while we spoke; I saw her face at

53

different planes and angles as she moved around, bending and straightening, lunging here and there with her arms bared to the elbow and her hands, white at the peaks of the knuckles, betraying like a tide-mark the steady presence of emotional frenzy, as though it moved in a body within her, now rising, now subsiding. I found her task obscurely threatening, for Rebecca was generally untidy and inconsistent in her habits and her fits of domestic purification were often significant and expressive of anger and intolerance, and a desire for change that did not augur well for those other residents of the *status quo* by which she had become so palpably infuriated.

'What about Hamish?' was what she said first of all, when I told her I was thinking of going away; the fact of my own absence having registered itself in an automatic neutrality of expression, as though it were a train passing through a station at which it was not scheduled to stop. It was left to me to feel the regret and anxiety that evidently did not suggest themselves to her, and which I noticed missing only when I spoke my plan out into the room and saw how indelibly rimed it was with controversy, and with the sordid expectation that by threatening to remove myself I would at least attract her attention. She did not feel it was required of her to explain what her question meant. Even so, it pained me as much to hear her ask it as if the plain fact that Rebecca could no longer be left alone with Hamish were new to me. Until now I had retained this knowledge as a form of generosity towards her, but I saw it become in that moment a dark tenet of our family life.

I said: 'I thought I would take him with me.'

At that a little wave of realisation broke uncontrollably over Rebecca's face, which she bent into the closet to hide. A few moments later she emerged holding a crushed shoe-box that disgorged bright pink tissue paper from its broken side. Excitement declared itself in two spots of colour on her pale cheeks.

'How long will you be gone?' she said.

'A week.'

'A week,' she repeated thoughtfully.

She maintained this quietly suggestive demeanour all the way to Wednesday, with the exception of one instance, when I wondered aloud whether in fact I hadn't better stay in Bath after all and arrange for someone to start clearing away the wreckage of the balcony. I might have been a dignitary contemplating the abandonment of some vital, long-planned mission for all the dismay this suggestion evoked; and she my zealous aide, promising extravagantly to take care of the problem herself, as solicitous for my absence as I was eager for the absence itself to effect some change in her. On the subject of the Hanburys she seemed to have trouble striking the note she wanted: she tried to find it both predictable and inexplicable that I should be going to see them, and when she referred to them at all it was as "your friends". At night I lay beside her and the presence of her still, coiled body was as exigent and declarative as that of a stranger on a long journey, someone dozing in a neighbouring seat; a person captured in a ceaseless act of self-manifestation, whose absence, when it comes, will be felt, in the failure to maintain a hold on even a remnant of her humanity, as a kind of death.

On Wednesday morning Rebecca drove us to the railway station and left us there an hour and a half before the departure of our train. She couldn't stay, she said, as irritated as though we had asked her to; she had so many things to do. Her manner was strikingly changed. She seemed now to find nothing of significance in our departure, to herself or to us. I felt that I could lie down on the pavement outside the station where she left us and not know whether it was in relief or despair. My heart was clenched like a fist in my chest. I watched her drive away, fast, and it was as though the little wavering car had streamers attached to it, which fluttered frantically around its vanishing form. Later, when our train pulled into its station and I saw Adam Hanbury standing on

55

the platform in a padded brown coat and a deerstalker hat, my eyes attached to him like the first object seen after waking from a dream. I looked at him, mesmerised by his solidity, until he saw us through the window and raised his hand.

THREE

Vivian said it was a good thing Caris was coming. She said she needed help with the dogs.

Out in the passage, the dogs were scratching at the kitchen door. Their claws pushed it and the wind pushed it back. The wood banged around in the loose frame and the banging sound made them bark, as if to alert themselves to what they had done. Through the door they could be heard rattling away down the passage. Almost as soon as they'd gone they came back again in a hurtling crescendo of tapping sounds and hurled themselves against the door once more.

'One feels like a stranger in one's own home,' said Vivian gloomily. 'It's a bit much, when you think that I'm the one who feeds them. Other people always seem to have something more important to do, don't they? They never used to come into the house,' she said, to me. 'Now they go sniffing around like a pair of policemen. I try to keep the door shut but I can hear them panting through the keyhole. It's quite sinister.'

'You wouldn't like being here alone,' Adam observed.

'We're not all as idiotic as Marjory Brice!' said Vivian. 'She thinks men are constantly trying to get in through her bedroom window.'

'Well, don't expect Caris to handle them,' said Adam. 'She hates those dogs. You'd get more help from the Queen Mother.'

'In Spain, a dog has to know its place,' Vivian informed me, in a significant tone. 'A dog has to work. People say the Spanish are cruel to animals because they don't let them sit on the sofa and lick the dinner plates but at least they know their place.'

Unseen by Vivian, Adam rolled his eyes.

'I have friends who own a ranch outside Madrid.' She pronounced the word 'Madrid' in an accent of severe authenticity. 'Alvaro has lurchers. Three of them, all black, terribly elegant. They're almost like people, though not the sort of people you ever meet. I asked him once how he'd trained them and he said he beat them. Beat them to within an inch of their lives! After that, he showed them nothing but respect. He never laid a finger on them again. I think that's rather dramatic, don't you?'

'Very,' I said.

'If you knew him,' she said, 'it wouldn't surprise you.'

She approached Adam and I where we sat at the table. In one hand she held a blackened frying pan from which smoke was issuing in a fast, grey, vertical stream. In the other she held a metal implement with which she proceeded to scrape furiously at the bottom of the pan, eventually detaching two ragged fried eggs which she added to what was already on our plates.

'Thank you,' I said.

Adam and I had been in the barns with the sheep since four o'clock that morning and it was now after nine: I was hungry, but in the gloom of the kitchen the food had a grey, indistinct appearance, as though it were very old. When I thought of the kitchen of Egypt Farm I thought of a place that was all light, yet I could see now that it faced into its own depths like a cave or a cathedral. The black hearth made a wall of darkness at one end. The flagstones on the floor were cold and the colour of discomfort. Daylight came through the small window that faced on to the yard and then stopped in a sort of obstructed oblong, as though we were looking at it from under water. Occasionally, the sun fell behind a bank of cloud outside in the tossing spring sky and the room would tilt and sway a little. Sometimes long shadows raced across the kitchen floor and flew up the far wall into oblivion.

I said: 'I'm surprised. I'd have had Caris down as an animal lover.'

'She used to cry on walks because the dogs chased the rabbits,' said Adam. 'Which I suppose makes her an animal lover of sorts. She said it was persecution. Something about the way they sniffed the ground.'

'She might have changed,' said Vivian, as though she hadn't seen Caris for years. 'She's always changing. The moment you've got the hang of what she's interested in she's interested in something completely different and can't stand the first thing. Then she seems to want to argue about it.'

Adam snorted. He had his mouth full. I watched him divide the fatty ribbons of bacon, the rough discs of potato, the blackened, visceral mushrooms, and place the sections one after the other in his mouth. *Bang-a-bang-a-bang-a* went the door. Around the walls stood the towering shelves holding the same items, pieces of china, ancient things made of copper and brass and iron, antique jelly moulds, jars and weights and scales, and mysterious yellowed cookery books with missing spines that were stacked together like a sorcerer's almanac. They looked reclusive, recessed into their dark wooden alcoves like strange icons. I wondered if any of them had been taken down and used since the last time I saw them. The dense black range crouched in a haze of grey, fat-smelling smoke. Vivian stood by the sink amidst the detritus of her culinary activities. I noticed how thin and hollow-looking she was. Her skin had a jaundiced appearance. Her eyes looked permanently aghast in their wrinkled beds of shadow. Her attenuated arms twitched lightly at her sides, yet her back and shoulders were so hunched around her concave chest that a great weight seemed to be hanging from them. In her dark clothes she had the look of a bloodless, exoskeletal creature.

'In fact,' said Adam, to me, 'you'll find Caris hasn't changed at all.'

'Good,' I said.

'She's still wondering what she wants to be when she grows up. Actually, I haven't seen her since last year,' he added bitterly. 'I haven't even spoken to her.'

'Doesn't she keep in touch?'

He laughed. 'By horoscope. By looking into her crystal ball.'

'What's she doing these days?'

'She lives in a commune. They call it an "artists' co-operative". Women only, of course. They've freed themselves from the male oppressor. Though to look at some of them I'd say the feeling was mutual.'

'In London?'

'She went off in a fit of pique,' he said, with his mouth full, 'about four years ago.'

'There was the most terrible argument,' added Vivian. 'She got very angry with everybody, I can't remember what about. There's always something, isn't there? The problem is that people don't say anything at the time. They get angry with you later, after you've forgotten whatever it is you're supposed to have done.'

'She said we were a disease,' said Adam.

'A what?'

'A disease.'

'The thing is, everybody does the best they can do at the time, don't they?' said Vivian. 'It's no good saying it wasn't good enough because it was the best you could do at the time.'

I noticed that Vivian was wearing a pair of sunglasses. She had taken them out of her pocket and put them on, in spite of the fact that it was almost dark in the kitchen. The large brown plastic lenses gave her big, bug-like eyes.

'Did she say when she was coming back?' said Adam.

'She talked about the myth. She said she was coming to inspect the myth.'

'And what did you say?'

'I said that of course she could come and inspect it if that was what she wanted,' said Vivian gamely, from behind her glasses. 'Only she mustn't expect to find it. It's the expectations that are the problem, do you see?'

Just then the dogs stopped scratching at the door and ran away down the passage. A car door slammed in the distance. Presently their muffled barks could be heard from outside. I laid my knife and fork side by side on my plate. I had managed to eat nearly everything and a feeling of extreme satiation oppressed me. The burnished wood of the table seemed to rise up before my eyes and slowly undulate. I saw little roads and rivers in the grain, and stripes, as though on the pelt of an animal.

'Who's that?' said Adam.

'I should think it's Jilly,' said Vivian darkly, 'wanting something.'

'Mum?' a woman's voice called from out in the passage. The kitchen door opened. 'Mum? What's wrong with the dogs?'

I wasn't sure that I would recognise Jilly but I did; though my first impression of her was that she was nothing like the poor rash-covered creature I remembered on the lawn at Caris's party. The impression she gave now was one of striking beauty which, curiously, solidified almost immediately into the certainty that she was not beautiful; at which point the awkward girl became visible once more. She was very tall and narrow, with a long neck and a small, lofty head, like a giraffe. She wore her hair, whose blonde streaks were being overridden by vigorous patches of brown, in an untidy ponytail and her clothes were unkempt too. The hem of her coat hung down and there were white stains on the jersey beneath it.

'It's dark in here,' she said, looking at us. She switched on the lights, which made it seem darker. 'There. Hello,' she said straight away, to me. 'I remember you. You were Adam's friend from university.' She spoke in a candid, child-like way that I found faintly disturbing. 'You didn't have a beard then, though.'

'I remember you too. You said you were going to have horses when you grew up.'

'Doesn't everybody think that?' said Jilly, with a costive expression. 'What's wrong with the dogs?' she continued.

'They went mad at me out on the drive.'

'There's nothing wrong with them,' said Vivian, looking innocently at her. 'They probably didn't recognise your car.'

'Well, they see it often enough. They must know that Paul's away. Animals are clever like that.'

'There's nothing for lunch, you know,' said Vivian.

Jilly looked beaky and offended.

'I didn't come to *get* anything,' she said. 'I just came to borrow Paul's big ladder. I need to put a tarpaulin over the barn.' She looked at her watch. 'Anyway, it's only ten o'clock. I couldn't possibly eat anything yet.'

'Where's Nigel?' said Vivian.

'He's gone over to Clatworthy. To see his mother.'

'Well, he won't get much out of *her*!'

'It's worth a try,' said Jilly.

'Listen to you!'

Jilly sat down at the kitchen table and put her head in her hands.

'The roof on the barn's about to fall in,' she said in a pinched little voice. 'What are we supposed to do, just let it go? We haven't a penny to spend on it. It's just been one thing after another.'

'It's hard to sympathise,' said Vivian morbidly, 'when you have to have your kitchen cupboards made by hand and brought from London.'

'Oh, when will you stop talking about that?' cried Jilly. 'I've told you, it was Nigel's cousin who made them! We got them for a fraction of the price!'

'And the tiles from Italy, and the leather chairs, and that crockery you're not even allowed to wash –'

'And why shouldn't we have them, when she's never done a day's work in her life! That great big house,' sighed Jilly. 'She's hardly ever there, you know. She stays in London – she's got another six empty bedrooms there!'

'I'm not surprised she stays away,' said Vivian. 'I always thought that house was unhappy. And it faces due north, you know. It can't get any light at all. I never understood why she went to such lengths to get it.'

'It's the family seat,' said Jilly indignantly. 'Her father built that house.'

'Wasn't her father mad?' said Adam.

'I remember he bred llamas,' said Vivian. 'They always looked very odd, standing there in the rain. He and his wife used to go about in the most extraordinary clothes.'

'What sort of clothes?' said Adam.

'I remember he used to wear a sort of chain mail outfit. And she wore a crown and these great medieval dresses with long sleeves. Everyone in the house did the same. The house was like a castle, a funny little castle there in the valley. They had a lot of servants and people just sort of hanging about and all of them had to wear these costumes too. I think they got a lot of people from London,' said Vivian, as though that explained everything.

'Why do you want to talk about all that?' said Jilly crossly. 'Nigel doesn't like people knowing. Anyway, he says it's all exaggerated. They probably had *one* fancy dress party.'

'She drowned in the river at the bottom of the garden,' said Vivian in a distant voice. 'He sold the house and no one heard anything from him again. They were using it as a nursing home. It had lifts on all the stairs.'

'You make it sound awful!' said Jilly. 'It's not awful,' she added, to me.

'Then one day Nigel's mother came and bought it. It turned out that her father had finally died and when she got his money the first thing she did was come back and buy that dreadful house. It's rather sad, don't you think?' said Vivian forlornly. 'Don't you think it's sad?'

'She probably paid five times what her father sold it for,' said Adam.

'She's got thousands in the bank,' said Jilly, 'and she won't use a first-class stamp. Can you believe it? She won't pay the money for a first-class stamp.'

'When you think of the people who must have died there!' said Vivian, distressed.

'It would be a drop in the ocean to her,' said Jilly. 'What we need for the roof. It's Nigel's money, anyway. It's his inheritance.'

Adam said: 'She might live till she's a hundred.'

'That'd be just like her,' said Jilly. 'Can't you do something about those dogs?' she added, turning around in her chair to address her mother. The dogs had started scratching at the door again. 'What's wrong with them?'

'I don't know,' shrugged Adam. 'They've been like this since dad went.'

'I can't imagine Paul in hospital. I can't even imagine him being ill,' Jilly said wonderingly.

'You should go in. He's desperate for visitors.'

'I don't think I could,' said she, shaking her head. 'I don't actually think I could. I'd find it too upsetting, seeing him like that.'

'He's bored stiff lying there on his own. He isn't actually that ill, you know – he's just waiting for the operation. He looks completely normal. I think they said they were doing it this afternoon.'

'I can't imagine what they make of him, the nurses and doctors!' cried Jilly. 'Do they all think he's disgustingly rude? You know,' she said, to me, 'all my friends were absolutely terrified of Paul. You'd be sitting there dreading the moment when he singled you out and yet wanting him to, because you felt so invisible if he didn't. Do you remember the time he threatened to kill Nell because Alice Beasley said she was allergic to dogs?' She laughed. 'He even got the gun out. Alice went completely white. I don't think she ever came back here again!'

'It isn't as though he's actually going to die,' said Vivian in a strange voice.

'It's a routine operation,' Adam agreed. 'There's nothing unusual about it at all.'

'But sometimes,' Vivian persisted, 'people are in the operating theatre having the silliest things done, like plastic surgery, and they just – *die*.'

There was a pause. Vivian was looking slightly wildly at us through her long black fringe.

'Why don't you come in with me later?' Adam said to her. 'Then you can see for yourself. There's no point sitting at home worrying about it.'

'I don't like hospitals,' said Vivian, to me. 'I always think I'm not going to get out of them.'

'What's wrong with you, mummy?' said Jilly crossly. 'You're being silly.'

'Look, why don't we go together?' said Adam again. 'We can go together in my car.'

'Have you ever noticed,' said Vivian, to me, 'that when you don't do what people want you to do they start treating you like an imbecile?'

'I'm only trying to help,' said Adam imperturbably. He stood up from the table. 'Let me know if you change your mind. We should be getting back.'

'I'm going too,' Jilly said. 'I'm expected at the Wattses. I'm helping Sarah move house.'

'Do they pay you?' said Vivian sharply.

Jilly laughed. 'Of course not!'

'It's just that I wanted to know if she paid you.'

'Why would she pay me?' Jilly put her coat on. As well as the loose hem, it had several buttons missing and a tear in the arm. 'She's a friend!'

'Why can't she move house herself – why does she need you to do it for her?'

'Friends help each other,' said Jilly, shrugging, as though she regretted this maxim but couldn't alter its truthfulness.

'I don't suppose she's anywhere to be seen when you need help. I don't suppose she's moving house for you – you probably can't see her for dust!'

Vivian opened a drawer and removed a chequebook, with

65

which she sat down at the table. She proceeded to write with a shaking hand.

'At least if she paid you the relationship would be clear.'

'All you think about is money!' cried Jilly, even as her mother carefully tore out a cheque and handed it to her. She looked at it and put it in her pocket. 'Thank you,' she said. 'Nigel and I are so grateful for this.'

She bent down and kissed her on the cheek with pursed lips. Vivian stayed sitting at the kitchen table. The rest of us left the house together. When we went out into the passage the dogs threw themselves against our legs. Startled, I half-stumbled over their writhing bodies. The air was full of grey, rank-smelling fur. Outside in the light Jilly gave us a fast smile.

'It works every time,' she said, indicating her ragged coat. She gave a little laugh and strode off across the courtyard. 'See you!' she called over her shoulder.

The dogs came part of the way with us across the yard. Then they turned together and ran back towards the house.

We crossed the sloping courtyard, where clumps of grass came through hillocks in the old cobblestones and numerous grey stone buildings were subsiding, showing their black, vacant interiors through the jagged gaps of missing planks and panes. Sheets of sunlight fell brilliantly on the uneven roofs and shattered. At the front the house was imposing but behind, where no one could see, it lapsed into a succession of flaws and pragmatisms. The side and back were harled and painted white and stained with mud and water. An assortment of doors and windows cluttered the rear wall. Puddles collected in the concavities of the courtyard floor.

We passed through a narrow stone archway out of the courtyard and down the steps to the track. The twin ruts meandered away across the hill. The cold blue vista of the sea stood in the distance. Earlier, at dawn, it had been the colour of mud. Now the light was very clear. The sea was like a

staring pair of blue eyes. The hill stood out as though electri-
fied, each tiny spear of grass differentiated from the next, the
branches of the trees fretful and naked. I could see the crenel-
lated mud around distant gates and the boundary of the
Hanburys' land as though it had been cut from a pattern,
with the two pyramidal hills lying mysteriously at its centre.
All around it the brown fences cast little heavy blocks of
shadow. It looked miniature, like a scale model. The grey
road looped up and over the hill and down the other side. Far
below, shiny cars moved noiselessly around the streets of
Doniford. Beyond that, towards the harbour, the old town
met the sea with a certain ramshackle grandeur. Some of the
houses there had been painted bright colours. Earlier, in the
rain, the effect was slightly demented, but in the sun it had a
cheering radiance. Beyond the town, along the coast, I could
see the pale brown frill of sand that edged the great folds of
land as they knelt down into the sea.

'You can see our house,' said Adam.

He pointed to the right, where the tiny grid of streets
fanned out into a big red delta of new housing that had
spread east from the compact centre of the town like something slowly being disgorged. I followed the direction of his
finger through the ranks of little boxes, each neatly summed
up on a square of green. From a distance it looked like a cir-
cuit board. I couldn't distinguish Adam's house from the others, though I wanted to: I had left Hamish there with Adam's
wife Lisa and their baby. I hadn't intended to do this. My
plans for Hamish had been vaguely incorporeal: I had imagined him following me around, unbodied, free of want, but as
soon as we arrived Lisa had placed him implacably under her
own jurisdiction, like an empire appropriating a small, suitable colony. It interested me to see how eagerly Hamish sur-
rendered himself to her highly regulated household, giving
the unmistakable impression that his was a life criminally
devoid of norms.

'I didn't know you could see it from up here when I bought

it,' said Adam. 'I don't really like the idea. I imagine dad standing here, looking down.' He paused. 'It's very convenient, though. I'm at work in less than five minutes. Actually, sometimes I wish it took a bit longer. Sometimes I'd like a bit more – scale. But it isn't for ever. That's what Lisa always says. We've given ourselves five years.'

'For what?' I said.

'For this. This phase. Then we're going to look at it all again. See where we are.'

The wind lifted our coats and tugged them from side to side. It was cold and exposed on the hill. Adam's nose was red and his eyes were watering. He breathed heavily next to me, as though with exertions that exceeded those of the present moment. The new red flank of the town maintained its unwavering hold on his attention. He looked at it with ambivalent fascination, as though he had built it himself. The fierce, staring blue of the sea reminded me of Rebecca's eyes.

'You make it sound like a military campaign,' I said.

'It is, in a way,' Adam replied, plunging his hands in his pockets.

He didn't seem offended by my remark but he didn't treat it as a joke either. His humourlessness caused me to feel a mild sensation of alarm, as though I had mislaid something, as though I had reached out for it, certain it was there, and found it wasn't. Adam looked at his watch.

'We'd better get back,' he said. 'Beverly times our breaks, you know.'

We set off again along the muddy track that led to the barns. Even from a distance you could hear the sound the sheep made in their enclosure, where they were penned up in a moving, baying mass behind metal railings. The disharmonious sound of their plaintive voices, lifted constantly in ululation, was interspersed with the percussive noise of the loose metal bars, which rattled frantically as the body of animals pushed them to and fro. The barns were freezing cold, and full of a sort of steam or vapour that rose off the sheep without warming the air. It was a harsh atmosphere, though not an unpleasant one: the promise of the lambs gave it a rich kind of urgency, a temporary beauty of illumination, as though a single ray of light were trained on this multitudinous place alone on the desolate hillside. Beverly was overseeing the lambing for the whole week. She lived on a nearby farm, but spent the nights in an old camper van she'd driven over and parked in the yard outside the barns. All night she woke every two hours to feed the ill or orphaned lambs. She performed this maternal service with better grace than Rebecca, who when Hamish was a baby used to tut and sigh and emit dramatic groans into the darkness when he cried next door. I did not like to think of those nights: I remembered them as the place in which Rebecca's unhappiness was conceived and made manifest, where it grew and gathered strength and was inadvertently nourished into autonomy. Sometimes, in those days, I felt angry with Hamish for his cries, though I never believed he was the real cause of Rebecca's distress; it was, rather, that he had exposed it, and as a consequence exposed me too, finding out my nascent reliability where it lay buried there in the dark.

When we got back to the barns Beverly was cleaning out one of the empty pens with a shovel. She didn't eat with us at the house; instead she produced a Tupperware box neatly packed with things segmented and wrapped, which she ate sitting on an overturned bucket in the yard. She kept the radio on, tuned to a station from which only the sound of human voices emanated, embedded in endless conversation. There were usually three of them talking, two men and a woman, or sometimes two women and a man, on which occasions I noticed a certain intimate aggression crept into the proceedings, so that the air was filled with the possibility that this verbal ping-pong could at any moment transform itself into something else.

'I'll finish that,' I said. I held out my hand for the shovel.

Beverly was the healthiest human I had ever laid eyes on.

She was twenty-five or so, and she looked as I imagined people were meant to look. Her broad, brown body was distinctly female and yet there was nothing slender or shiny about her. She was like a piece of oak. Her hair was light matt brown and curly and her eyes were bright, friendly lozenges of green. I didn't think she was married. I imagined her associating only with a menagerie of animals, like a girl in a children's story.

'Suit yourself,' she said. 'You can dig a hole for that when you're done.'

She tapped a big yellow bucket in the straw with her boot. Inside it was a dead lamb. Its eyes were closed. Its woolly muzzle was pursed. Its rigid legs were all crossed like poles.

'What happened to him?' said Adam.

'I expect it was a heart defect,' said Beverly flatly. 'He's one of triplets. The mother's too ill to take them. I'm going to try fostering the others out.'

She shrugged, having delivered herself of this tale of woe. She wore men's clothes, big canvas jeans belted at the waist, a checked shirt and an oversized padded waistcoat. I noticed the shirt was ironed. I wondered how she managed to look so neat, spending her nights in the camper van.

'Well, it wasn't your fault,' said Adam. He had his back to her and hence missed the look Beverly gave him, which signified that she found his remark idiotic.

'Round by the fence at the back is a good place,' she said to me, tapping the bucket with her boot again.

I started shovelling dirty straw into a mud-spattered wheelbarrow. The straw gave off a deep, rancid smell and sent up yellow clouds of dust and flaky matter that slowly sank back down through the inhospitable, cold air to the concrete floor. After that I stood in the wind at the back of the barn and dug a hole for the dead lamb. The crumpled body had shrunk from its exposure to air and light. It looked embryonic, as though it were reversing out of existence. Beverly said that the lambs were usually born at night: most things were, she said, and they died at night too. I thought of the dawn we had seen hours earlier: the strenuous emergence of light, the reconfiguration, the recalculation of the sum of what there was. I upended the bucket and the body rolled out into the dirt. Closing my eyes I shovelled more dirt on top of it. Presently I went back to the barn, where Adam was filling the big trough for the ewes that were still pregnant. They barged into one another to get to the food, as broad and brainless as sofas.

'There's another just been born,' called Beverly from the far corner. 'It's ever so sweet. I'm going to call it Muesli, because it's all speckled. Come and have a look.'

We went to look at Muesli. It was staggering gamely around in the straw and fixed me with the accusatory eyes of the new-born. In the next pen was a ewe with a black lamb like the one I had just buried. The ewe's shaggy coat was matted with dried mud. She was butting her head against the wooden door and making the metal bolts and hinges rattle. The lamb was angling at her underside and trying to nip her teats. Every time it got hold of her she threw herself against the door and finally rolled around the pen to shake it off. The tiny animal followed her automatically round and round, pecking her belly with its soft little muzzle. I found its persistence more disturbing even than the mother's aggression. She bent her head and shoved it away so that it fell against the side of the pen. It levered itself up on its knees and shakily unfolded its rigid sections of leg. It darted for the mother's belly again. The sound of her big body bruising around the pen and causing the hinges to rattle was deafening.

'You've got a problem here,' I called to Beverly.

The ewe had packed herself into a corner and was showing her hind quarters to the lamb like a closed door. Beverly didn't come over. She barely even looked up.

'I know,' she said.

'For some reason the mother doesn't want to feed it.'

'She's not the mother,' said Beverly. 'I'm trying to get her to foster. It's not working, though.'

'What shall we do?'

'Not much you can do.'

'What about feeding it by hand?'

'Maybe. Then you've got to feed them all night too. It's a lot of work. Sometimes it's best just to let nature take its course.'

Hamish had a story in which a child looked after an orphaned lamb. The story made it clear that compared with everything else, the nurture of small animals ought to be rudimentary.

'I probably will, though,' continued Beverly flatly. 'Those black ones are sort of cute.'

I took another load in the wheelbarrow and pushed it out into the open yard. Adam was there raking the pile up against the wall in the wind. Little scratchy shreds of matter were whirled up into the air and came barrelling against our faces.

'We drew the short straw, you know,' he said in a low voice. 'All this shovelling and tidying up – the nights are much better. Brendon got them, of course. Him and Beverly light all these candles and sit in the straw drinking beer.'

I was surprised.

'I didn't know Brendon was still here.'

'He never left. He lives in the lodge. They'll give you hot water at the house, you know,' he called over to Beverly.

Beverly was sitting in the yard lighting the little gas burner she'd brought with her in her van. It made a hoarse noise of great exertion against the wind. She had a tin kettle she stood on it to make tea.

'I'm all right here,' Beverly called back.

'Brendon,' Adam continued in a discreet voice, 'isn't viable.'

'What do you mean?'

'He isn't capable of independent life. He's never even had a job! He just sits there talking to his chickens. And for that,' Adam concluded grimly, 'he gets all the perks.'

I found that I felt defensive of Brendon: something in the

72

way Adam spoke about him made me think of Hamish. I remembered the little white face of the forgotten boy I had glimpsed in the chicken house the first time I came to Egypt.

'I remember he liked chickens.'

Adam laughed and shook his head.

'Incredible, isn't it? No one's ever lifted a finger to help me and Lisa. Everything we've got, we've got for ourselves. Some people have to be carried through life,' he added, looking at me significantly, as though to ascertain whether I was one of those people. 'I'm going over there now, actually. I've got to ask him to help Vivian with the dogs. Should be entertaining – he's got some kind of dog phobia. We're just going down to the lodge,' he called to Beverly.

'See you,' she said, lightly but with resignation. 'Tell Brendon I'll see him at the pub.'

I followed Adam out of the barn. He raised his arm beside me in assent but when we got out on to the track he said:

'That's the first I've heard of her seeing him at the pub.'

'What's wrong with it?'

'There's nothing morally wrong with Brendon seeing a woman,' admitted Adam after a while.

'Is this where the artist used to live?'

We were going down the track towards the stone gates.

'Which artist?'

'The one who painted Caris.'

'Oh, him. I don't know what happened to him. He sort of disappeared.'

'I thought he was going to be the next Frank Auerbach.'

'Well, he wasn't.'

A single-storey grey stone building appeared on the side of the hill. A feather of wood smoke came out of the chimney, bent sideways by the wind. As we approached I saw that a big wire structure was attached to the side wall. It was like a tunnel or hangar following the line of the building. There were three large wooden hen houses inside. A number of fat, ruffled birds were pecking the ground around them.

'You've been busy,' said Adam when his brother opened the door.

A set of bamboo wind chimes hung from the lintel. They made a crazy knocking noise and writhed about in the wind. Brendon wore an expression of astonishment. He regarded us, wild-eyed, for a full ten seconds.

'You mean the new run,' he stated.

'It's pretty close to the house.'

'Right by it,' nodded Brendon, emphatically.

He was taller and more slender than Adam. His pale blue eyes were startled and round. His blond hair stood up in spikes. He looked like a doll that had been too energetically played with. I had last seen him as a child and I could still see that early version of him within the man he had become. It was like seeing someone imprisoned in a very small cell. On his feet he wore big lace-up boots that had been clumsily hand-painted in the colours of the rainbow.

'This is Michael.' Adam gestured towards me.

'H-hi. Welcome.'

'The birds'll scratch a trench along the wall,' Adam said.

Brendon stared at him.

'Thought of that,' he gasped, nodding. 'I l-lined it with bricks. Want to see?'

We followed him round to the side of the house, where the wind desisted a little.

'They love the s-s-space,' stammered Brendon, red with pride. 'My yields have sh-shot up.'

He was wearing a shirt which had on it a pattern of buxom, dark-haired women with garlands around their necks.

'You should change your cartons,' said Adam. 'You'd get more business.'

'I don't think I can. I've got a new customer that likes them.'

Adam lifted his head suspiciously.

'Who's that?'

'Sh-shelby's.'

'You can't supply someone like Shelby's from here,' said Adam. 'There isn't the infrastructure.'

Brendon moved his mouth, as though he were ingesting the word.

'Come inside,' he said finally. 'You look a bit stressed out. Beverly says it's pretty manic up there.'

We followed him through the door of the cottage and into a cramped sitting room. The ceiling sagged perilously in the middle. On one wall a large dark patch of rot was smeared across the plaster. A decrepit-looking sofa and a malformed armchair were the only furniture. The room smelled of damp and wood smoke. It didn't look like a place where a person could live. I remembered what Adam had said about Brendon receiving perks, and wondered if this was meant to be one of them.

He went through a doorway into a lean-to that housed the kitchen. I watched him pick up a hot-water bottle that lay on the counter and unscrew the plug. With his back to us he emptied the contents into the kettle and switched it on.

'We should sort this place out,' said Adam, looking around. 'People are getting a fortune for this kind of thing. They rent them out as holiday cottages. The Brices say theirs is booked nearly the whole year round.'

'You can't do that here,' said Brendon from the kitchen.

'Why not?' Adam demanded.

'You can't. Dad w-wanted to. He got someone to come and look at it and they found, you know, asbestos. In the roof. So officially the building's a, um, health hazard.' Brendon appeared in the doorway. 'It isn't harmful so long as you don't touch it.'

'What isn't?'

'Asbestos.'

The kitchen was so small that when the kettle boiled it sent a jet of steam out into the sitting room.

'Bloody typical,' muttered Adam. He seemed to think Brendon had put the asbestos there himself. 'How much is

75

that going to cost to sort out, I wonder?'

'I d-don't know. A lot. Dad decided it wasn't worth it. It would have h-halved the price.'

'What price? We're talking about renting it out, not selling it.'

'No.' Brendon shook his head. 'No, it was to s-sell.'

'I don't believe it.'

'He wanted to sell it,' repeated Brendon. 'With some land. Half the l-little field down the hill and –'

'I don't believe it,' said Adam again.

'The problem was,' Brendon continued, tentatively coming further into the room like something being slowly lured out of its burrow, 'they'd have knocked it down.'

'Who would?'

'The new owners. And built something else. An eyesore.' Brendon tugged at his eye with his middle finger and disappeared into the kitchen again.

'Brendon doesn't know what he's talking about,' said Adam, to me.

Brendon did not contradict this, although he was now standing right beside his brother with two cups trembling in his hands. Some of the hot, light-brown liquid spilled over the brim of one of them and pattered over the carpet.

'It's not as if he needs the money,' Adam persisted. 'He'd never let a piece of the farm go, not in a million years.'

He seemed distressed, as much by the fact that he hadn't been told about it as by the inadmissibility of the idea itself. I felt sorry for him: this was a state into which I was frequently thrown by Rebecca.

'I was glad,' Brendon said. 'I didn't want them to knock it down. This place stands on a l-ley line, you know. It's a s-sacred site. Bad luck to harm it. Did you know Caris is coming?' he added.

I sat down in the armchair. It was covered with a length of cloth, like something in a morgue.

'I had heard,' said Adam.

'She'll tell you. She's s-seen things here.'

Adam put a hand to his head, as though he were in pain.

'What sort of things?' I asked.

'E-emanations. Lights. Do you know Caris?'

'A little.'

'She's very porous. She's always seeing things.'

'Well, she hasn't seen Isobel,' Adam said. Isobel was the name of his baby. 'She's had distinct trouble seeing her. She's never once laid eyes on her.'

Brendon stared at him with his mouth open.

'I know she got someone to do her solar chart when she was born,' he said reasonably. 'She's bringing it with her from London. It's, ah, good news apparently.'

The windows of the little room were wet with condensation. A pall of odorous steam was suspended at its centre. There was a dirty, boiled-roots smell.

'What's that smell?' I asked.

'Hot mash,' Brendon replied. 'For the birds. Apparently it stops them pining for a cockerel.'

'Who told you that?' said Adam.

'M-mum.'

'I thought so. Show Michael your cartons.'

'Oh. All right.' Brendon hopped off the sofa and vanished into the kitchen. He returned with a carton and handed it to me. 'Th-there you go.'

The carton was bright pink. It had a turquoise label which read 'Funky Chickens'.

'A friend of mine makes them for me,' said Brendon proudly. 'They s-stand out a mile in the shops.'

'You should have seen dad's face when he saw them,' said Adam, to me. 'He thought he'd never be able to show himself in Doniford again.'

'He just had to get used to them,' said Brendon. 'He likes them now. He saw Lady Higham buying some and she said they were the l-latest thing.'

'The latest thing,' Adam repeated, shaking his head. He put

his hands on his knees and stood up heavily. 'The latest thing in eggs. That reconciled him, did it?'

I stood up too. The dank steam was much thicker towards the top and centre of the room so I went and stood by the cast-iron fireplace. On the mantelpiece there was a small brass Buddha, grinning insanely. Next to it was an inlaid incense holder with a little grey worm of ash lying beside it.

'I came to ask you a favour,' Adam said.

Brendon looked frightened. 'Go on,' he said.

'Vivian needs the dogs walking.'

'All right,' said Brendon doubtfully. 'They don't like me, though.'

'She can't see to the end of her arm. They're spending all day shut in.'

'I'll t-try,' said Brendon.

'They're a bit temperamental with dad away.'

Brendon looked aghast.

'It's all right,' Adam said. 'It's only for a week.'

'What am I supposed to do with them?'

'Just take them to the top of the hill and back.'

'But what if they run away?'

Adam opened the cottage door and let us out on to the windy hill. A belch of steam was let out with us and was instantly drawn upwards into the sky.

'If they run away you'll just have to go and find them,' he said.

We set off back up the track towards the barns.

FOUR

Adam's house stood in a delta of tarmac, new, black and pristine. It lay at the end of a black, pristine tarmac river that meandered grandly out of the east side of town, beyond the old grid-patterned streets of residential Doniford, which looked infirm by comparison. There, the coast road passed through a fuming, hooting, rattling cascade of metal the narrow, decorous terraces struggled to contain. Great lorries like dinosaurs manoeuvred on the small roundabouts. Dirty trucks freighted with skips and scaffolding roared past, driven by men who gazed blankly through their spattered windscreens. Beside them the pavements and brick walls of front gardens looked miniature: the gardens and the facades of the houses shook like toys as the lorries passed and the daffodils seemed to jolt from side to side in the grass. The houses looked so vulnerable next to the pounding road that it was difficult to believe in the world in which they had been constructed. Some of the terraces were only fifty or sixty years old but they seemed rooted in a past that had become meaningless. Great weights hurtled back and forth at high velocity past the little, unaccustomed rows of houses, four feet from their front gates.

Adam's road, the new road, branched away from this spectacle towards its fresh green site in the fields between the town and the sea. There were perhaps a hundred houses there, all like Adam's. In spite of the exertions of the tarmac, which wound and circled graciously amidst the properties as though to give the impression that each was distinct and difficult to find, the development had a somewhat regimental appearance. When you glimpsed it from the town, its roofs and top-floor windows resembled the impassive heads of an invading army coming over the hill. Once there, however, a pleasant, almost dreamlike atmosphere prevailed. It was an atmosphere that arose from the expectation that absolutely nothing untoward was going to occur. This expectation was well founded, in that as far as I could see none of the factors – natural or man-made – that might constitute, or even precipitate, an event were present. There were no shops or strangers or meeting places, no through-traffic or litter or noise. Even the sea, which was less than half a mile away on the other side of a small rise, was soundless, invisible and without odour. There were merely people, curiously motiveless in their identical red-brick houses, each with their fenced rectangle of grass that was indistinguishable from the grass outside the fence. I hadn't been there long before I noticed the habit they had, of coming out of their houses and standing there beneath the wadded grey sky, looking around. They would look around for a while and then they would go back in again.

I said to Lisa:

'It's a shame you can't see the sea from here.'

She said, 'I don't really want to look at the sea all day.'

I supposed she might have taken offence at my remark, which to be honest I half-thought I was making to Adam. I have found there to be roughly two types of men, those who take offence at everything I say, and those who don't. Adam was the second type.

'I wouldn't want to have it there day in and day out,' continued Lisa, 'just sitting outside my window. Why would you want to have this great big thing outside your window? I mean, why would you?'

I wasn't entirely sure why I would: she made it sound slightly depraved.

'People make such a fuss about a sea view,' she sighed.

The view from Adam and Lisa's house was densely patterned and, because everything you saw had been created at roughly the same time, strangely depthless. From my window in the spare room I could see the homogeneous red brick of other houses, the straight beige lines of the unweathered pallet fence, the lurid blades of new grass, the neat black ribbon of tarmac. I could see clean cars and bicycles and white garage doors. It was like looking at a collage: nothing shaded into anything else but rather seemed cut out and pasted into place. The window was so well sealed that it created a sort of vacuum in the room. In Nimrod Street our windows rattled and let in noise and draughts, and the presence of these things was like that of an audience, bored, judgmental, companionable, suspirating in the anonymous dark. In Adam and Lisa's spare room the silence and stillness were such that I became almost intolerably aware of myself. When I opened the window there was a small sound of compressed air being released, a hesitation, before the outside world ran in in a tepid stream of babbling air.

The house had four bedrooms, which Lisa showed me. She did this with some gravity in the afternoon, while Adam went to look in at his office over in the town. It was as though she had waited for us to be alone. Also, she had waited for daylight, she explained, rather than showing me the house when I might, if ever, have expected to see it, on arrival the night before. She gave the confusing impression that her interest in these matters was not unsatirical. It was a distinct possibility that she believed herself in addition to be gratifying some sordid but well-established impulse on my part, and had elected to do it, if it had to be done, in broad daylight.

'This is the baby's room,' she said on the square landing, pushing open a door so that it made a hoarse sound as it ran over the thick, resisting carpet. The baby's habitation of her room was faint and sketch-like. I glimpsed a cot and various padded items. 'And this is Janie's room.' Janie was Lisa's daughter from her previous marriage, whom I had not yet met. Her room was a little more substantiated than the baby's, though overwhelmingly similar in colour, shape and texture. She had already been installed in it asleep when we arrived, and was now apparently at school.

'This is the spare room, which you know,' said Lisa, whose liturgy nonetheless required that she complete the ceremony by opening and shutting the door to my room. 'And this is our room.'

Adam and Lisa's room, being the *pièce de résistance* of the tour, we were permitted to enter. Lisa stepped ahead of me into its cream-carpeted spaces, as enchanted as a fawn entering a sunlit clearing. I saw the mystery of their bed, immaculately made.

'Very nice,' I said.

'And this is our bathroom.'

I ducked my head into the bathroom – tiled, with gold taps and white porcelain appurtenances – and received a startling impression of multitudinous cosmetics, randomly marshalled like the skyline of a fast-growing city over every surface. A large chrome-plated hairdryer with an intimidating vent on the end hung from a hook on the wall. A prod-like object with an electric flex hung beside it. On a shelf sat a tray of miniature forensic items, tiny picks and blades. The bottles and jars of every conceivable size and shape suggested a world suspended partway between medicine and magic. I caught a glimpse of something called 'breast-firming cream'. I tried to imagine the orgy of self-improvement that routinely occurred here.

'Everything is so efficient in this house,' Lisa remarked. 'Everything works. You can just get on with your life.'

I found myself wondering what, according to these terms, life actually was. We were still in the bathroom – Lisa sat down on the white, rounded edge of the bath. I contemplated the gleaming toilet, from which the suggestion seemed to emanate that unknown to me the problems of human putrefaction had recently and happily been resolved. Lisa was dressed for the temperate climate of the house, in a sleeveless T-shirt and a pair of sandals. Her toenails were painted red.

'We did look at a few old houses,' she said, with the

emphasis – derogatory – on 'old'. 'We though it might be fun to buy a wreck and, you know, do it up, but in the end, I thought, what's the point? What is the actual point of *period features*? What's it *for*, all that arty-farty stuff? I think it's pretentious,' she concluded, 'living somewhere with fireplaces when you've got central heating.'

'That sounds like our place,' I said, simulating a rueful expression.

'I grew up in an old house,' said Lisa, consideringly, after a moment, as though she had decided to disclose her roots to me in order to prove that her opinions were not the fruit of mere bigotry.

'Whereabouts?' I asked.

'Oh, you wouldn't know it,' said she mysteriously. 'It's in the north-east. But our house was really old. When you got into bed your sheets would be wet from the damp.'

'Do you come from a big family?'

I wanted to hear more of this tale of woe.

'Oh yeah,' she said vaguely. Now I could detect her accent. 'There's lots of us.'

She was still sitting on the edge of the bath. She folded her arms over a bare, unblemished section of her midriff and jiggled her foot to and fro so that the sandal slapped against her sole. She was a large-limbed, rounded, well-finished woman with blonde hair so straight and symmetrical there was no doubt of it having been ironed. I wondered if the electric prod was what she did it with. I did not dislike her, though I saw she was suffering from a madness of convenience. She had decided to concern herself with the morality of inanimate objects. I had encountered this affliction before, but only in the denizens of those arty houses with superfluous fireplaces. Rick and Ali, for example, were quite capable of allowing their evangelism in matters of taste to interfere with the run of social play. I had seen Ali complain to someone whose house we were staying at for the weekend that she could not possibly sleep in the sheets with which she had been provid-

ed because they were made of the wrong material. I understood that people did and said such things because they were
in some sense incapable, but I could not have said exactly
what constituted this incapacity in Lisa, unless it was a background of such dreariness or deprivation that it had made her
obsessed with her own comfort.

'Adam's family are really strange,' she continued. 'They
spend all their time talking about each other. Often they're so
horrible I wonder if they actually hate each other. My family
aren't like that at all.'

I sensed she found this habit of mutual discussion as pretentious as a liking for period features.

'They didn't use to be like that,' I said in their defence.
'When I first met them the thing that struck me was how
friendly they all managed to be.'

'Really?' Lisa's neat, even-toned face assumed an expression of distaste. 'My family are just a really close family,' she
said.

'The Hanburys have never been able to acknowledge their
divisions,' I said grandly, somewhat surprising myself.

'What do you mean?' Lisa visibly perked up.

'They're so socially and materially conformist, yet so terrified of seeming conventional,' I continued, finding that it was
not about the Hanburys but the Alexanders that I was speaking, 'that they violate the laws of emotion as a substitute for
real acts of rebellion.'

'Adam's stepmother is a very dark lady,' Lisa presently
agreed, apparently inspired by my talk of laws being violat-
ed. 'She's a very dark, unhappy lady. Did you know that
when they were younger she used to deny the children food?'

'Did she?'

'She denied them fruit!' Lisa looked me in the eye as she lev-
elled this obscure charge. 'Adam told me that once she put
some beautiful peaches in a bowl on the table and every time
the children asked if they could have one she said no. Then one
day they found that the peaches had gone bad. Also,' she con-

tinued in a low voice, carefully hooking her hair behind her ears, 'she tried once to stop Adam and me getting married.'

'Why?' I said, surprised.

'Because of my – you know. My previous life.' She leaned forwards on the edge of the bath. 'She told Adam,' she continued discreetly, speaking only with her lips, 'that he shouldn't saddle himself with someone else's child. I don't know if that's exactly how she put it, but that was the gist, you know. She offers to have Janie sometimes but Janie won't go. The first time she met her Janie thought she was a witch.' Lisa sat back and looked at me triumphantly. 'It was quite embarrassing, actually. The thing is, the baby isn't even related to her,' she concluded irrelevantly. 'I have to keep reminding Adam that Vivian and the baby aren't actually blood relatives.'

I had a pressing need to get out of the bathroom, whose close, tiled walls seemed to be amplifying but not ventilating our conversation. Besides, we had left Hamish and the baby downstairs in the richly carpeted sitting room, whose dense furnishings would no doubt absorb any sounds of alarm. Lisa rose from her seat on the bathtub as though I had spoken this thought aloud: I followed her through the bedroom, lapped suddenly by warm sensations of gratitude which caused my personal powers of discrimination to cleave to my skin like wet clothing. It was not the first time in our brief acquaintance that Lisa had caused me to feel this singular form of discomfort. Not only had she elected to look after Hamish in the mornings while Adam and I were up at the farm, but already she actually claimed to feel some fondness for him. When we came back from the farm I had found him sitting on her lap on the sofa in a synthetic-coloured swamp of baby toys, watching television; and while I questioned her methods I was overwhelmed all the same by relief. Nevertheless, I sensed that Lisa was a person who could say anything, and would, given sufficient time. I was no closer, after our conversation in the bathroom, to understanding her relationship with Adam: in fact, if anything I was more mystified, now that I knew he had not only 'saddled' himself with the encumbrance of a child but winkled its mother out of the humble but tenacious bosom of her family in the distant north-east, for the express purpose of being with her. It seemed to run contrary to his sense of personal destiny, not to mention that of geographical limitation.

Hamish and the baby were exactly as we had left them, seated on the carpet with their faces lifted, transfixed, to the television screen. They sat in its blue light as though in the light of an icon. Their submission was slightly sinister. I noticed that Lisa, with the use of various aids, was adept at plunging children into immobility or, if required, rousing them to action. She could get them from one state to the other in seconds, guiding them on their criss-crossing paths through the hours like someone in a control tower directing air traffic. Similarly she appeared able to do several things at once, as though her body were inhabited by more than one consciousness. She had the unnerving habit, when speaking to another adult, of removing sweets from their wrappers with her hands without her eyes ever leaving your face, so that when a child came to interrupt she could insert one directly into its open mouth. While preparing to take me on her tour of the house she had placed the children in front of the screen, switched it on, and then, like an anaesthetist, waited for a count of ten, before the end of which they had happily vacated their bodies.

'A hot potter,' Hamish said when he noticed us.

This utterance, which I had to conclude was more or less meaningless, was nonetheless typical of a recent advance in Hamish's development: I hoped, at least, that it was an advance, consisting as it did of phrases of verbal nonsense spoken earnestly, as though they contained coded information of the highest importance. This scrambled form of communication was slightly distressing to me. I felt sure that Hamish did have important things to say, particularly about his mother, whom he saw on the eve of our departure repeatedly smashing my watch against the kitchen wall while it was still attached to my wrist. Rebecca had never censored her outbursts for Hamish's sake: on the contrary, I sometimes thought she needed to have him there, as the courtroom needs the stenographer, in order to see the precise record of her actions detailed on his blank little face. Rebecca claimed to believe that it was better for him to see her as she really was, while feigning a certain blindness to the effects of these exposures. I sometimes felt that Hamish was closer to madness than Rebecca herself, though I did not endear myself to her by saying so.

'A hot trotter,' he said.

'What's that he's saying?' marvelled Lisa, deceived by the mysteriously accomplished tone of his delivery.

'I'm not sure,' I said. 'But at least it's in English. I used to worry that he might be tuned into a different station.'

Hamish had started doing something strange with his hands, which involved holding them above his head and rotating them very fast, as though he were spinning a dinner plate on each one. This was a relatively new habit, which I had noticed with a sinking heart.

'Are you saying you think there's something wrong with him?' said Lisa.

I had by now grown used to the way she leaned forward in order to communicate something she considered to be private. The movement caused the blade of her hair to swing disconcertingly towards my face. Lisa gave the impression that it was of no interest to her whether there actually was something wrong with Hamish or not. What concerned her was whether I thought there was. The sitting-room window extended almost the entire width of the room: it faced on to the back garden, and hence gave an unconfined view of a confined space. The effect was distinctly odd. The room was saturated with grey daylight. The fenced rectangle of the garden lay unbearably exposed in every detail.

'Not at all,' I said.

'He's just a little delayed,' she continued, as though he were a train. 'He's obviously very bright.'

I had heard these two statements juxtaposed so many times that their true nature was beginning to make itself known to me. Taken separately they were relatively harmless, but together they functioned like the converging arms of a pair of pliers bent on working Hamish loose from his happy entrenchment in obscurity. He turned his head and looked at us over his shoulder. His large, highly modelled face was startling and slightly grotesque in the room's relentless neutrality. Hamish looked good against a more gothic background. He said something that sounded like 'Derry doctor' and returned his attention to the screen.

'That's Adam back,' said Lisa, although it was unclear how she had deduced this from the torpor of the house. A minute or two later, though, the front door banged and Adam called out from the hall. Lisa sat on the sofa, plump, almost mystically calm, as though directing him in with rays from her unblinking eyes. I sat on the thick carpet with the children. In the warm, well-sealed room we were like dumb creatures waiting in a nest.

'Sorry I'm late,' said Adam. 'I had to call in at mum's.'

'Would you mind going to pick up Janie?'

Adam was slightly breathless and his cheeks were red from the wind. He looked alarmed at Lisa's request, which she made from the imperturbable depths of the sofa.

'I've only just got in,' he said.

'You've got your coat on,' Lisa observed.

'Do I have to?'

'She'll be really pleased,' said Lisa flatly.

'I'll come with you,' I said.

'It's only down the road,' they both replied, whether by way of encouragement or the reverse it was unclear.

I picked up Hamish from where he sat in front of the television. He was like someone in a trance. His legs remained neatly crossed in front of him as he rose through the air.

'How was your mum?' Lisa said.

'A little frayed,' said Adam. 'She'd drawn her eyebrows all wrong. One of them went up and the other one went down. The effect was –'

'Oh, leave the poor woman alone!' cried Lisa unexpectedly. 'The thing is, Adam,' she enlarged, after a pause, 'she's probably worried sick about your dad. She probably hasn't got the time to think about herself.'

She put her finger on her chin and looked at him interestedly, as though by this Socratic pose hoping to draw him into a counter-debate.

'She kept talking about money,' said Adam. 'On and on. Something about her allowance.'

'You make her sound like a senile old lady!' shrieked Lisa. 'Go on, what did she actually say?'

'I'll tell you when I get back.'

'What did she say?'

Adam lowered his voice.

'She said dad and Vivian had stopped her allowance.'

Lisa's blue eyes went very wide at this admission.

'Christ on a stick,' she said. 'What do you make of that?'

'It's the first I've heard of any allowance. Dad never told me he still gave her money. I didn't know what she was talking about.'

'What d'you mean you didn't know what she was talking about? How do you think she lives if your dad doesn't pay her alimony?' She pronounced it to rhyme with 'pony'. 'It's her entitlement. After all,' said Lisa significantly, 'she's the original wife.'

'I never noticed you getting any alimony.'

'Don't start on all that,' said Lisa.

'They've been divorced for twenty-three years.'

Out in the hall I bent down and fastened the buttons of Hamish's coat. We opened the door and went and stood outside on the gravel drive.

'– bloody life sentence,' said Adam.

'How can you say that about your own mother?' I heard Lisa say.

Presently Adam came out to join us. We set off down the cul-de-sac. I felt again the strange candour of the saturating grey light. I was aware of the grain of the beige mortar in the new brick walls, the spongy black surface of the road, the toothpick legs of the little brown birds that landed weightlessly on car bonnets and fences and then lit off again. A bit of twig detached itself from a bare branch somewhere near by and whirled slowly to the ground in front of us, and the world seemed paused for the moments of its spinning descent. I watched it make contact with the grey slab of the pavement.

All around us women were emerging from the front doors of houses. One of them greeted Adam and fell into step beside us.

'How are you?' said Adam, in a way that suggested he had forgotten her name.

'Not too bad,' she said. She had a large mouth that turned down at the corners when she smiled, so that she looked as though she were about to make irreverent commentary on her own pleasantries. 'Yourself? We don't usually see you around at this time of day. Doing the *school run*.'

'Oh, fine. We're fine. We're lambing up at my father's farm this week.'

'Really?' She gave the ironic smile again. Her plump lips were slathered in a grainy, bubble gum-pink lipstick. 'That must be fun.'

I wasn't sure whether she meant it was fun or not fun at all. I wondered if she knew. Several women were now moving with us along the pavement, singly or in groups of two or three. They appeared peculiarly burdened: with their bags and coats and pushchairs they had the processive bulk of a column of refugees. Their hair was whipped to and fro by the wind. I saw the short hair of one woman, dyed red, riven into furrows of colour like the pelt of an animal. Most of them had children with them and they were padded too – they staggered behind like small astronauts or stared out of their pushchairs paralysed by zip-up suits that made their arms and legs stick out stiffly. The woman beside us wore a tight, padded coat. It made a creaking sound when her arms swayed back and forth.

'Chris is off work too,' she said. 'Sick leave.'

'Oh dear,' said Adam.

She laughed out of her pink, downturned mouth.

'He's feeling *very* sorry for himself,' she said. 'He had the snip on Monday.'

She made a scissors motion with her fingers. A cold feeling suffused the back of my neck.

'Oh, right,' said Adam uneasily.

We were approaching the school. The mothers were congregating in the grey playground, each arrival being integrated into the mass so that it had the appearance of an avid, fast-growing organism seething with noise and movement.

'He's taken the whole week off,' she continued, 'to convalesce. Typical male behaviour. I told him he should try having a ba–'

Her attention left us like a scrap of paper whipped up in a sudden wind. She was waving frantically. The coat creaked faster.

'Hi! Hi!' she called, her head periscoping on her neck.

'How's Chris?' someone shouted.

'Furious!' yelled the woman, to whoops of female laughter.

In the classrooms that bordered the playground the children were pressing their small, indistinct faces to the window.

'There she is,' said Adam. 'I'll go in. You wait here.'

Hamish and I ambled around the playground in the mêlée, amidst the calling mothers and the screaming, running children, who appeared to be either fleeing an event or ecstatically approaching one, it was unclear which.

'You're going to school soon,' I said to Hamish, who did not reply.

Adam came out holding the hand of a small girl who was crying hysterically. I saw him say something to her and point towards Hamish and me, at which sight her desolate mouth opened wider and tears ran in sheets down her face.

'Sorry about this,' he called. 'I think she was expecting Lisa.'

'I want my mummy!' the girl shrieked. 'I want my mummy!'

'All right, Janie,' said Adam.

'Where is she? I want my mummy!'

'You can have her in just a minute.'

'I want her now!'

'Janie,' said Adam, 'you're embarrassing me. Please. What's Hamish going to think?'

Janie's crying rose a key.

'Let's just get your coat on,' Adam persisted. 'It's cold. You need to wear your coat.'

Janie was permitted to work herself into a sort of fit over the coat, lying down on the playground and kicking her legs and turning her head from side to side so that long, wet strands of her fair hair were webbed across her face.

'You're going to get hurt,' puffed Adam, bent over her with his hands gripping the tops of her arms. 'I'm going to hurt you if you don't let me put your coat on.'

This statement of intent had the effect both of incensing Janie and of bringing about, at the heart of her tantrum, a form of submission. Somehow Adam got her coat on and then we were walking back up the road. Several of the women looked at us as we passed. They appeared to disapprove of us.

'You'd think it would be easy, but it's not,' Adam said, when Janie was walking ahead. 'It's not like it is with your own child. You get all the responsibility and none of the pleasure. Lisa says I try to control her too much.'

'I want my mummy!' bellowed Janie, activated by the mention of her mother's name.

'The problem is, if you can't be in control, what are you left with? You're left with being a saint. You become a sort of victim in your own life. Every time I look at her,' he added in a low voice, 'I see her father. I can't help it. I see his face looking out of hers. I feel like I'm living with a rival.' After a while, he added: 'The baby's been really good. It's helped us all to feel we're more of a family.'

When we got back to the house Janie stepped over the baby in order to get out into the manicured back garden, where she spent the rest of the afternoon jumping over a broomstick she had laid horizontally across two chairs, her ponytail bobbing, tapping her own flank with a little riding crop each time she made the approach. I took Hamish down to the harbour to look at the boats. The tide was out and so they lay on their sides in the mud. Their naked, round underbellies dried helplessly in the wind. Rope and rigging and faded orange buoys clung to their sleeping forms. There was a little stone pier and I sat there on a bench while Hamish played with some green fisherman's nets that were lying tangled against a wall. Because the tide was out there was no water around the pier either, just a vacant drop on all sides. The wind blew relentlessly. Presently Adam appeared on the esplanade. He waved his arm, clutching his coat around himself. As he came up the pier the wind blew his clothes flat against his body and I noticed how broad and formless he had become, as though he had grown rings around himself, like a vegetable left too long in the ground. His coat was square and brown and padded. His fair hair stood sideways in the wind. He looked like a less fortunate relation of the Adam I had first known. He sat down beside me on the bench.

'Lisa's back at the house. She's made some food for Hamish.'

'That's nice of her,' I said.

'She's a rock,' Adam stated, into the wind. After a while he said: 'Do you mind if we stop at mum's on the way back? I want to see if she wants a lift to the hospital. It's visiting time at six. There's no point in all of us going separately.'

'Not at all.'

'I can't get hold of Vivian. She must have set off on her own.'

We walked back up the pier and into the middle of Doniford. The shops were all closed. Most of them were charity shops: as we passed their darkened windows I could see the shapes of old furniture and shelves indistinctly cluttered with bric-à-brac, and ghostly racks of clothes, all in deep tents of shadow like little museums of abandonment. We turned down an alleyway and then emerged on the seafront again, where a terrace of grand Regency houses looked out over the brown, drained harbour. Adam stopped at one of these houses and banged the brass knocker. I noticed in the window a little poster facing out on to the street, fixed to the glass. It said '57% Say No!'

'No to what?' I said.

'What's that?'

I pointed at the poster.

'Fifty-seven per cent say no to what?'

The door opened. A man stood there.

'Well, well,' he said.

It was Adam's uncle David. He was wearing a plum-coloured silk robe tied around the waist with a shirt and tie and trousers on underneath.

'We won't keep you,' Adam said. 'I just wanted a word with mum.'

David arched an eyebrow. Behind him I could see a very elegant hallway, whose most striking characteristic was that everything in it was white. The walls were white and the floor was tiled with white marble and a white chandelier hung overhead. There was a little antique bureau and chair, also white, on top of which stood a bowl of white roses.

'Actually, she's flown the coop,' he said, standing back to allow us in. 'Some guru she knows about is talking at the town hall in Taunton. The five pliers of something, what was it, there's a leaflet about it somewhere – did I say pliers? I meant pillars. Five of them. Something to do with a quest for enlightenment. Self-esteem and whatnot. She's gone with all her friends. No doubt there will also be a quest for refreshments afterwards.'

He led us through the hall into a large room where, again, everything was strikingly white, the sofas, the carpets, the curtains, the tables and chairs. There was a bowl of white stones in the fireplace.

'What an extraordinary house,' I couldn't stop myself from remarking.

'You not been here before?' said David. 'Yes, well, it's not everyone's thing. A friend of mine says it's like being inside a marshmallow. It's the same upstairs, you know. Audrey did it all herself. She says she likes it because it doesn't remind her of Egypt – take that how you will. It isn't a house for children,' he added, glancing at Hamish. 'At least, that was the idea. Audrey rather blanked out thoughts of the next generation. She's got away with it so far but she can't keep them out for ever. I think we'll be fine so long as nobody calls her "granny".'

'I thought she might want to see dad,' Adam said.

'What? Well, you'll have to thrash that out with her. I try to keep out of her plans. I've got work of my own to do. I'm writing a book,' he said, to me. 'It's fascinating stuff, but you really have to pull up the drawbridge, if you take my meaning, otherwise it never gets done. Audrey and I are ships in the night. Marvellous phrase, that, isn't it? I wonder who came up with that. Some scribbler who couldn't pay the gas bill no doubt.'

I was standing by the white-painted mantelpiece, where white-framed photographs stood in a line. I looked at the photographs in turn, all of which, I presently realised, depicted Audrey. In most of them she was laughing. In one of them she was lying on a bed shrouded in white lengths of gauze.

'Do you think she might have gone to the hospital on the way?'

'No idea,' said David delightedly. He tapped the side of his head. 'Not a clue! Have we met before?' he asked me.

95

'A long time ago.'

'Thought so. It was the beard that foxed me. I never forget a face. You were one of Adam's university chums. Chemistry, wasn't it?'

'History.'

'That's it! I'm an historian myself, you know.'

'I remember.'

Hamish had squatted down beside the fireplace and was removing the white stones from their bowl and placing them on the carpet.

'Call him off, will you?' said David, with a tormented look in his eyes. 'Only Audrey's such a stickler – I'll get into all sorts of trouble.'

'Sorry,' I said. I detached the stones from Hamish's warm hands and replaced them in the bowl.

'To resume,' said David. 'I'm doing a little work into family trees at the moment, absolutely gripping stuff, you can imagine, Doniford having once been an active port. We've got all sorts here, Jews, Slavs, Albanians who jumped ship, half the East End of London. I'm trying to make a link between racial ancestry and violent crime, of which Doniford has a *particularly* high incidence. It's amazing what I've uncovered – you could almost spot the villains at birth! The Hanburys have a Latvian link,' he said, in my ear. 'Real slashers and burners. Have you boys got time for a drink?'

'Afraid not,' Adam said.

'That's a pity. While the cat's away and all that.'

He followed us back out into the white hall. A white-carpeted staircase swept up one side of it. I noticed that a chain of little lights had been woven all the way up through the wooden railings. They reminded me of the lights that guide aircraft on and off the tarmac.

'Tell mum I'm going again tomorrow if she wants a lift.'

'Best to tell her yourself,' said David. 'Saves wires getting crossed.'

His passivity grated on me: I had the sense of it as the

casing for a parasitical nature. I remembered how David had formed an incidental part of the pleasing picture of eccentricity I had taken away with me from Egypt Hill all those years before: now I discerned something hard and unyielding in him that struck me as being more central to this world than I had thought, though not more instrumental. He was like a deposit, a residue, by which the composition of the greater body could be read. I wondered what it said of the Hanburys that this should be their imprint; and of me that I had failed to take the measure of it.

'I saw your pa myself today,' David said.

'I'm glad somebody did.'

'Funny place he's in – it's like a hotel. The old boy seemed quite put out by it all.'

'It was his choice,' Adam said. 'He could have gone to a normal hospital.'

'I left him some magazines – strictly educational, of course. I thought they'd do him good. He's never paid enough attention to his grey matter, that's part of the problem. You've got to, in a place like this,' he said, to me. 'There's no theatre or art or music here. There was a bookshop, but they closed it down for lack of use. Sometimes I look at the people here and wonder what possible motivation they can have for staying alive.'

He opened the front door with its gleaming brass handle to let us out.

'As far as cultural activities go,' he said, peering out into the grey, windy evening, 'we might as well be on the moon.'

At ten o'clock Adam and Lisa went to bed, making their apologies as they backed towards the stairs, like a pair of sheepish politicians sent to the scene of a tragedy; that tragedy being, I supposed, that we had all got older. I phoned Rebecca, as it seemed she was not going to phone me. When she picked up the telephone she was laughing.

'Hello?' she said presently, in a garrulous voice.

The man who had been laughing with her continued to laugh.

'It's me. Is that Marco with you?'

Marco laughed a lot, excessively in fact, particularly where the world struck you as least funny. I realised it sounded as though I considered her brother to be the only suitable, indeed the only possible, male for Rebecca to be entertaining at home, late in the evening, in my absence.

'No,' she said. Her voice was stranded somewhere between coldness and levity. 'No, it's Niven actually.'

I had a sudden pain in my stomach, which sheared off into a feeling of indifference.

'We're just going through the layout for his show,' Rebecca continued. 'You know, the Art in Nature show we're doing in the summer. We've had this fantastic idea of arranging the canvases to make a sort of walk, a country walk.'

'A ramble,' interposed Niven boomingly in the background.

'Sorry, a ramble. We could do it with partitions and – and –' For some reason the mention of partitions caused Rebecca to succumb once more to hilarity. 'We had this brilliant idea,' she presently resumed, more soberly, 'of covering the floor of the gallery with leaves.'

'Don't forget the sheep,' boomed Niven.

'Niven wants sheep,' Rebecca relayed to me. 'Just one or two, sort of – wandering around . . .'

A gale of laughter blew tinnily down the receiver.

'Hamish is having a nice time,' I said, enunciating clearly through the noise.

'Is he?' laughed Rebecca. 'That's great news. No, really, Michael,' she said, her voice descending the ladder of mirth, 'that's great. I'm really, really pleased.'

In the warm, airless spare room I lay on the bed in the dark. I stared at the side wall of the house opposite. There were no windows in that wall. On the floor beside me Hamish rolled around in his sleeping bag. Every time he moved the sleeping bag made a dry, rustling noise. The noise was like something emanating from his sleep, from his unconsciousness. It was like the constant expression of a need. I lay listening to it for the rest of the night until Adam came in to wake me at four and we went up in the dark to the farm.

FIVE

I knew that Caris had arrived, but I didn't expect to find her sitting at the table in the kitchen when we came up to the house for breakfast.

'Hello, Michael,' she said.

She spoke in a rich voice, and looked me straight in the eyes as though to mesmerise me.

'Caris. It's been a long time.'

As I said her name the thought occurred to me that perhaps she wasn't Caris: her penetrating air, as well as the distinct theatricality of her appearance, seemed to raise the possibility that she was an impersonator, or a passing fortune teller who had mysteriously divined my identity. She was wearing an embroidered peasant blouse with voluminous gathered sleeves and had large gold hoops in her ears. Her hair was a wild bonnet of coarse, springy-looking black curls.

'It's been a long time,' I said again. It was the sight of Caris so changed that made a sort of geological reality of the fact.

'Not *so* long,' she said, still pinioning me with her eyes, into which a quizzical light had stolen. 'Seeing you, it's as though it were only a minute. I feel as though I could just walk outside, and find my party still going on.'

Were this the case, the uncharitable thought crossed my mind that Caris would discover she no longer fitted into her dress.

'But of course,' she continued, perhaps seeing something disbelieving in my expression, 'this is the *new* Michael, the grown-up Michael. I don't know this Michael at all. I don't know why he should be here, the week that I decide to go home. All I know is that for some reason he's come around again.'

The mere mention of coming around turned my innards to stone. Caris continued to fix me with her dark-brown gaze as though to prevent me looking at her in return. I discerned a certain weariness in her, with a compulsion of her own from which she was unable to free herself, to invest everything with significance. Her face had become longer and squarer and a resemblance to her father had emerged, like a second face behind the first. Parentheses were etched deeply into the skin around her mouth: again, they gave an impression of fatigue, almost of disillusion. But her eyebrows were militant, fierce and thick and black, and from where I was sitting I could see a coarse shadow of black hair on her upper lip. She had grown much larger and fleshier in the parts of her that I could see, her shoulders and neck and arms. She had acquired a striking, almost sculptural, solidity. The effect was not unimpressive.

'It's so strange being here without dad!' she observed gaily, looking around her. 'I can't remember a single time that I was here without him. Adam, don't you think it's strange being here without dad?'

This was her greeting to Adam, who had stopped in the yard on the way up and hence had only just entered the room. I recalled the fact that they had not seen each other for almost a year, and thought that Caris's opening salvo showed a certain steel.

'He always sits just *there*,' continued Caris, pointing at the high-backed wooden chair next to the vast black hearth, 'usually in his riding things, swearing like a trooper and drinking port at eight o'clock in the morning.'

This, at least, I did recall of the Caris of old, a certain coquettish habit of asserting universal truths where her father was concerned. It had seemed more charming at eighteen than it did at thirty-four.

'His port-drinking days are over,' Adam grimly observed. 'The doctor put him on a strict diet of white wine and shandy.'

'Now that I *can't* imagine,' said Caris. 'Dad drinking – what did he call them? Women's drinks. Do you remember that about dad, Michael? Women, poofs and Jews. The unholy Trinity.'

'How did you get here?' asked Adam.

'How did I get here? Let me see – I took the bus to the tube station, then I took the tube to the railway station. Then I took two different trains to get to Taunton. Then I took the bus to Doniford, and I was about to walk the rest but Clifford spotted me and gave me a lift in his taxi. I rather liked the idea of arriving on foot, like a pilgrim, but he wasn't to be put off.'

'Lisa would have picked you up. She wouldn't have minded.'

'I found out the most extraordinary things about Clifford! Did you know he used to live in a castle? He grew up on the west coast, somewhere near Braunton, and apparently there was this big castle on a hill that he always used to look at when he was a child. He decided that when he was older he'd buy it, and one day it came on the market and he did. He was a builder at the time, he said. He raised an enormous mortgage and scraped together every penny of his own, and he and his wife moved in and installed some kitchen units!' She sat back in her chair and laughed rousingly. 'I think that was all they could ever afford to do. Then a couple of years later the market crashed and the mortgage company took it away from him. He lost all his money, so he came to Doniford because his brother lived here and they started a taxi company. And do you know what he did as soon as he'd made a thousand pounds? He bought a little field, right in the middle of Doniford. Apparently it's now worth a million pounds to a developer, but he can't sell it because there's a right of way across it, which the council are always on the verge of overturning and then don't. I got the impression he doesn't actually want them to. If they did he might have to go and buy another castle. He's still haunted by his kitchen units. He built them himself, he said.' She looked for someone to whom to address her next remark and settled on me. 'This is the sort of thing you find out when you don't drive a car.'

'Don't or can't?' I said.

'Won't,' she replied triumphantly. 'Can, but won't. I used to drive. I was a very dextrous driver. I especially liked going fast. I used to come right up behind people and flash my lights at them.'

'At least you admit it,' I said.

'Oh, I admit everything,' said Caris. 'I've made a full confession. I despise my former idolatry. I used to love cars, and now I can hardly bring myself to get in one. They disgust me – the smell disgusts me, the smug moulded seats, the seat-belts, that great big idiotic steering wheel, the whole phallic enterprise. I feel as though I must have had an early traumatic experience in a car but in fact it was only that I liked them. Work *that* out,' she said, lifting her palms upwards. 'In London I tap on people's windows and wave at them. I can't help it. When I see them sitting all in a row staring straight ahead I can't help it. People get so frightened when you touch their cars. It's as though you've put your hands down their trousers.'

'Do you do that too?' I joked, nevertheless making it clear that I had forgotten the pale, superior nymph-Caris who lived somewhere in this trenchant Caris.

'No, Michael.' She gave me a sour look. 'No, I don't do that.'

'Oh, you're all here,' said Vivian from the door. She smiled rather rakishly, with one side of her mouth. The other side remained downturned, as though half of her were perpetually reminding the other half of occasions on which an optimistic approach to things had not paid off. 'I wasn't expecting you to come up for another half an hour or so. I don't know why I wasn't,' she said, in a rambling manner, shuffling out of a large brown garment that was half coat, half cape. 'It's silly of me in a way to expect you always to come up at the same time. There's no reason why you should, is there? I don't know why,' she continued, so that it was impossible not to form the impression that she was slightly drunk, or in some way afflicted, 'I always think that everything has to happen according to a sort of timetable. I suppose it's all the years of following what the men were doing. There *is* such a timetable, that's the thing, on a farm – other people simply aren't flexible, so I suppose in the end you become rather like that yourself.'

Having shed her cape, Vivian retained a hat with a drooping brim that almost obscured her eyes, which were themselves shielded by her large brown sunglasses. She did not look particularly like she had spent her life adhering to a timetable. She looked distinctly cavalier.

'Beverly needs to go somewhere later,' said Adam. 'She asked if we minded breaking a bit earlier so she can get away.'

'Well, I do think she could have told me,' said Vivian from beneath her hat. 'She obviously thinks I just sit here all day waiting for people to go in and out. I know the lambs are important, but other people have lives too.'

'Oh, the lambs!' cried Caris. 'The little lambs! I must come down and say hello to them – do you remember how dad used to take the old record player out to the barn and play music to the ewes? It was the funniest thing – do you remember, Vivian?'

'He claimed it took their minds off it,' said Vivian, giving us her rakish smile again. 'I suppose there was no way of knowing whether it did or not.'

'Of course,' continued Caris, 'it was a different thing altogether when it came to human beings. Dad was notoriously unsympathetic,' she said, to me. 'His own capacity for pain is enormous. I once saw him put a pitchfork through his own foot. He went completely white. Then he just pulled it out again –' she imitated this manoeuvre with her robust arms '– and walked back to the house.'

'I don't remember that,' said Adam.

'You weren't there,' said Caris. 'I was the only one there.'

'I suppose I never really believed that a sheep had the capacity to know its own suffering,' said Vivian. 'I suppose that was it, really.'

'They make a lot of noise,' I said. It was a noise my head was still full of. 'But they don't seem to suffer much.'

'I don't see how you'd know,' said Caris. 'Anyway, the noise suggests they do suffer. Why would they make it otherwise?'

'Yes, it would help to sort of drown it out, wouldn't it?' said Vivian. She was holding a frying pan out in front of her as though preparing to hit a tennis ball with it. 'The music. Perhaps that's why he did it.'

'They all make the noise,' I said, to Caris. 'Communally. At the same time.'

'I imagine they're frightened,' she replied presently, giving me a wide-eyed look that accused me of some unspecified tyranny.

Adam said, 'Vivian, is that the dogs upstairs?'

Vivian was now at the stove, breaking eggs into the frying pan. She did this by holding the egg high above the pan and then crushing it amidst her shaking fingers, creating a long, glaucous fall of matter. She did one and then picked up another and held it what seemed to be rather too far to the left. As I watched, the innards of the egg fell not into the frying pan but all the way down to the floor with a flop. Vivian appeared not to notice.

'Vivian?' Adam repeated. 'Are the dogs upstairs?'

'What did you say?' said Vivian, apparently startled. She turned her head and I saw that she was still wearing her sunglasses.

'I think I can hear the dogs upstairs.'

I too could hear scratching sounds travelling in patterns over our heads.

'They went up there,' said Vivian. 'I couldn't get them down.'

'What do you mean?' said Adam.

'I went out into the hall and they came down the stairs and barked at me.'

'They barked at me too,' said Caris. 'They were lying on my bed.'

'Oh, for heaven's sake!' said Adam. 'They never go upstairs.'

'I shut them out last night and they went wild,' said Vivian. 'Marjory Brice could hear them all the way down the hill. She telephoned to see what the matter was. In the end I let them in and they just ran upstairs into our room and got on to the bed.'

'So how did you get them out?' demanded Adam.

'I didn't. I locked them in and slept in the spare room. All night I could hear them panting through the keyhole.'

'What about Brendon? Didn't Brendon come?'

'They wouldn't go with him either. He managed to get their leads on – the problem was that then we couldn't get them off again. They got all tangled around his legs and then they sort of each ran off in different directions and pulled him over. He hit his head on the chest of drawers. Then Nell bit him on the hand. He was terribly upset.'

'This is completely ridiculous,' Adam said.

'It's a bit much, really, isn't it?' said Vivian, to all of us. 'Don't you think it's a bit much?'

We listened to the tapping sounds, running in rapid figures of eight over our heads.

'It's as if they know dad isn't here,' said Caris.

'Of course they know dad isn't here,' said Adam. 'They can see he isn't here.'

'But it's as though they're worried. They know something's wrong. Dad has an amazing rapport with animals,' she informed me. I noticed that her early, impressive contralto had now risen by several tones. 'They speak to him, they really do. They'd defend him to the death.'

The black fumes of Vivian's breakfast were billowing across the kitchen. With a feeling of submission, almost of defeat, I felt my palate rise in anticipation, not just of food but apparently of repetition itself. It seemed that the quality of Vivian's breakfasts was insignificant, compared to my willingness to make a habit of them. For some reason this caused me to think of Hamish. It was both sad and relieving to imagine him adjusting to each new latitude, each substitution of day for night, with a physiological routine bent not on understanding things but merely acclimatising to them. Already he seemed perfectly happy living with Lisa at 22 The Meadows, which in terms of time zones was as Sydney to Rebecca and Nimrod Street's London. Whatever feelings spilled out of him at the transits of his fate the mechanism of his body set about busily mopping up. Caris had risen from her chair and moved to the window, giving me the opportunity to examine the other half of her outfit. Below the peasant blouse she was wearing a very full dark-red skirt with beads sewn around the bottom, a pair of white lacy tights and high-heeled red shoes. She looked as though she were wearing the national dress of a small, high-spirited country. I wondered how she had planned to climb Egypt Hill in this attire. The skirt emphasised the solidity of her hips in a way that was more intimidating than unflattering. She folded her arms and stood with one leg thrown out to the side, contemplating the grey prospect of the courtyard. Vivian put my plate in front of me. I looked down at the steaming, gory spectacle and experienced a return of the previous day's aversion, along with the feeling that by eating amongst the Hanburys I would in some way implicate myself, confer a solidity upon myself that might make it impossible for me ever to leave; that by this complicated, laborious act of ingestion I would surrender not only something of my impartiality but some of the space, too, in which my loyalty to my own life was housed.

'Thank you,' I said.

'It's so strange being back,' said Caris, from the window.

'Is it?' said Vivian vaguely. 'I expect it is. It's rather a shame the weather isn't better. If you'd waited until the summer we could have used the terrace. Not that we ever get the evenings they get in Spain of course. At Las Pitunas they sit out half the night, with people turning up at the most extraordinary hours in just a T-shirt and a pair of flip-flops. Nobody seems to mind,' she said gloomily. 'They're all terribly *free*. There's none of this calling up and arranging Sunday lunch in three months' time. By the time you've thought about it for that long you don't actually want to do it, do you? The other day someone rang and invited us to dinner next autumn! She claimed they didn't have a free weekend until then. I didn't know whether to accept or not. It seemed a bit presumptuous. I thought, well, who knows, I might be dead. I suppose if I am someone will let them know.'

'But we were never like that!' exclaimed Caris. 'There have always been people at Egypt, always, without anyone arranging it or planning it! Do you remember the time that man stayed, and after he'd gone everyone admitted they hadn't got a clue who he was?'

'I think he'd come to fix the boiler,' said Vivian. She gave a snuffling little laugh.

'Yes!' shrieked Caris, delighted. 'And someone offered him a drink!'

'Didn't he end up getting off with Fiona Lacey?' She pronounced it 'orf'.

'No – no! He can't have!'

'She was still married to Dan in those days. God!' she expostulated, gloomy once more. 'He was the most terrible pig.'

'I remember their daughter,' said Caris. 'She went to our school. The two boys were at some boarding school where you wore black tie and got to have your own horse, but she went to Doniford Middle because she was a girl.'

'Yes,' said Vivian vaguely, 'I think Fiona's a bit like that.'

'It's incredible, isn't it,' said Caris. 'In this day and age – do you remember her? She had red hair. I wonder what happened to her. She might as well have gone around with it branded on her forehead, you know – "I'm not important".'

'Maybe they just couldn't afford it,' said Adam. 'It might have been nothing to do with her being a girl.'

'In that case,' said Caris, 'none of them should have gone.'

'So if everybody can't have everything, nobody should have anything, is that what you're saying?'

'It's called justice, Adam,' said Caris sarcastically. 'You may not have heard of it.'

'I'd just like you to explain where the justice is in denying two people a decent education.'

'There was nothing wrong with the education you got at Doniford Middle – in fact, they'd probably have been better off there.'

'Well, what are you complaining about then?' said Adam, sitting back in his chair triumphantly. 'In that case she got the best deal.'

'I just happen personally to regard being manufactured by a patriarchal institution as a handicap in life. Not everyone agrees with me.'

'I suppose I should never have sent Jilly and Laura away,' interposed Vivian. 'When they came back they were never quite as I remembered them. They seemed very big and sort of frightening. I remember they were always looking in the cupboards. Almost the minute they came home they'd start going around the house opening everything and looking inside. It was like having burglars to stay.'

'You don't really regret sending them, do you?' said Caris.

'I didn't at the time,' said Vivian. 'But now they say I did something awful to them, although I don't see how I can have done, when I wasn't even there. I had quite fond memories of school. The nuns were always terribly nice, although I don't think they taught us anything.'

'What did you do that was awful?' asked Caris reprovingly, as though it were inconceivable that anyone could accuse Vivian of whatever it was.

'The problem was,' said Vivian, looking vacantly at something over our heads, 'that there simply wasn't room for them here.'

'Vivian,' said Caris carefully, 'that isn't actually true.' She smiled. 'They took my bedroom.'

'Well, they'd had rooms of their own at Ivybridge, you know –'

'Yes,' said Caris, still smiling, 'but it was my room. The boys kept their rooms, of course,' she added, speaking to me. 'The sons and heirs were not to be inconvenienced.'

'This was the problem, you see?' said Vivian frantically, also to me. 'There was all this fighting! In the end Paul just said, you know, bloody well enough!'

Caris had turned to the window and folded her arms tightly across her chest, so that discord radiated from her back.

'It's not really surprising that we fought,' she said, in a cold and faraway voice. 'When you consider the circumstances.'

'Bloody well enough, he said, I can't stand women fighting! If there's one thing I can't stand it's women fighting, that's what he said, you know.'

'So Jilly and Laura were packed off,' said Adam, shaking his head and laughing.

'He said, "I don't care who it bloody well is, just get them out of here,"' cried Vivian, who appeared still not to know what to make of it all. A dark animation surged in her face. She gyrated with emotion. '"Just get them all out! "'

'All?' said Caris in her small, cold voice.

There was the sound of a car horn out on the drive.

'That's Jackie,' said Caris, after a long pause. 'She's giving me a lift down to mum's. I'll see you later.'

And she picked up her coat and left the room, without once turning to face any of us.

'I'd better sort out those dogs,' said Adam, rising and scraping back his chair. His face was red with a mixture of shame and amusement. 'I'll put them in the shed for you. My advice is that you don't let them back in, no matter how much they bark. They'll take the hint eventually.'

He stamped out of the room in his boots and down the hall, perhaps thinking that if he made enough noise he would erase the uncomfortable atmosphere Caris had left behind her. Her head drooping, Vivian stood forlornly beside the raw egg on the floor, as though it were something that had fallen out of her, like an eye, that would be virtually impossible to put back. Unexpectedly, she looked up and gave me a roguish smile.

She said, 'My first husband was an awful bore, you know, but Jilly and Laura talk about him as though he were a plaster saint. He lives on the Isle of Wight now. He has a flat.'

'Oh,' I said.

'When we left Ivybridge,' she said, 'he picked up a rock and threw it through one of the windows. Don't you think that's awful?'

'Was Ivybridge the house you lived in before?'

'He always hated it because it wasn't his, you see. It belonged to my parents – it was my childhood home. He took me to court to try and get half the money from the sale, but he didn't get it. Paul fought him tooth and nail. In the end I didn't really see why he *shouldn't* get it since he seemed to have lost everything else, but Paul wasn't having any of that. He said, you know, that's your inheritance. That's your birthright, don't give it away. It was a lot of money, you see, because it wasn't just an ordinary sale, a private sale. We'd got permission to develop the barns and the outbuildings, and a Change of Use, which is very difficult to get, but Paul is on the planning committee and that sort of smoothed the way.'

She appeared to expect me to speak.

'A developer bought it, if you must know,' she confessed presently. 'I rather expected my parents to, you know, rise from their graves when it happened.' She gave a strange little laugh. 'But in the end the fuss died down and everyone forgot about it. You know, sort of life goes on. I've no idea what it looks like now, of course. I never go there, even though it's only just in the next valley. You can walk there from Egypt in,

111

oh, twenty minutes I suppose.' She looked at me almost gaily. 'They call it Ivybridge Holiday Village. What do you think that is, a "holiday village"? Jilly says they've put up a big red-brick wall all the way round it with these sort of Victorian street lamps on top. She says they look like policemen's heads! And she says the most ghastly people go there, you know, all sandals with socks, and men with tattoos and great fat bellies, and there they sit, you know.'

Adam's footsteps were creaking rapidly overhead. I could hear his voice, rising and falling harshly, and the excited sliding, skittering sounds of the dogs' paws.

'I couldn't bear to see what they've done to the garden!' cried Vivian, grasping my arm suddenly with her bony hand. 'They must have taken up all mummy's rose bushes! And the apple orchard, with twenty-six old varieties, some of them virtually extinct! And the tree by the pond where I used to have my swing, and my little vegetable patch that daddy made me!'

'Vivian,' I said.

'All gone,' she cried, 'all destroyed! I'll never see any of it again! And I'm to be punished for it – as if I haven't been punished enough! Every winter that I've sat up here on this hill it's got worse!'

'What's got worse?'

'They hate me,' she said in a low voice. 'They've always hated me – you don't know what it's like, to be so hated!'

She rose abruptly from the table and moved with the light, disjointed speed of a spider to the kitchen cupboards. She opened a door and removed a half-pint bottle of whisky, from whose neck I was startled to see her take a long, determined swallow.

'Joan and Alvaro say that I should leave him, you know,' she gasped, giving me a dramatic look. 'They say that but then they don't know, do they? He's always here, that's the thing. It's hard to leave someone if they're always there. They never let you alone. It all seems very simple to them, in Spain.

To them it's just a matter of staying where you are and missing the flight home. They think that would solve everything, don't they? The problem is that then there'd be two messes where there was one. You can't just go around making more and more messes, can you? Mummy and daddy would be horrified if they knew,' she said, folding her arms and retracting her chin into her bony chest. She looked up at me through her fringe. 'They'd tell me to pull myself together. "Where's your backbone?" they used to say. "Where's your spine? " That's what they would have said, you know.'

The door opened and Adam came in holding the dogs by their collars. They made high-pitched mewling noises and their feet skated over the cold stone floor. They writhed around their own necks where he held them.

'They've been on all the beds,' he puffed. 'They wouldn't come. I don't know what's got into them. It's a bit of a mess up there, I'm afraid. They've been in the sheets and everything. I'll take them to the shed for you.'

Vivian looked at him mutely with her cheeks puffed out, as though she had her mouth full. I got up and opened the back door for him.

'We'll go home after this,' he said over his shoulder. The dogs were tugging him down the passage. 'We're done for the day. Tell Vivian, would you?'

I went back into the kitchen to tell Vivian but she wasn't there – she had vanished. I felt the presence of something sinister in the empty room, as though it had swallowed her. I went outside again to find Adam.

'You compare Egypt to Don Brice's land,' said Adam, 'and it's amazing really, the difference.'

We drove out of the track and turned down the empty road to Doniford. I saw the deserted vista of the hillside, with its descending waves of green and the glinting heap of the town at its feet.

'What *is* the difference?'

'He's farmed all the life out of it. There's no love.'

I was surprised to hear Adam talk of love.

'Dad does things the old-fashioned way. People respect him for it. I don't know whether I'd be able to keep it up.'

'Keep what up?'

'He wouldn't even let the council run electricity cables over his fields. There's a house beyond the farm that's still powered by a generator because it's too circuitous to run it along the road and Dad won't let them go over his fields. The family tried to bribe him.' Adam laughed. 'They offered him a whack of money. It's depressing the value of their house so much they reckoned it was worth it.'

We had passed the boundary of Egypt: the rudimentary litany of what I now knew to be Don Brice's fields flowed past my window instead. It was an untidy patchwork of electric fences and half-dug pits and pawed segments of earth. Everywhere, decaying lengths of plastic sheeting anchored by old car tyres waved their tatters in the wind. Adam slowed down to look at the sheep. The pregnant ewes were penned into a muddy square steeped in their own dung. The smell came through the open window like a fist as we drove by. Half a mile down the road, a man was driving a mud-splattered four-wheeled motorbike along the verge with two scrappy dogs twisting around him, one on either side like a pair of apostrophes.

'That's Don,' said Adam. 'He's always on that bike. I can't remember the last time I saw him standing on his own legs.'

The man craned his head around and squinted at us over his shoulder. He was smoking a pipe. He raised his arm. Adam pulled up alongside him and the dogs jumped yapping at the window. One of them had a yellow eye. The other dog was brown and white and ran around barking at its own tail.

'You done midwifing for the day, then?' said Don. His lined mouth opened like a wound around his pipe.

'You don't look far off yourself,' said Adam.

''Nother three weeks yet. It's your dad likes to get them in

114

early, so's the frost can kill 'em off.'

'We're having a good year,' said Adam. 'A few twins.'

'Is that so?' said Don.

'We've kept them all so far except one.'

Don laughed and folded his arms as he sat astride his bike.

'He's saved you the price of the petrol, then,' he said.

'Beverly's running a tight ship.'

'Surprised that girl can run a tap. *Sharrup*!' Don scooped the barking brown and white dog on to his boot and forked it into the verge.

'Yours aren't looking too bright for that matter, Don,' said Adam. 'You should try rotating them. That way they don't have to stand in their own leavings.'

'Oh, those old birds,' said Don, turning his mean little blue eyes to the muddy horizon. 'This is their last year. I'm just seeing 'em to market is all.'

'I didn't know that,' said Adam. He sounded surprised.

'I only just knew myself. I wouldn't have bothered with them otherwise.'

'Are you selling?'

'My planning's come through. Call came just yesterday.'

'What planning?'

'For my barns. The barns down the hill along the road.'

'I didn't know you had any barns there,' said Adam.

'Barns as was,' said Don. 'I think once they used them for something but I never did. They just sat there. They're no more'n a couple of old sheds to be honest. They think they can get three four-bed dwellings out of them, though dwellings for what I don't like to think.' He laughed around his pipe. 'Dwarfs, it'd have to be. They're taking my old beet fields too as acreage. I know your dad was against it and he'll be none too pleased, but there it is,' he added. His little eyes were now hovering around Adam like a pair of flies. 'It went through at the meeting and he weren't there.'

'How could he have been there?' said Adam. 'He's in hospital.'

'Can't be helped,' said Don. 'I told him before, you've got to live and farming ain't no living any more. He's all right – he's got her to keep him, and as far as I can see she made her money the same way I'm making mine. Like I say, there it is. It won't make no difference to him anyhow,' he added. 'It's just a couple of old sheds. You can hardly see 'em from up there. In his condition things like this don't matter, do they? It comes down to what's important, don't it, family and that, not whether there's houses or not on some old field. Don't it, eh, son?'

'I suppose so,' said Adam.

'Niver understood why he was so dead against it in the first place,' Don continued, wrapping his fingers around his pipe as though in meditation.

'That's the way he is.'

A grimace of understanding crossed the farmer's face.

'I suppose you'll be boss up there yourself one of these days,' he said meaningfully.

'I'm my own boss already.'

'Course y'are. Got your own little place. And a wife and kiddies too.'

'I'll see you, Don.'

We pulled away with Don holding his pipe at his lips while he opened his mouth to laugh. The lane plummeted downwards in shuttered flashes of brightness. Big black birds hopped on the verge around a smear of blood and fur. Thin lines of wires zigzagged overhead, veered off across the fields like things taking flight, then emerged from their tributaries again and coalesced, swooping upwards in formation to crest the giant grey peaks of pylons that passed along the bottom of the hill in their march down the coast. We passed a new bungalow being built on the side of the road. I glimpsed the raw slash of gravel in front, the military row of dwarfish green conifers, the still-exposed flanks of grey breeze block.

'Look,' said Adam, 'they're coming up the hill. For ages the first house you saw on the way down was that one.'

We were in the outskirts of Doniford now. He pointed to the end of a plain, white-harled row of old council housing which stood forlornly impacted in a ring of bigger new red-brick houses that bristled with ornamentation. The garden was a small rectangle of green with nothing in it except a bare metal climbing frame in the shape of a beehive.

'I used to be friends with the boy who lived there,' said Adam. 'We were in the same class at school.'

'Really?'

'I used to go there to play. I sort of liked going there. It was cosy and his mother was always there, and no one ever asked you to do anything. And compared to Egypt it was so small! I couldn't believe how small it was. Once when Vivian came to collect me I said to her in front of Ian and his mother that I liked Ian's house because it was so small.' He laughed. 'I think I thought I was being interesting. Vivian went wild afterwards. She said some pretty strong things in the car. I remember thinking, God, she really hates me. Of course, I understand that better now,' he added stiffly. 'I understand how difficult it was for her.'

'Does he still live here?' I asked. I wanted to hear more of Adam's feelings for this boy.

'He manages the petrol station. We always say hello. It's funny, we were such good friends,' he said, as though it made no sense to him now. 'I used to think that one day Ian might come to live with us at Egypt. He'd just appear and we'd save him. I suppose I couldn't believe he was happy where he was. His mother used to cook this awful food. Everything was white and soft and bland. It was like hospital food. Ian used to eat it up.'

His telephone rang in his lap.

'We're just coming down the hill,' he said into it.

I looked out of the window at Doniford, which had changed so much and yet was still regarded as itself, like a person grown older, thicker, coarser. My memories of it, and of the Hanburys themselves, were in a sense homeless: they

117

could not dwell in reality, so changed. They wandered around the occupied spaces, mournful as ghosts. I had not realised that time would move in this way over my life, would fill its lacunae as brown saltwater filled Doniford harbour until it brimmed.

'What for?' said Adam.

We stopped at the traffic lights on the high street, where a woman stood on the pavement waiting to cross. Her hands were folded in front of her and the straps of her leather handbag were looped over her forearm, which she held very still. She had permed, mouse-coloured hair and the round, pallid face of a Delft maiden. We looked at one another blankly before she crossed the road, stepping carefully in front of our car.

'She can't be,' said Adam. 'I only just bought a pack.' After a pause he said: 'I don't need to come home and see. Either she has or she hasn't.' After another pause he said: 'I'll see what I can do. I'll see what I can do, okay? Sorry,' he said to me. 'I've got to stop and get some you-know-whats.'

Adam parked the car on the pavement outside the Spar. I stayed there while he went inside. I looked at the milling high street, whose grey prospect was occasionally riven by slanting sheets of spring sunlight. I looked at people's legs and at the wheels of passing cars. A girl of sixteen or seventeen tried to get her pushchair through the space between our car and the shopfront and couldn't. People waited behind her. Presently a new stream of people forged itself on the other side of the car, in the road. An elderly man tapped on my window and I rolled it down. He said:

'You can't park here.'

'Okay,' I said.

'People can't get along the pavement,' he said, indicating it with his hand.

'Okay,' I said.

He shook his head and walked away. After a while Adam came out of the Spar and we drove back to the house.

SIX

Lisa said:

'I don't have a really good relationship with Caris.'

'Don't you?' I said.

'I'll be honest with you, I don't actually like her. She's the only one of the family I don't actually like.'

We were in the Spar while this admission was being made. Lisa had Isobel and I had Hamish. We were like members of some particularly burdened species that favoured talk and inaction. Lisa went very slowly down the aisles and chose things as though the choosing of them, rather than the putative cooking and consumption, were the point.

'Hamish,' she said, 'do you like these Potato Faces thingies?'

'No,' said Hamish.

'I think that means yes, don't you?' she said, to me. She hurled the frozen bag into the cart with a thud.

We stood in the cold parabola of the freezer section while Lisa looked everything over. The Spar hadn't changed much since I had searched it for Caris's *cassis* all those years before, except in the unnerving particular that I was certain its aisles once ran along its length rather than across its width as they did now.

'The thing about Caris,' said Lisa in her 'discreet' voice, putting her head very close to mine and her mouth beside my ear, 'is that she's stuck in the past.'

She said it to rhyme with 'gassed'.

'She's full of bitterness and resentment about the things that happened and yet she can't stop herself idealising it, you know, her family and how it all was. And so when she comes down here she feels this *contradictory* set of emotions. I

119

haven't met her very many times, actually,' said Lisa. 'She hardly ever comes here, I think for the reasons I say. She and Adam aren't very close.'

We arrived at fruit and vegetables, where Lisa picked up a large shiny pepper that looked as though it were made out of plastic.

'Which do you prefer,' she said, turning it in her hand to get a good look at it, 'red peppers or green? I used to hate the green ones but now I quite like them. Do you ever find that happens to you?'

I felt that I was as far as I could be from actually eating the pepper, without having to grow it first. It seemed to me that Lisa should choose something a little more advanced in its evolution towards the plate.

'Rebecca was a vegetarian,' I said, 'and then one day I found her eating a packet of salami. She ate the whole packet. I did find it very disturbing seeing her eat it.'

'Why?' said Lisa, amazed. She stopped turning the pepper. I realised that I had caused us to grind to a complete halt.

I said, 'It was slightly frightening, that's all. It seemed very bloody. I think I must have respected her more than I realised.'

'You haven't told me about your wife,' said Lisa. 'What's she like?'

'I don't think I can describe her,' I said, after a pause.

Lisa laughed. 'You must know what she's *like*,' she said.

I looked at the bank of fruit and vegetables, where bananas lay with bananas and tomatoes with tomatoes, neat forests of broccoli and apples in straight lines, all even-coloured, all unblemished, and which Lisa stood beside as though she had created it for me herself, as a model of categorisation. It struck me that I did not find her bent for simplification actually irritating. The reason for this was that I believed she did it on purpose – that she had settled on it as the best way of presenting herself under the circumstances. I didn't think, either, that it had arisen out of a need to distinguish herself from the

Hanburys, or even as a sort of criticism of them. I guessed that Adam had found her literal-mindedness attractive, and that one way or another it had become her means of survival. The problem was that she was stuck with it, while still having to get her pleasure and satisfaction from somewhere.

'What's anybody like?' I said.

Lisa immediately looked crestfallen. I didn't mean to be cruel, exactly, but I didn't see that it was my responsibility to humour her either.

'I only meant,' she said, 'that you must know her better than anybody else. You said, for example, that you respected her more than you realised. What did you mean by that exactly?'

I was conscious of the Spar's strip lighting overhead, which rained nakedly down from the synthetic panelled ceiling.

'That I sometimes failed to see the value of the things Rebecca believed in.'

'Are you a vegetarian?' said Lisa.

'No.'

'But you wanted her to be one, is that what you're saying?'

Lisa seemed prepared to find this idea amusing. I saw her beginning to take pleasure in what she considered to be my quirks, as a child might begin to discern in an object the possibility of play. Rebecca had consumed the salami standing beside the sink in our kitchen. Watching the meat fold itself into her pale pink mouth I had felt revolted. Yet in the past her refusal to eat meat had irritated me, not only because I regarded it as an affectation but because it galled me to see her impose a discipline on herself that profited nobody. If she wanted reforms, I had numerous suggestions for them. In fact, I had come vaguely to feel that she abstained in order to spite me, which made my sense of her betrayal, almost of her infidelity, as she stood there at the sink, seem so sad and self-defeating that I was unable to speak to her about what she had done.

'Not really,' I said.

'My sister's a vegetarian. She says she can smell the meat on people now. She says sometimes it really turns her stomach. Hamish, will you get us some of those Hula Hoops? I know we shouldn't eat them but I can't help it. The ones in the orange packet, that's it.'

Lisa took out her purse, which was large and creased, and stuffed with cards and banknotes and receipts. She withdrew a piece of paper on which she had written a shopping list and went through the items, murmuring aloud. She wore sunglasses pushed back on her head and sandals, although outside the Spar the street was grey and turbulent and people walked past the big windows as though they were moving through water, with their heads bowed and their clothes pressed in wrinkles against their bodies. In her chair the baby began to make a plaintive sound. Little ropes of saliva were running over the ledge of her lower lip and paying wetly down the front of her coat. Without taking her eyes from the list, Lisa pulled a dummy out of her pocket and plugged it into the baby's mouth. I experienced a feeling of surrender to her methods and to her sense of time, which ran along like a slow train making no stops at which you might be permitted to disembark. While I had come to Doniford with the undefined expectation of surrendering to something, it was certainly not to this. It was as though I had arrived carrying some unwieldy, burdensome object – a standard lamp, say – of which I had confidently hoped somehow to discharge myself; and finding, to my vexation and surprise, that there was nowhere to put it, nowhere to leave it in safe keeping, I had become used to just lugging it around with me. Everywhere I went I had the sense of myself carrying around the standard lamp, setting it down beside me to eat or speak to people, who were of course too polite to mention that it was there. What I had expected to surrender to, I suppose, was the state of dispossession, but it appeared that it was no longer permissible to be unencumbered, to be free. At my age you had to belong somewhere, even if it was on Lisa's train. I had noticed that she was reluctant to leave me in the house alone, as though this were inappropriate, even scandalous.

'To get back to Caris,' she said, 'I think she's very distrustful of other women. Sometimes I think she doesn't actually want to *be* a woman. I think that's why she doesn't have children. Also,' she said, 'I think she's got a real father complex. Paul's quite a manly man. He likes men to be men and women to be women – he's quite vulgar in a way, actually. But then you realise that in fact he's very principled. He's not like most people; he's not at all interested in money. Adam says he could get hundreds of thousands for his barns and for some of his land around Doniford, where the council are letting you build. He's not like that at all, though. He sits on the planning committee and tries to get everything overturned. Adam says he's made a lot of enemies in the town. Caris wants Egypt,' she said, putting her mouth next to my ear, 'but Adam'll get it because he's the son.'

'Surely he'd leave it to all of them,' I said.

'Oh no,' she replied, 'not Paul. He's too canny for that. He knows they'd fight over it. Anyway, they couldn't *all* live there. They'd have to sell, or buy each other out. He's not above playing games, though,' she said. 'He likes to say he's changing his will every now and then. He likes to get them all running around. I think it makes him feel powerful.'

'Maybe he will change it one day.'

'Oh, I shouldn't think so,' said Lisa. 'It's always gone to the eldest son, down three generations. You wouldn't get away with that in my family, I'm telling you! We're three girls and a boy, though. My dad wouldn't dare. We've got a female advantage.'

Lisa was flinging things in plastic bags as the cashier slid them along. She spoke so carelessly that I didn't entirely believe her.

'As I say, it's Caris that really wants it,' she said. 'Me and Adam aren't really bothered one way or the other. It's sad, isn't it, the way things work out?'

'Maybe you'll give it to her,' I said.

'We can't do that!' shrieked Lisa jovially. 'Anyway, we're more likely to sell it and maybe give her a share of the proceeds. I can't really see myself living up there, can you, miles from anywhere, with all those sheep and no proper driveway – I'd go crackers. Once,' she said, lowering her voice, 'Adam and I had to stay the night up there and we were woken up by this noise in our room, and do you know what it was? A bat! Don't you think that's disgusting? I can cope with wasps and even mice at a pinch – but bats!'

In the afternoon I tried to persuade Hamish to come with me again down to the harbour.

'Hamish, shall we go and see the boats again?'

Hamish said something that sounded like 'nofuck'.

'Shall we go down to the harbour?'

'Nofuck.'

'What are you saying?'

'No. Not not. No.'

'We can look at the boats and find some nets,' I said, wheedlingly.

Hamish was sitting cross-legged on the carpet in the sitting room. He kept turning his head away from me, like someone distracted at a party.

'He's all right if you want to leave him here,' called Lisa from the kitchen. 'There's the Teletubbies about to come on.'

'I'll take you down on the rocks and we can find some seaweed and pebbles and things,' I said. 'Then we can make some pictures like the ones mummy used to make when she was little, and wait for the waves to come and wash them away.'

Rebecca had two ways of talking about the world of her childhood. One of them was as a place where everything was wrong. The other was as a place where everything was right.

'Tick crot,' said Hamish, turning his head away from me in a manner I was beginning to find infuriating. 'Ya ya ya.'

I realised that it was one of the features of our unpre-
dictable family life that Hamish generally chose not to be
refractory. He had been stubborn only in his refusal to speak,
which now that I thought about it was almost the only area of
his existence that fell entirely within his control.

'Stop talking nonsense,' I said crossly. 'Come on, let's go.'

I held out my hand but he disdained it like a duchess, with
his nose in the air, so I grabbed his arm and tried to yank him
to his feet. So solid was his resistance that he appeared will-
ing to allow his arm to be torn from his body rather than
move. He wanted no part of my scheme, to leave this warm
room and go out there in the grey day, with the cold, tea-
coloured sea brimming at the harbour wall, and the cars and
the boats and the people and the wind, all nagging like things
heard in sleep, pricking the unconscious and dragging it into
wakefulness. I, too, began to doubt that it would be entirely
pleasant, and like a little blade my doubt nicked my anger
and it all came running out, hot and bilious. I would go on my
walk, I would! And Hamish would accompany me, if only for
the reason that there was no one on earth except him whom I
could compel to do anything! I tried to wrestle him to his feet
and discovered that it was much more difficult than wrestling
him *off* his feet. He kicked me and started batting at me with
his hands. I picked up his squirming, vigorous body and
started walking with it towards the door. He roared in my
ear. I felt the hot, wet spurt of his tears on my cheek. Holding
him I experienced, suddenly, a longing for the time when he
was a baby and I used to walk him up and down the creaking
floorboards at Nimrod Street, holding him upright just as I
was now, with his hot face buried in my neck and shoulder.
He, too, seemed to recall those uncomplicated interludes, for
as I walked with him towards the door he ceased to struggle
and his body adhered to mine, grasping me as though with
tentacles of ferocious need. His face, though bigger than it
was, still fitted in my neck and shoulder. In Lisa and Adam's
well-carpeted hall I walked him about while he sobbed. It

seemed truly a pity to me that he'd had to get so big, and yet retain the naked ability to feel. In the end I had to go back into the sitting room and sit down with him plastered over my front, while Lisa tiptoed reverently around us. After a while I looked down and saw that he had passed silently into sleep. His big, beaky face lay abandoned an inch or two from mine. I looked for a while through the rectangular window at the motionless vista of the garden and then my gaze contracted to the beige walls, so that in the silence I was conscious of nothing but the hot body that lay on my chest; and my consciousness of it grew labyrinthine, interior, until I became lost in the red folds of physical proximity and wandered about, asleep, in the drama there.

When I awoke the room was dim and full of shadow, as though it were being stealthily colonised by the natural forces of neglect. A long slice of light showed around the edge of the kitchen door. Behind it I could hear voices. There was a smell of cooking and the clattering of pots and pans. I heard Adam say:

'Don't put the garlic in now. It'll burn.'

Janie said, 'I hate garlic. I won't eat it if it's got garlic.'

'Shall I not put it in then?' said Lisa.

'Yes, in a minute.'

'No!' wailed Janie. 'Don't!'

'Is there any point putting it in if she's not going to eat it?'

'She's not the only pebble on the beach. You're not the only pebble on the beach, young lady.'

'But hon,' said Lisa, 'think about it, it's only one tiny thing. You probably won't even notice the difference.'

'Neither will she then.'

Hamish stirred on my chest and sat up. There was something seismic in our parting, like the crusty parting of the surface of the earth when the underlying plates force themselves violently upwards.

'Anyway, didn't she eat earlier?'

'No, I thought she could eat with us tonight.'

'What are those green things? I don't like those green things.'

'You see?'

'Those are peppers. They're just peppers.'

Hamish looked around the shadowy room silently, as though trying to remember where he was.

'– the spicy kind. The green kind. They're there to make it look pretty.'

'Once you let her get the idea that it's up to her –'

'I don't like them.'

'You've never tried them, Janie. Have you ever tried them?'

'No, because I don't like them.'

'They don't actually taste of anything,' said Lisa.

There was a clattering sound.

'– tell her that. Why are you telling her that?'

'I'm just saying that they aren't actually offensive.'

The room was filling with a blue, underwater light. It was like a reflection, a displacement: it seemed to have rolled in off the placid, darkening sea that lay out of sight nearby. Adam told me that the land these houses were built on had once lain under water. Hamish and I were sitting below sea level. The headlights of a passing car fled in a brilliant arc up the walls and across the ceiling, illuminating the empty pieces of furniture.

'Look,' said Lisa, 'I'll take the peppers out of yours, all right?'

'That's completely ridiculous.'

'All right?'

'Oh, for heaven's sake don't start crying.'

Mewling sounds came from behind the closed door. Hamish turned his head towards it.

'Oh, honey, what's the matter?'

'Nothing's the matter,' I heard Adam say.

'What is it, sweetheart?'

'I don't like peppers!' wailed Janie.

'Look, she just said she was going to take yours out!' said Adam. 'It's completely ridiculous.'

'I don't like them!'

'Why don't you just give her something else? What's the point of wasting good food on her? It's completely ridiculous.'

'You're repeating yourself.'

'Your mother isn't a slave, you know! She's got better things to do than cook three separate meals every evening!'

'People are allowed not to like things,' said Lisa.

'I don't like peppers!' wailed Janie.

'I know you don't. Mummy'll take them out.'

'But I want something else! I don't want that – I want something else!'

Hamish got off my lap and set off into the gloom. Presently I saw his shape passing in front of the large window.

'But you said!' said Janie.

'Nobody said.'

'They did!'

'No they didn't!'

'Look, it's nothing. I'll just do something else quickly. I'll do some fish fingers. It won't take a minute.'

'You're giving in to her.'

'I had fish fingers for lunch.'

'I'm not giving in! I just happen to think it's cruel to force children to eat things that disgust them.'

'We had fish fingers at school for lunch.'

'Well, in that case she should eat earlier. She should eat with the baby. It isn't disgusting, you know, just because you don't like it. Adults don't eat disgusting things. Why would I eat something if it was disgusting?'

'You don't like tomatoes. Nobody forces you to eat tomatoes, do they?'

'I do like tomatoes.'

'I hate tomatoes,' said Janie.

Their voices seemed to agitate the surface of a torpor at whose bottom I lay, untouched, like some sunken object that had slipped out of the bounds of light and fallen far beneath the reach of a commotion now both meaningless and mysterious. I wondered where Rebecca was, and the thought of her paid out above me, winding and waving upwards through the blue light until I could see its end, far short of any grasp. If she came to look for me, I thought, she would never find me.

I heard Lisa say:

'That's a lie.'

'What?'

'I said that's a lie. You're lying. You don't like tomatoes.'

Adam said: 'I can't believe you'd accuse me of lying.'

He appeared to wish to confer on this accusation more seriousness than the dislike of tomatoes alone could sustain.

'I'm just stating the facts.'

'There aren't any facts. I know what I like and what I don't like.'

'When I don't like something,' said Janie, 'I put it in my pocket.'

'What, food? You put food in your pocket?'

'I take it out later and throw it into the bin.'

'You put it in your pocket?'

'When I don't like something I do. Like stew – it's got all those bits in it.'

'You put that in your pocket?'

Hamish bumped into the darkened television set. It rocked on its stand and he cried out in alarm as a cascade of videos fell to the floor. Immediately the kitchen door opened. Hamish stood as though naked in the new path of light, his face petrified.

'Oops-a-daisy!' cried Lisa, before I could speak.

She trod swiftly over the carpet and gathered Hamish into her arms, and without a glance in my direction she carried him into the kitchen.

At ten o'clock, as I did the night before, I phoned Rebecca before it could be established, definitively, that she was not going to phone me.

129

'I just got in,' she said. 'I just walked through the door.'

This, at least, was ambiguous: she might have been accusing me of pestering her, or she might equally have been mentioning her absence as the excuse for not having called earlier. There was a third possibility, which was that she meant to convey both things, irritation and guilt, at once. I envisaged these three interpretations as a sort of diagram, like a drawing of the chambers of the heart. In such drawings there were always little arrows to clarify the direction of flow, in through the blue veins and out through the red. Then there was the heart itself, which in spite of its centrality to all those veins, in spite of the appearance it gave of turning bad blood to good, was remarkable only for the intricacy with which it maintained separation between them. In those neat little chambers the blue and the red dwelt side by side, not mingling but merely proximate. It was the closest possible arrangement, like marriage, for contradictory traffic.

I distinctly remembered that when Rebecca and I first began our relationship we were possessed by the need to maintain spotlessness in our dealings with one another. As soon as a smear or mark appeared we cleaned it up, and although it was usually clear which one of us had, by error or accident, put it there, there was no sequel of recrimination or blame, merely the mutual desire to reinstate order. We were like two people running their separate businesses out of shared premises. I don't know precisely when this decorous era ended, but by a certain point our modest, hopeful square footage had been abandoned for a different, more sprawling joint enterprise. I remembered that when Hamish was a very small baby Rebecca became distraught with him one afternoon, actually angry, and I was surprised that after six weeks she thought she knew him well enough to carry on like that. It suggested to me that her good conduct at the same stage in our own relationship was the result of a great and uncharacteristic exercise of self-restraint, an exercise that could be considered somewhat fraudulent, given that as far as I knew it was repeated nowhere else in her history. Rick and Ali were always pleased to fill me in on the parts of that history that predated my arrival. It sometimes occurred to me that Rebecca had seen in me the possibility for reform, if not outright escape from herself; that she saw me as some new, prosperous, unhistoried country, like Australia, to which she could emigrate and forget her problems. She discussed those problems with me, which mainly had to do with her childhood and her family, and owing to my inability to solve them, or perhaps merely to hear and respond to them correctly I soon superseded them and became the problem myself; leaving her, I suppose, with strong but muddled feelings of what appeared to be homesickness for the original problems, compounded by the sense that in allying herself with me she had effected some sort of betrayal of the things she loved. The real problem, in the end, seemed to be that I wasn't related to her. If I had been her cousin, or even some old family friend, she would not have suffered so from divided loyalties, nor found herself to be carrying the disease of my difference from her, my innate hostility to the organism that was her life. That was as close as I could come to solving the problem – or rather diagnosing it, for there was of course no actual cure for this particular difficulty.

'Where have you been?' I said. I said it with lively curiosity rather than accusatory grimness, but there was only so much camouflage the words themselves would accept.

'At mum and dad's,' she replied, somewhat stonily. She didn't say anything else. Again I had the sense of two unambiguous meanings combined to make a force of highly systematised confusion. This time it appeared to me as the coloured tubes of copper filament, one live, one neutral, that lie side by side in the white plastic vein of an electric flex. Either she had gone to her parents as a place of refuge from me; or she had gone there and been made unhappy by them. Or both: her refusal to elaborate left the question charged.

'Did they give you something to eat?' I said.

'Oh, I don't know,' she replied. 'They were just in a complete state.'

'What about?'

There was a second of tinny silence.

'Mum found a lump on her breast. Or rather, dad found it, as he kept telling everyone. I'm sure it'll turn out to be nothing.'

'When was this?'

There was another pause. I heard Rebecca take a drink of something and swallow.

'This morning. They went down to the hospital and had some tests done on it.'

'When will they get the results?'

'I don't know. A few days, I think. I'm sure it will be nothing.'

'I'm really sorry,' I said.

'I'm sure it will be nothing,' said Rebecca again. 'Anyway, they've gone completely wild over it. They've really gone for the amateur dramatics. There's no, you know, let's wait and see what the test says. Dad won't let her out of his sight – he even followed her to the toilet and stood there talking to her through the door. They sat there all evening holding hands as though mum had just been told she'd got a week to live. What's really annoying,' she continued, 'is that dad's already wanting to scale things down at the gallery so that he can look after her. He's even saying he wants to cancel Niven's show.'

'That's a shame,' I said.

'I told him, you know, wait until we've actually got a diagnosis before you start cancelling things! Whatever happened to, you know, positive visualisation?'

'I'm sure it won't come to that.'

'Oh, they're still in the dramatic phase, you know, big statements, big gestures, the whole roadshow. But that's exactly when they can decide to make an example of someone. It's right when they're in the middle of an emotional trip that they suddenly need something to bite on, you know, just to show that they're not all talk. What I hate,' she continued, 'is the fact that they think their world is more real than anyone else's. I know we all think that in a way, but with them it's all *about* other people. It's in being witnessed that their life becomes real for them. Have you ever noticed,' she said, 'how they're always losing friends and making new ones? Everywhere they go they find more people. You turn your back for a second and they've collared someone else and started telling them about their sex life. Then when they've done that they tell them about *your* sex life. Then eventually everyone gets into the habit of this frankness thing and they all start to behave badly, and then they fall out. People like that shouldn't have children. All they want children for is so that they can have more material, more life, more things to talk about, more actors in their pathetic domestic drama –'

'I think you're being a little hard on them.'

'It's no wonder that none of us have had children of our own,' said Rebecca. 'We know what they'll be made into – victims, food for the predators!'

'Except you, of course,' I said.

'What's that?'

'You. You've had a child.'

Rebecca gave a strange little laugh.

'I was thinking about something else,' she said vaguely. 'Anyway, they're sort of down on Niven at the moment.'

'Why?'

'Oh, I don't know, something to do with dad giving him money to get something for him and him not getting it and not giving dad the money back. It was grass, I bet. They make a big point of never mentioning drugs in front of me. They think it atones for something.'

I said nothing. I steadily extended my silence forwards like a hydraulic arm with which I intended to push Rebecca over the precipice of enquiry.

'How are you, anyway?' she finally said.

Now that she'd asked, I found that I didn't want to tell her anything about myself. I found myself thinking about Ali's lump, identifying with it almost, with the lump itself. Wrongly, I suppose, I attributed to it qualities of vulnerability that I felt myself in that moment to share. I realised presently that it was the prospect of its excision that caused me to feel this.

'I miss you,' said Rebecca.

Still I did not speak. A little surge of adrenalin caused my heart to thump. This did not signify excitement exactly, more a feeling of fear. I did not in that instant make a native connection between Rebecca's missing me and the possibility of mercy or benevolence or love. It seemed, rather, to hint at the possibility of violence.

'Though I think it's good,' she continued, 'for us to be apart.'

'Do you?'

'Oh, absolutely,' she said. 'It was what you always used to say, that the loosest ties are the strongest.'

'I never said that.'

'You've always said,' reiterated Rebecca, 'that we should lead more separate lives. I can hear you saying it now.'

'I didn't mean that we shouldn't see each other.'

'Letting go has been the hardest thing for me.'

'I never said anything about letting go! I only meant that we shouldn't hold each other responsible for all our problems.'

'I've been very angry with you, Michael, *really* angry, but I've adored you too. Never forget that. And you're also the father of my child. You always will be.'

'I only meant that there's a limit to how much you can relate to another person. Beyond a certain point it just becomes chaos – chaos!'

I found that my skin had drawn very tight around the top of my head. This was an effect Rebecca could have on me.

'You're afraid of passion, Michael. You're afraid of blood on the floor. But the thing is, I've always been a very passionate person and if you won't allow me to express it then you know I'll just turn on you. I'll turn on you.'

In a way, I admired her for this kind of talk. Even when I'd listened, agonised, to her regaling that terrified boy with it in the pub, I felt too a sort of anarchic thrill at her lack of shame. To me, these fits of self-description were the closest she came to a creative act. It was herself she was creating, yet I felt sure that her state while she did it was not so distant from that which she yearned to attain, in which she would find herself enabled to make something that could actually stand apart from her.

'All my life,' she was saying now, 'all my life I've been looking for something straight and fixed, something dependable, something I could pour myself into that would hold me.'

I guessed she was going to say that I was that thing.

'And you were it, Michael. You were that vessel. You said to me, come on, I'll hold you. I'll contain you. I'll give you routine and stability. I'll give you a home, I'll give you a baby if you want one. But don't think that you can grow. Don't think that you can move, or change. Because if you do I'll crack. My nice strong walls can't take pressure from the inside. I'll crack and I'll break and in the end I'll shatter.'

'*You* will?' I said, confused.

'You – you! I think maybe you needed to be broken. I think maybe that's why you chose me.'

'I thought you chose me. I thought I was the vessel and you were the –'

I couldn't remember what she was. It had started out as some kind of fast-setting liquid, and ended up as an exuberant house plant.

'You could have found some nice girl. Some nice, predictable girl.'

'Why do you keep saying things like that?' I shouted. 'You're the only thing that makes me predictable, because somebody has to be!'

'You don't know how hard it is for me,' she said presently, in a trembling voice, 'to stand on my own.'

'I'm not asking you to stand on your own.'

'You are. You just don't see it yet.'

'I think I'd see it if I were asking it.'

My mouth felt as though it were stuffed with something dry, like bread.

'We're married,' I said finally. 'Doesn't that mean anything to you? For all their faults, at least your parents stay together.'

'That isn't a marriage,' said Rebecca. 'That's a mutual dependency.'

'Of course it seems like that to you! At least they touch each other!' I said. It seemed I was shouting again. 'You'd have to have a lump on your breast the size of a football for me to stand any chance of even noticing it!'

I went to bed and lay listening to the sound of Hamish rustling in his sleeping bag. I lay awake for so long in the airless, featureless spare room that I began to feel like something in a specimen case, being lightly tormented where I lay pinned behind glass by the sounds my son made, which summoned me constantly to awareness and to the state that precedes activity. I felt that if only I could hear or smell the sea this sensation would pass. I felt I could be comforted by the existence of something animate but impartial. In this place of fences such intrusions were apparently considered hazardous. It occurred to me that Doniford had succumbed to a sort of partitioning, a spoliation, out of its inability to adhere to its true nature. Like me, it had admitted ugliness because ugliness asked to be admitted.

SEVEN

'Where are the women?' Paul Hanbury wanted to know, when Adam, Hamish and I opened the door to his room. 'Stand aside – let me see! Where are they? Where are my bloody women? Three days I've been in this bloody room and not one of them has come to see me!'

In its spacious sparseness and beige diffidence, the room was more like a room in a hotel than a hospital. Paul Hanbury lay on the grand, plinth-like bed at its centre. He wore a white smock and looked very small and tyrannical, like a child emperor. I would have recognised him by his voice alone, yet it was hard now to believe that it had emanated from him – it travelled around the room in great rings of sound that dwarfed his body. He had never been large, but lying in that bed he looked wizened – except for his head, which retained its distinctive scale and grandeur, and which he barely moved when he spoke, so that in spite of everything he had the poised appearance of a statesman, or an actor. His hair rolled back from his forehead in thick, steel-grey waves and his face had darkened and deepened into creases since the last time I saw him, especially around his eyes, which were small and black and glittered like buttons. He opened his large, well-shaped mouth wide in order to talk, revealing straight, strong, even yellow teeth and the resilient, plump pad of his tongue.

'That's not true, dad,' said Adam. 'Vivian came last night.'

'She did not – not a soul has come since you showed your face here yesterday! And before that there was only that poseur David, who came with some bloody stupid periodical and wouldn't sit down in case he creased his trousers, and apart from that there's been nobody.'

137

'I don't understand,' said Adam.

'Where's it gone? It's called the *Wankers' Review* – or the *Wallies' Review*. Where the hell is it? Ah yes, here we go – the *Wolsey Review*. "Solitary Sex: A Cultural History of Masturbation". I think that's David's idea of a joke. D'you see what they've done to my dong? They've gift-wrapped it, do you see?' He folded back his covers to reveal part of a hooped wire contraption that stood in an ominous arch over his hips, and then drew them quickly up again before it could be established what was underneath. 'And what else is there – "Mary Wollstonecraft and the Feminist Imagination"! I think I'll save that for Vivian, if she ever comes.'

Beside me Hamish made his bell noise. It sounded particularly loud in the well-insulated room.

'What's that?' said Paul amusedly, looking around. 'School's out?'

'Vivian definitely said she was coming in last night,' said Adam. 'I don't understand why she didn't say something this morning.'

'Michael! Come over here where I can see you.' This was bellowed as though from a great distance, although I was standing six feet from the bed and the room was full of daylight. 'Is this fellow yours?'

'Yes.'

'He's a funny little bugger, isn't he? What's his name?'

'Hamish.'

'Put him up on the bed, will you? Put him here, next to me, if he'll come. Has he got a mother?'

'Rebecca. My wife.'

'Well, I hope he doesn't get his looks from her. How does life treat you, Michael? With its gloves off, judging by the bags under your eyes.'

'I'm very well.'

'If you say so. Where are you living? Have you got some nice place in the country where your boy can stretch his legs?'

'We live in Bath.'

'Ah, Bath. I always liked the idea of Bath. The reality never quite lived up to it, though. I'd take the women there and you wouldn't see them for dust. They'd be off and into the shops like rats up a drainpipe. And how do you earn your crust in Bath?'

'I work for a charity.'

'Of course you do. Paying your debt to society – I'm glad somebody is! And you're taking some leave – or rather, you're down here for a week's babysitting while the missus exercises her feminist imagination. I wouldn't leave a woman alone in Bath for a day, let alone a week, but I suppose she's acclimatised. Or is she the enigmatic type as well?'

Hamish seemed happy enough sitting on the plush bed, but I was worried that he might knock the wire hoop. It would be very painful, I imagined, if he did. I furtively grasped the back of Hamish's shirt.

'Caris is here,' said Adam.

'Not as far as I can see she bloody well isn't,' said Paul.

'She came down yesterday on the train.'

'Well, don't leave her alone in the house. She'll have packed everything up and sent it to the Donkey Sanctuary or the IRA or whoever the hell else she's feeling sorry for this week. Have you seen Caris?' he asked me.

'Yes.'

'Nuts, isn't she?' he said delightedly. 'She's getting fat, too. Her mother never got fat, but then she never had to. All she had to do was sit on her little arse in Doniford reading magazines and drinking diet milkshakes until they came out of her ears. But Caris won't have anything to do with all that – her mother shoved it down her throat and now she won't have anything to do with it. And more's the pity,' he continued, settling back into his pillows, 'because she was a good-looking girl, a fine-looking girl. Her mother competed with her, that was the problem. She could be very cold. Caris got the idea that it didn't do to be so pretty. Of course, she'll tell you it's all my fault,' he concluded cheerfully, with his arms folded behind his head. 'Women stick together in the end – ask Mary Wollstonecraft.'

'I've been up at the farm with Adam,' I said, by way of a diversion.

'Oh you have, have you?' He looked slightly discomfited, as though I had revealed myself to be untrustworthy. 'What are you doing up there?'

'We're lambing, dad,' said Adam, loudly.

'All right, all right,' said Paul irritably, flapping his hand. 'I'm not some old fart in a home – I just didn't know what he meant, that's all. So you've been up at Egypt, have you? What do you think of the place? Marvellous, isn't it? I always say that as the rest of the world gets worse, Egypt gets better. The principal of entropy does not apply. You've no idea, the torture it is to me to be in here, with spring coming on to the hill and everything waking up. I tell you, I can hear the grass growing! I only hope this isn't what death is like, you know, an empty box and a view of the car park. I should have gone to a normal hospital,' he said petulantly. 'I'd have been far happier on a ward, with a fat black lady taking my temperature.'

'You didn't want to go on a ward!' protested Adam. 'You *wanted* to come here.'

'Thought I'd never come out of one of those places alive, didn't I?' muttered Paul. 'Now I don't know which is worse, dying with the riffraff or living alone in this hell. Besides, I thought the nurses would be better looking. The nurses are absolute dogs,' he said, to me. 'They send them to me specially. I'm not allowed to be stimulated.'

I made to remove Hamish from the bed but Paul shot out a hand from behind his head and gripped his arm with it.

'Oh, leave him be,' he said. 'I like the feel of a warm boy next to me.' He cackled delightedly at himself.

'I don't want him to hurt you.'

'You mean you don't want him hearing my filth – are you another of these protective parents? None of them will let me lay a hand on their babies, you know. I think Laura hoses hers down with antiseptic after they've been at Egypt. As for the new one, I have to request audiences with her, like Vivian did with the Pope. And she's a Hanbury – my own flesh and blood!'

'I didn't know Vivian had seen the Pope,' said Adam, from the bathroom, where he had gone to fill his father's water jug.

'That's because she hasn't,' called Paul. 'He wouldn't have her. The Pontiff turned her down.'

Adam laughed. 'Did he?'

'He took the view,' said Paul, 'that dissolving Vivian's marriage would be like dissolving a set of functioning molars. I think he's a very sensible chap. You can't go saying a marriage didn't happen when there are two strapping children to show that it did. So he stood her up. She went all the way to Rome and he stood her up. At least, that's where she said she was. She could have been anywhere. She was probably getting pissed on sangria with that hippy friend of hers and her dago shopkeeper husband. Now that I come to think of it, she did come back with her tan. Do you know Vivian's tan?' he asked me. 'It's very amusing. She looks like she's been embalmed in salad dressing.'

'Dad, do you want me to turn up the pump?' said Adam. 'The dial's set lower than it was yesterday.'

'The funny thing,' said Paul, to me, 'is that after His Holiness rebuffed her she kept going back for punishment. To *Mass*.' He pronounced it to rhyme with 'arse.' 'And because she'd had the gumption finally to leave her miserable drunk husband she wasn't allowed to take the holy Host. She was considered to be excommunicated. For some reason she didn't know she was, though. One day she was standing in the queue and when she got to the priest and stuck her tongue out he wouldn't give it to her. He popped his wafer right back in the bowl and put his hand over it, as though she might steal one! Some interfering old bitch had told him that Vivian was excommunicado. So after that she went along and sat at the back and when everyone else got up to join the queue she stayed where she was and pretended to read the hymn-book. I said to her, how can you bloody let them do that to you! How can you let them win, do you see? I'll bet they loved seeing her sitting there all contrite, while they were busy rogering the altar-boys – leave that bloody thing alone!' he said to Adam, who was scrutinising a plastic valve from which a pale tube led to the hard delta of veins in Paul Hanbury's brown, hairy wrist.

'It's just that it seems very low.'

'I don't want that bloody stuff in my veins!'

'Dad,' said Adam heavily, 'all you're doing is subjecting your body to unnecessary pain.'

'I wouldn't walk around with a blindfold on either.'

'There's nothing vital about pain.'

'What do you mean! How will I know what's happened to me if I don't feel it? Answer me that! That's how you walk over a cliff in life! You can't go around numbing yourself and sedating yourself against half the things that happen to you and expect to get any sensation from the other half – that's what it means, to do things by halves! Do you know,' he said, to me, 'I've been going to the dentist in Doniford all my life and I've never had an anaesthetic. While this big fellow –' he pointed to Adam '– has to be unconscious before he'll let them so much as clean between his teeth.'

'I think you'll find, dad, that most people have an anaes-thetic when they go to the dentist.'

'What do I care what most people do? Most people live lives of such surpassing inanity I don't know why they both-er! Most people want to sit in their little red-brick boxes on their little estates watching television, or drive around going nowhere in their cars, or stuff their faces with junk, or go shopping – and I'm not saying that's any worse than what people have always wanted to do. The difference is that now they've got everything laid on for them. The world's been wrecked, laying on their houses and their cars and their

142

cheap holidays and their cheap food – and a hundred years ago, most of them would have been pushing a plough with not a thought in their heads, and be none the worse off for it!'

Through the great pale window the distant skeletons of trees were faintly picked out against a wad of sky. The hospital was half an hour's drive from Doniford, I didn't know exactly where, just that we had driven directly away from the coast and the green hills and become gradually mired in a flat, grey, nondescript landscape cluttered with buildings and petrol stations, and street lamps with nothing human to light, and warehouses behind wire fences. This clutter was not, it appeared, to amount to anything so definite as a town: like a tundra, its formlessness was its single geographical feature. The hospital was a low red-brick building that stood like an island in the sea of its car park. Inside, in the foyer, it blazed with light and with wood-veneered surfaces. The foyer was carpeted, as was the lift. The woman at the reception desk wore a tailored black suit and high heels and the nurses wore vague white uniforms, so that the whole place had an atmosphere of discretion that bordered on secrecy, as though the question of sickness were inadmissible; as though, were a drama ever to unfold here, it would manifest itself in the spectacle not of disease but of celebration of life itself.

'We were at mum's yesterday,' said Adam.

Paul assumed a peevish expression. 'Yes, David says she's got the hump about something. I suppose I've said something I shouldn't have, have I? Is that it?'

'She'd better tell you about it herself,' said Adam.

'The first Mrs Hanbury,' said Paul, to me, 'is a very sensitive creature where her own thin skin is concerned. She's like the princess who can feel the pea through twenty mattresses – I believe she considers it to be the mark of good breeding. She's what they call "high maintenance". So's the second, now that I come to think of it, though in a different way. The second gets the blues. Vivian's blues are like those fogs you get in Scotland that last for two weeks. They sort of envelop you and quietly soak you to the skin.'

'I don't understand why Vivian didn't come in,' said Adam, for the third or fourth time. He was still holding the plastic valve in his hand. He had something of the butler about him, the castrated quality of a male given over to a life of service. He seemed to me just then to be completely without what I could only describe as poetry, or heroism; to lack, in any case, the promise or the threat of unpredictability.

'I tell you, she's got the blues. The first Mrs Hanbury's got the hump and the second's got the blues. What's your woman like, Michael? Is she cheerful? I hope for your sake that she is.'

'Sometimes she is.'

'What does she make of that fur on your face? Does she like it?'

'She doesn't mind it,' I said, although the truth was that Rebecca's attitude to my beard was entirely ambivalent, and for that reason I maintained it, partly as a sort of doorstop to prevent our relationship swinging shut. For some reason, I felt that as long as I kept this semicircle of dark hair on my face I could never be said to have succumbed: I could not be negated, by love nor by hate.

'Only doesn't mind?' he said. 'I'd have thought she'd be one way or the other, if the women I know are anything to go by. The women I know like to take a definite position. As a military tactic it doesn't work, that's what I'm always telling them. If you take a position you're open to attack. You're better off keeping on the move. I always wondered whether women liked a beard,' he said, consideringly. 'But I could never get mine to grow. Does it increase sensation? Does she tell you that?'

I smiled in what I hoped was a mysterious fashion.

'Oh, I see. That's how it is. That's how it is, is it?' Paul looked around the featureless room impatiently. 'Well, someone's got to humour a sick old man – where's Lisa? Why hasn't she been in to see me?'

144

'She doesn't want to bring Isobel into the hospital,' said Adam.

'Why, does she think it's catching, cancer of the dong? You see what I mean about protective parents,' he said, to me again. 'Have you been to their house? You have to take your shoes off before they'll let you in. I feel like a horse with nothing on its hooves when I'm there. And my socks are always squiffy. That's why Audrey won't go there, you know. Her stiletto heels were soldered to her feet at birth. She'd go up in a puff of smoke if she ever took them off. Have you met Lisa? She's a good girl really. She's rather a solid girl. Very house-proud, isn't she, Adam? Her father sells bathtubs.'

'Jacuzzis,' said Adam. 'Don't pretend you've never been in a jacuzzi, dad.'

'The first Mrs Hanbury was fond of that sort of thing. I couldn't stand it – it was like being boiled alive. And on the subject of hygiene, they're an absolute breeding ground for germs – all sorts of people pile into them, you know, all together. You try to stretch your legs out and you find you're playing footsie with the hairy calves of some overweight middle manager. Still, we've all got to earn our living, I suppose. Adam says he does rather well out of it. The problem is, you never know when that sort of craze will pass, do you? He might find himself out on his ear in a year or two, when people find some other way to waste their time and money. Do you see what I mean? It's not like a farm, is it? You can never say, this is my patch of the earth, my place. This is where I have my being. You can't say that about a bloody bathtub, can you?'

'They've got a perfectly good patch of the earth,' said Adam. 'They own an eight-bedroom house in Northumberland with twenty acres of land.'

'But it's all in hock to the bathtubs! If the bathtubs go, so does the land!'

'That's how life is, dad. That's how life is for most people. We're not all as lucky as you.'

'Luck has nothing to do with it,' said Paul. 'The best luck I've had is to be given the good sense not to meddle with what I have. I could have ruined it in a million different ways – look at Don Brice! Look at Si Higham, driving around in that big jalopy with the white leather seats, pleased as punch with himself, and for what? For selling all his land to the highest bidder and turning Doniford into suburbia!'

Paul was becoming quite exercised – his wiry neck and chest were dark red where I could see around the collar of the white hospital garment. I picked up Hamish, who had sat beside him on the bed all this while virtually motionless, looking straight ahead with a superior expression on his face. This time Paul let me take him with an exasperated gesture.

'I don't see what's so wrong with that,' said Adam. 'He wasn't farming the land – he wasn't using it for anything. Anyway, where are people supposed to live?'

'If they've got nowhere to live then they shouldn't have been born.'

'It's a bit late for that,' said Adam calmly.

'You people,' said Paul, 'you people don't understand how to desire what is actually yours – you're always scheming, the lot of you! Always dissatisfied! Even that layabout Brendon, turning the lodge into a chicken farm when he thinks I'm not looking – a bunch of hangers-on, a pack of vultures is what you are!'

I carried Hamish to the window and together we looked down at the car park, with its symmetrical rows of shiny, unpersoned vehicles.

'No one's scheming, dad,' said Adam behind me. 'Brendon's doing the chickens as a way of being more financially independent, that's all. And Caris is never here – you can hardly call her a vulture.'

'I'll call her what I like,' said Paul morosely. 'She's been a great disappointment to me.'

'As for me, I'm just trying to help you. I've taken a week off work to do the lambs – even Michael is here to help you.'

'Why?' snapped Paul. 'Why haven't you got your own lives to lead? Michael, haven't you got a family of your own? Parents of your own?'

'Yes.'

'And where are they?'

'They live in Surrey.'

'What are they doing there?' said Paul, as though there were something outlandish about it.

'They're doctors,' I said.

'Doctors – are they really? Both of them?'

'Yes.'

'I suppose *they* don't need much help then. I suppose they're quite able to doctor on their own. Are they busy – out a lot? Don't have time for you?'

'Something like that,' I said.

'And all they'll be leaving you is their surgical instruments, I suppose, and the house in Surrey. Mind you, that could be worth something.'

'I don't expect them to leave me anything.'

'Well, they probably will, but you're a good boy anyway. The problem with my brood,' he said confidentially, 'is that they've come in to land a bit early. They all think I'm going to pop my clogs before I'm seventy – even Caris shelled out the money for the train fare as soon as she heard I was hospitalised.'

'Oh, for heaven's sake,' said Adam.

'She wouldn't miss it for the world! And nor would Brendon, if he could only work out how to get here. As for the eldest son, he hasn't let me out of his sight in years – the heir presumptive, if you know what I mean. Mind you, there's always the jacuzzi salesman to consider. They're bad for the heart, you know, those things. Eight bedrooms and twenty acres in Northumberland, don't forget. He could be taking his leave any day.'

In spite of myself, I laughed.

'Tell me what your mother's got the hump about, there's a good boy,' said Paul to Adam, who was putting his coat on.

147

'I'd rather she told you herself. I don't really understand what the problem is.'

'Well, she can't tell me if she doesn't come.'

'There's a phone beside the bed, dad.'

'I can't talk to her on the telephone. I never could – she uses it as an instrument of torture.'

'Something to do with money. She says she hasn't got her allowance. I didn't know what she was talking about.'

Paul was silent. He held his head up in a soldierly fashion, as though bravely contemplating some doom-laden enterprise.

'Tell Vivian to come in, will you?' he said presently. 'Tell the old girl to come in. Tell her I'm not too good. Put her in the car and bring her yourself if you have to. Will you do that for me?'

'All right,' said Adam. 'She said she was coming anyway. She'll probably be here before I even get a chance to speak to her.'

'I don't expect she will. Just do as I ask. Get the old girl in here where I can see her.'

'It'll probably be tomorrow rather than today.'

'Make it as soon as you can, there's a good boy,' said Paul. 'Has the consultant been in yet?'

'What? Oh, yes.'

'What did he say?'

'He was an Asian fellow,' said Paul. 'Knew his stuff, though, I'll say that for him,' he added. 'He said he came from Kerala in the south of India – a beautiful place apparently, he told me all about it, white buildings and trees, hot as hell. The Christians colonised it in the fifteenth century. Now he's living in a suburb of Taunton. I said to him, if you know what beauty is, how can you stand to live without it? And he said, "Beauty is secondary, Mr Hanbury."' Paul put on an accent to relay the consultant's sentiments. 'I said to him, don't they need consultants in Kerala? Yes, he said, they do. So I said, well, tell me why you're here then. He looked a little taken aback, you know, a little superior. Then he started yakking on about skills and training and equipment, and suddenly I thought, here it is again! Selfishness! Greed! So I said, admit it, you're here because they pay you more. And he admitted that he was!'

Paul gave a bark of laughter and sat back against his pillows with his arms folded. His expression was morbid.

'When did he say you could come home?' said Adam.

'Monday. Tell Vivian that too. Tell her not to bring out the fatted calf. Tell her I'm on a hospital diet. Have you experienced Vivian's cooking?' he asked me. 'Awful, isn't it? The first Mrs Hanbury wasn't bad, but she never ate the things she cooked, which used to make you wonder what she'd put in it.'

'I'll be back tomorrow,' said Adam.

'Don't forget, will you? You've got to bring Vivian in. Actually in, do you hear?'

'Goodbye, Paul,' I said.

I held out my hand and Paul grabbed it and pulled me nearly on to his chest. Hamish, whom I was holding, clung to my neck as we went over and Paul put his arms around my neck too, so that I lay across the bed like a fallen tree being strangulated by vines.

'Kiss me,' said Paul gruffly, and I obeyed by kissing his leathery cheek. 'You're a good boy,' he said. He released my neck and gripped my face between the vice of his hands instead. 'It's rather soft, your fur,' he said. 'Do you put anything on it?'

'No,' I said, with difficulty.

'I never petted mine enough,' he said hotly, into my ear. 'You've got to pet them and stroke them every day, then they'll never give you any trouble. Every day, do you hear? The day you forget is the day they'll get it in their minds to turn against you!'

He released my head and turned to Hamish, who was regarding him close to with a certain alarmed curiosity. He ruffled Hamish's fair hair, before making an unexpected and not inaccurate attempt at Hamish's bell noise.

'Goodbye, fellow-me-lad,' he said, laughing loudly.

In the car on the way back to Doniford I kept turning around and talking nonsense to Hamish and tickling his toes as he liked them tickled, aware as I did so that I was harbouring a feeling of guilt about what suddenly seemed to me to be the unsatisfactory state of his circumstances. As we drew into The Meadows, a mild feeling of oppression settled over me. In the flat, late-afternoon light which cast no shadows, unstirred by wind or rain, there was something actually inhuman about the place. I noticed that several of the houses had caravans parked in their driveways, white and rounded, like the babies of the stolid, red-brick adults, as though the big dwelling had mechanistically spawned the small. The caravans were the only things here that were neither square nor triangular, though I supposed that if they stayed long enough they might become so. The houses stared dumbly out of their windows.

'What I like about this place,' said Adam, steering us with conspicuous smoothness around the tarmac, 'is the fact that it doesn't remind me of anything.'

'On the phone you described it as hilarious,' I observed.

'Well, it is, in a way,' he said. 'If you were going to be a snob about it.'

We passed a group of children in spotless tracksuits and baseball caps, who lifted their white faces to us as we went by.

'I'm not saying we're going to stay here for ever,' said Adam. 'But for now it actually suits us really well. At least it isn't pretentious. It doesn't pretend to be something it's not.'

I heard the voice of Lisa speaking through this remark.

'With some of the houses they're building now, they're trying to make them look as though they haven't just slapped them up. I think that's worse, in a way. Actually, the houses here have gone up fifteen, twenty per cent since we bought, and that's partly because you're not paying for some mock-Georgian porch over your front door, or a carport with a cupola. You're paying for the location and the outside space. There are houses in Doniford now that are twice the size of ours with half the garden. Lisa gets itchy feet sometimes,' he added presently.

'Does she?'

'She'd like more, you know, grandeur. But we're just going to have to wait. We'll have to wait and see what happens. This is a pretty solid investment.' We both contemplated the house, in whose driveway we were now parked. 'Tony's offered me a job,' Adam disclosed, with his face sideways to mine. 'Lisa's father. He's offered me a share in the business.'

'Are you going to take it?' I said, surprised.

'I don't know. Lisa's pretty keen. She'd like to be near her family. I can't quite see myself up north but in a way it's a fantastic opportunity. Tony's thinking of retiring. They've got a place in Portugal, you know, and they want to spend more time there. So I'd basically be running the show. It would mean giving up my practice, of course,' he said, 'though I don't feel particularly sentimental about that. It would be a relief, actually. I just did it for something to do until dad needed me to take over the farm. But that's all changed a bit.'

'What do you mean?'

'Well –' Adam rubbed his face with his hands sheepishly. 'I've been going through some of the accounts this week. I was just being nosy, actually. Dad's never really said any-thing specific about what the farm earns – there's just been, you know, this impression of money, but in fact he's been running it virtually at a loss. He makes five, six thousand a year, most of it from subsidies. It's incredible – I don't know quite how he's done it. The new barns alone cost a fortune, plus the tractor and all the new fencing. In fact, if he sold his whole herd he wouldn't begin to cover the cost. I suppose Vivian must have paid for them.'

151

We sat there in silence for a moment.

'Anyway, it did start me thinking, you know, about Egypt, about what it actually was. I mean, dad's always talked about it as a working farm, as something that had to be nurtured and worked at. Pretty much from the minute we could walk we had to be out there helping, with the sheep and the hay harvest and the fencing, and hearing him talking about it all day and night, and now I'm beginning to wonder whether it wasn't just a bit of a con. You know, whether he didn't use it as a way to control us. I mean, if it isn't a farm then what is it? It's just a nice house, that's all. A nice house.'

I tried to think of what the answer to his question might be.

'I don't understand why he didn't tell me!' cried Adam, thumping the steering wheel. 'All these years it's been, you know, when Adam takes over the farm, when I hand over the reins to Adam, Adam the son and heir – and in fact there's nothing to hand over! There's just Egypt, where he lives, and which he'll only leave, as he's fond of saying, in a wooden box. And I'm not waiting for that – it could take years! Even if I did get the house I couldn't afford to maintain it on what I get from the practice. I'd have to sell. It's worth more than a million pounds, you know. I got an off-the-record valuation from the agent in Doniford.' He looked askance at me. 'Incredible, isn't it?'

'Perhaps you should tell him that you've seen the accounts.'

'I don't think I can do that,' said Adam after a pause. 'I know dad. He'd cut me out completely. He'd leave everything to Brendon. Laughable as that may seem.'

Adam's front door opened and Lisa appeared, mouthing and beckoning frantically. Finally she picked her way in her bare feet across the gravel. The soft shapes of her breasts jiggled beneath her T-shirt.

'Caris is here,' she said discreetly through the window. 'She's been here absolutely ages. We're running out of things to talk about.'

She turned around and slowly picked her way back again.

Caris was sitting on Adam and Lisa's sofa with her legs curled up beside her and the baby on her lap. Immediately I felt a certain kinship with her, as I had the first time I met her all those years ago, when she had wound the impermanent ivy around herself for adornment. I guessed that she, like me, held back from definitively securing the territories of her existence. Sometimes, when I looked at the people I knew, I saw them as the generals of invisible armies, always advancing and expanding. Their lives seemed to bulk out around them like pyramidal structures by which they were lifted higher and higher until they became almost impossible to see, and when they spoke it was of the next campaign and the one after, so that they appeared peculiarly more burdened by the future than by the past.

'Hello, Michael,' she said. 'Still here?'

'Still here.'

'What is it you want from us?' she said jovially. 'What is it you're after?'

'Entertainment, I think. Or perhaps just distraction. I've forgotten which it was.'

'Michael's here to see Adam,' interposed Lisa, who looked slightly alarmed by this exchange. 'They're old friends from university.'

'I know Michael,' said Caris grandly. She looked large and rather unruly in the tidy, pale-coloured room. 'I know what's under that beard, that's how well I know him. Who's this?' she added, with a fluting note of suspicion in her voice, when she caught sight of Hamish. She looked around her, as though expecting someone to come and claim him, or at least to offer an explanation.

'My son. Hamish.'

'Your son? Well! I didn't know!'

I didn't see particularly why she should have known, but she seemed nonetheless slightly peeved at the fact of Hamish's existence.

'How old is he?' she asked, looking from him to me and back again.

'He's three.'

'Well!' she said again. 'Three years – so I was –' she did a mental calculation '– yes, I had just moved to London then.'

I wondered if she would explain the way in which these two events were related. Today she was wearing a sort of beatnik outfit, with a black beret pressed down over her coarse, springy hair and a frayed black leather jacket.

'You wouldn't have heard, then,' I said. 'Not in London.'

'I know you're teasing me, Michael,' she said, mock-reprovingly. 'But I like to get things in order. I like to see the whole picture. There's you over there –' she illustrated my position, which was on the left side of the sofa, with one hand '– and here's me over here –' the right side of the sofa '– and we're both travelling at the same speed on our separate roads.' She lifted her arms while the baby wobbled precariously on her lap and together we were slowly precipitated forwards over the edge of the seat.

'And the strange thing is,' she continued, enlightened, 'that exactly when you were increasing your estate I was shedding mine.'

'Were you?'

'I walked away from everything,' she said dramatically. 'I just walked away. My place, my relationship, even my family.' The last she uttered furtively, out of consideration I supposed. 'I left the money economy, and the sex economy, and the patriarchy of the home – it wasn't easy.'

'No, I don't suppose it was.'

'Are you being sarcastic, Michael? Because I know it's tempting to be. But I happen to regard sarcasm as a vice, a crutch. I had to hurt a lot of people to be free.' She stroked the baby's feathery hair with her hand. 'Some of them were innocent people. But I did it. And I don't regret it.'

'Free from what, exactly?'

'I was sick,' she said. 'It was as though my body were full

of poisons. But in fact it was full of lies and misconceptions, about who and what I was. A woman, hence secondary; a daughter, not a son; a sex object, a servant, a parasite. Someone who wasn't capable of seeing past the end of her pretty nose, let alone of doing any good in the world. But I'll tell you what, you're never safe, you're never really free from it – I haven't been back here in eighteen months and yet it's already started, the shame, the jealousy, the anger, the feelings of guilt.'

'You haven't left the money economy,' interposed Adam from the kitchen, where he had withdrawn with Lisa on some nebulous domestic business. 'You get money for those pots.'

'Yes,' said Caris, composedly, with her head held high, 'we do. We have rent and bills to pay, like everyone else. And necessities, and some luxuries too. We're a community, not a penitentiary. We're just a group of women who've chosen to live together and support one another and pool our talents in the hope of doing some good, whether at home or elsewhere.'

'I don't think I could live with lots of other women,' said Lisa, drawn from her sanctuary in the kitchen by the turn the conversation had taken. 'Don't you find you just fight all the time? I grew up with sisters and I'm telling you, we were awful. We were always nicking each others' things and having great screaming rows, and we were ever so competitive, you know. Everyone says it's men who are competitive, but I think women are much worse.'

'Can men join your community?' I asked.

Caris laughed. 'Why? Are you tempted?'

'I just wondered why freedom from society is something women can be seen to want but not men.'

'If you have men,' said Caris coolly, 'then you *are* society. We'd be deferring to them and offering to do their laundry inside a month.'

'Then you don't have a very high opinion of yourselves.'

Caris smiled. 'That's why we're there.'

'I don't understand what you're talking about,' said Lisa.

'Michael's saying that he thinks we ought to be able to be what we want to be in a world that includes men,' said Caris. 'Perhaps he thinks we're storing up unhappiness for ourselves.'

'I just don't think you can last,' I said.

'There's no reason why we should. Needing to hang on to things is part of the problem.'

'What about love? What about affection?'

'You see!' said Caris triumphantly. 'That's why we don't let in men – they'd be telling us to *relax* –' she assumed a collapsed position on the sofa '– and to stop being so uptight!'

'But what about it?'

Caris sat up and smiled mysteriously. 'I love my sister and my sister loves me,' she said. 'Besides, there are plenty of people who don't get love and affection in their marriages. Look at Vivian, for pity's sake.'

'If you ask me,' intervened Lisa, 'Vivian's brought that on herself.'

'Anyway, what does it matter?' said Caris. 'We're more than just our sex, you know – we campaign, we do environmental projects, we get involved in justice issues.'

'It sounds like a laugh a minute,' said Adam from the kitchen.

'Right now,' said Caris, for some reason consulting her watch, 'loggers are ripping down primeval rain forest in Tasmania and dousing the land with napalm. Does that not mean anything to you?'

'Not really,' said Adam, who had joined Lisa at the threshold. 'Why should it? It's happening on the other side of the world.'

'Well, it matters to me. We're petitioning everyone in our area and sending the signatures to the Australian government.'

'Somehow,' said Adam, 'I don't think you'll stop them.'

'We might!'

'All you're doing,' said Adam, 'is causing yourself unnecessary pain.'

I wondered where I had heard him say this before, and remembered it was in the hospital.

'And you'd know all about that, wouldn't you? On the list of things that have caused me unnecessary pain, you'd come out just about at the top!'

'I think I'll go and get the children's tea on,' said Lisa, in her 'discreet' voice. 'Are you coming, Hamish?'

'Oh come on,' said Adam. 'Not that again.'

'He broke my arm,' said Caris, to me. 'He knocked out two of my front teeth. He gave me a cracked rib and concussion, not to mention bruises all over my legs.'

'It wasn't broken. It was fractured.'

'It was broken, damn you! From the age of three to the age of sixteen,' said Caris, fixing my eyes with hers, 'my brother systematically physically abused me. From before that, for all I know.'

'Caris,' called Lisa distantly from the kitchen, 'I really don't think you ought to make those sorts of accusations.'

'He locked me in the wine cellar where there were rats. He pushed me down the stairs. He tied me to a tree and threw tennis balls at me.'

'That's just what children do!' protested Adam.

'He shut me in the boot of dad's car. He hit me with his cricket bat.'

'Caris, I think you should stop,' said Lisa from the doorway. She crossed the room and took the baby from Caris's lap and returned to the kitchen. 'Everyone's mean to their brothers and sisters,' she said, from the doorway. 'I really think you should just get over it.'

'Well,' said Caris, 'he's your problem now, not mine.' She rose from the sofa. 'Sorry to mess up your evening,' she said in a strangled voice. 'You obviously don't want me here so I'll go.'

'Do you want me to call you a cab?' I said.

'Oh, it's still light,' she said. 'I'll walk.'

I followed her into the hall.

'Don't be angry,' I said.

She stood outside on the drive with her arms folded and her head tilted away. I felt sorry for all the time that had passed.

'It's all true, you know,' she said. 'I'm always surprised when that doesn't make a difference.'

She was gone in a few smart crunches of gravel before I could say anything. I closed the front door behind her. From the kitchen I heard Lisa say:

'Do you think Caris is a lesbian?'

I went upstairs and for the first time since my arrival in Doniford I took my violin out of its case and began to play. I played most of the repertoire we went through during our Friday evenings. At first the sound was loud and harsh but gradually it grew more rounded, as though it were working itself into the stiff walls and carpet and rendering them pliant. I must have lost track of time, because when I became aware of Lisa standing in the doorway the window was full of the purple light of evening. She was smiling. In the dusk her face had a bronzed look from which her hair and teeth glowed with an avid, slightly sinister whiteness. She had her arms folded and her head cocked to one side.

'That's really nice,' she said. In her 'discreet' voice she added: 'The thing is, I've just put the baby down and I'd really like her to go to sleep.'

'Sorry,' I said. 'I'll stop.'

EIGHT

The next day was Saturday. Beverly was taking the day off, so we agreed to work the late-morning shift while she and Brendon did the night. This meant that we didn't need to get to the farm until eight o'clock and had to stay through until noon, which is how I came to witness the extraordinary scene that took place amongst the Hanburys that day.

For the first time, I was left to sleep until it was light. It was a luxury for which I expected myself to be grateful after the days of hard, dark, four o'clock risings, but when I opened my eyes to the grey, established daylight I discovered instead that I had been served with the unmistakable summons of despair. It was as though thoughts of my wife had formed a sort of crust or skin around me while I slept. On opening my eyes I received a startling impression of my own bondage to these thoughts; I was encased by them, to a point that apparently precluded physical movement. I realised that by getting up early all these mornings I had cheated the part of my constitution that needed time and stillness to form the fog of feeling. Lying helpless in bed I let the grey light run in its doomy legions over me. Eventually I heard Hamish rustling in his sleeping bag, and for some reason I prayed for him not to wake up yet, for it seemed unbearable to me that I should have to confront him in this state: but he did wake up. I was aware of him laboriously getting to his feet, as though he were the first human. The quivering top of his blond head and then his face appeared beside me.

'Hello,' I said.

'Hi,' he said.

I said, 'We're going home soon. Tomorrow maybe. We're going home to see mummy.'

159

Hamish assumed a neutral expression, like a priest hearing a particularly gruesome confession.

'I bet you've missed her, haven't you?'

He nodded. As far as I knew Rebecca had not once telephoned to speak to Hamish; nor to me, as it happened, although I had been able to mask this omission by telephoning her myself. I had tried vainly to reach her the night before, which was doubtless one cause of my current prostration. The message on her mobile phone annoyed me so much that it caused feelings of actual hatred to course through me, not for Rebecca but for the phone itself, as though it were holding her hostage and repeatedly releasing the same fragment of her. I imagined smashing it, banging its square little face against a rock until its casing fell apart and then prising out its metallic innards.

By the time Adam and I drove up the hill, the day was windy and bright and the naked trees cast moving shadows on the grass and on the road so that sometimes their bare arms seemed to be flailing the windscreen while shards of cold sunlight hailed down from the sky. Great clouds foamed at the top of the hill, grey and white, like something beaten out of a distant ferment. I said:

'I think we'll be off tomorrow.'

In the shuttered, discontinuous light I waited for his reply.

'That's a shame,' he said. 'We expected you to stay longer.'

'There are some problems at home I've got to sort out.'

A moment earlier I had felt a pressing need to make this disclosure. Now that I had, I felt vulnerable and ashamed.

'We thought that might be the case,' said Adam presently, with ostentatious care. He stared keenly through the windscreen.

'The balcony fell off our house,' I said. 'I should really go and sort it out.'

There was a silence, during which Adam failed to recognise his obligation to enquire about the dramatic event to which I had just referred. Like some predatory animal my anger left off the trail of Rebecca and swerved hungrily towards this new source of affront. Did he think I was lying? That 'we'!

'It nearly killed me,' I said. 'It missed me by a foot.'

Still he did not speak. I thought that I might hit him. I wanted to – there was a hot feeling of excitement in my chest that made the prospect of hitting Adam seem infinitely satisfying, like the prospect of taking flight. I did not, however, hit him. I began to feel jittery and light-headed, and my hands trembled on my thighs. I looked out of the window to the side of me at the rushing hedgerows. There was a leaden sensation in my stomach. It seemed that Adam and I were no longer friends. I felt certain that he would agree, but what perplexed me was how our brief conversation, in which we had taken such different parts, could have led to both of us forming this conclusion. I supposed that he could have decided it at some earlier point in my visit. I felt then that I had exposed myself to him in every particular. I felt his solidity, his self-satisfaction, in opposition to my transience. I imagined him and Lisa laughing at Hamish and at me; I imagined, ashamed, the clarity with which they had perceived that I scorned their suburban existence, and though I scorned it still, this idea, along with their beige carpets and their aspirations and the fact especially of their hospitality, put them somehow in the right. It was one of Rebecca's criticisms of me that I was judgmental, as though I were the last advocate of an otherwise extinct morality. What she meant was that the disapproval made me immoral myself, by which I had always understood her to be saying that her lack of discrimination made discrimination a crime.

'Lisa's bringing the kids up at lunchtime to see the lambs,' said Adam, as though further to assert the simple virtues of his existence, as opposed to the snarling, duplicitous chaos of mine.

'Will she bring Hamish?' I said.

Adam smiled.

'Well, I don't think she can leave him at home,' he said.

'That's nice of her,' I said, more petulantly than I'd meant to, so that as we were bumping up the track Adam turned his head to glance at me.

There were only six pregnant ewes in the pens. I left Adam to sit with them while I loitered around the barns in a pretence of efficiency, slowly shovelling dirty straw into the wheelbarrow. Sometimes I went out and looked at the vivid blue sea below, its surface creased by wind. I saw little boats charging madly up and down. The hours passed, forced through the tiny aperture in my angry feelings of subjection. I gave the orphaned lambs their milk, sickened by the greed with which they jostled and slobbered at the teat. They kept pulling it nearly out of my hands. I saw that Adam had moved two of the ewes to their own stalls.

'Can you take one of these?' he called.

Reluctantly I plodded to the stalls. The ewes stood panting rapidly and staring straight ahead with their close-together eyes. Adam was sitting on a stool in one of the stalls. I went into the other.

'Good girl,' I heard him say over the divide.

I sat on the stool, where the ewe's broad, woolly haunches presented themselves to me. Her sides moved in and out quickly. I stared at her livid, quivering genitals. The smell of straw and muck was pleasanter in this enclosed space than when it was mixed with the wind outside. I sat and waited, as I had seen Adam and Beverly do.

'Is there something I should be doing?' I called.

'Not unless her insides start coming out,' said Adam ominously.

'What do I do then?'

'I don't know,' said Adam after a pause. 'I get Beverly to do those. I think you have to sort of shove them back in.'

I stared around the battered wooden sides of the stall and then put my head back and looked up at the rafters. A group of pigeons were up there and they looked quizzically down at me.

Outside the wind banged the gates and rattled them against their hinges. The ewe panted. Time passed. Her little sharp breaths seemed to buffer me; they broke on me like little waves on a smooth, empty beach. I marvelled at her containment. It seemed incredible to me that anything would issue from her impassive bulk. She was without sensibility; she was like a rock, a boulder. In the presence of her rudimentary life I had a sense of the superfluity of certain things and the necessity of others.

'Were you given a cause?' said Adam from the other stall.

'For what?'

'For the balcony collapsing.'

'Frost damage,' I said. 'A plant grew through a crack in the stone.'

There was a pause.

'You'll have problems with insurance,' he observed.

'I know.'

'If I were you,' he said, 'I'd look at reinforced concrete to replace it. It's far cheaper and much easier to secure into the outside wall.'

'It's a listed building,' I said.

'That's no problem. There's no problem using a concrete slab. As long as the appearance is the same. Was the lime-stone painted?'

'Yes.'

'Well, there you go. There's only so far a listed buildings consent will go in specifying the nature of the materials. You want to find someone who'll run it straight into the wall rather than taking out sections of the stone. Don't listen if they say they can't do it. You'll save yourselves three or four thousand pounds.'

'Thanks,' I said.

I leaned back against the frayed wood and thick splinters pushed against my shirt. The ewe shifted a little on her deli-cate hooves. I closed my eyes. The wind descanted distantly.

'– continual maintenance, that's the problem,' Adam said from next door.

'What's that?' I said.

'I was saying you're constantly having to maintain them. Old buildings. It can be a real headache. The maintenance costs on an old building can be a real drain. Personally I'd rather spend the money on something else.'

'I think mine's coming,' I said.

A rounded, shiny-blue protuberance, like a knuckle, had appeared amidst the ewe's red, fleshy folds. It kept receding and returning, each time a little more substantially.

'Mine too,' Adam said. 'I worked out that the equity on a new build is actually more stable once you factor in the running costs.'

The ewe was panting even faster: while not moving at all, she was like something running at full tilt. The knuckle edged its way out. Now it was a parcel, mottled and tightly packed, being forced through a letterbox.

'Should I pull it out?' I said.

'No,' said Adam. 'She does it all. There, mine's out.' I heard a rustle of straw from his stall. 'In Bath, though,' he continued, 'I should say you'd get a lot of value added just from the heritage point of view. It's the Georgian factor – you can't go wrong, really, in Bath. Ridiculous, isn't it? The money people will spend on something that's basically just an illusion.'

I turned back to my ewe and saw the parcel, greasy and bright, suspended in a long moment of obstruction before it suddenly slithered out in a rush and fell with a thud into the straw. There was a smell of old blood. I watched as it woke itself, unfolding its legs and nosing blindly at the remnants of the bag it had come in, before scrambling unsteadily to its feet. It stood there, quivering, while the ewe licked it and carelessly shoved it around. I realised my heart was thumping. I met the ewe's depthless brown gaze. The four ewes left in the pen bayed and barged against the metal poles with their massive bodies. I inched around the edge of the stall and let myself out.

*

Later I saw the gilded figure of Hamish running across the yard with his hair flying crazily in the wind and a smile on his face so large and unaccustomed that at first I thought he must be in pain.

'Look!' he shrieked. 'Look!'

He was clutching something in his hand. Lisa and Janie and the baby were behind him, moving through the yard looking this way and that, like tourists. Lisa was wearing sunglasses.

'Look!'

'What is it?' I asked. It was a piece of paper but I couldn't prise it out of his fist.

'You got a letter from mummy, didn't you, Hamish?' said Lisa, tucking a strand of hair sympathetically behind his ear as though he were a poor orphan.

'Did you?' I said, simulating pleasure. I was surprised to feel a little stab of jealousy at this revelation. Why should she be glorified for writing, when she was forced to do it simply by the fact of her absence? And why, if she was in the mood for writing letters, didn't she write one to me?

'It's been a long time, hasn't it, pet?' Lisa continued, pityingly.

'He can't even read,' said Janie. 'Why is she sending him letters if he can't even read?'

Had Hamish not been there I might have applauded this line of questioning, and perhaps hazarded the explanation that the letter had been sent out of a confused sense of guilt, mixed with a craven liking for showy, attention-seeking gestures which required the minimum of effort and carried high parental prestige.

'Why doesn't she just come and see him?' Janie added.

'She's busy this week,' I said, because Lisa was listening closely. 'She's working. She's got a big exhibition she's putting on at an art gallery.'

'Clever mummy,' said Lisa, with a meaningful intonation.

'We did two this morning,' said Adam heartily. His face

was red and his jacket was covered in wisps of straw. 'I had to get Michael in there at gunpoint. He thought he might have to put his hand up something.'

'Men!' exclaimed Lisa, tutting. 'It's perfectly natural, you know,' she said to me. 'There's nothing disgusting about it.'

'There wasn't much to do,' I said. 'I don't know what all the fuss is about.'

'Try saying that when you've got a prolapsed ewe, or twins, or the cord tied round somebody's neck,' said Adam grimly. 'You'd know what the fuss was about then.'

'Laura's up at the house,' said Lisa. 'I said you'd pop in and say hello.'

I remembered Laura very vaguely, as a laughing, self-possessed girl with no particular lack of grace or attractiveness, who nevertheless advanced common sense as her chief characteristic and virtue. I remembered her round, flat, white, well-modelled face, like the blank, unpainted face of a Venetian mask, from which she wore her fair hair pulled back by an Alice band. When we passed through the courtyard next to the house we saw two children playing, both extremely fair and unkempt, a boy of about eight and a slightly smaller girl. Adam greeted them, which did not prevent the boy from raising what appeared to be a small crossbow and pointing it directly at him.

'Put that down, Rufus,' said Adam, quite angrily. 'Can't you see there are children around?'

'I'm not pointing it at them,' said Rufus. I couldn't tell whether he liked the fact that nobody had accused him of being a child himself, or not.

'You shouldn't point that thing at anybody,' said Adam. 'Where did you get it from?'

Rufus shrugged.

'Mum gave it to me,' he said.

'I'm sure she didn't.'

'She did!' squeaked the little girl.

'Good God,' said Adam. 'What will she think of next?'

I guessed that these were Laura's children. Common sense was clearly no longer something she went in for.

'Take it out to the field, will you?' continued Adam. 'I don't want it anywhere near the house.'

'You really shouldn't be playing with things like that, Rufus,' said Lisa. 'It's actually not very nice.'

'It's none of your business!' shouted Rufus.

'Well, it is my business if one of my children gets hurt,' she said. 'Isn't it, Rufus?'

'No one's got hurt! I haven't done anything wrong!' yelled Rufus furiously. 'We were just playing!'

He stormed out of the courtyard and a minute later, with a look of uncertainty, his sister followed him.

'Honestly,' said Lisa, rolling her eyes, 'I only have to come up here and I start to think I've gone mad.'

Inside the house Laura was nowhere to be seen. Vivian and Brendon were sitting hunched at the kitchen table peeling potatoes. After the sunlight outside it looked as though they were sitting in a great cavern, or in the belly of a gigantic animal with the ceiling beams as its black, huge ribs. I noticed that Brendon had a large piece of gauze taped to his forehead.

'Oh, hello,' said Vivian presently, lifting her eyebrows. 'I didn't know you were still here.'

'We've just knocked off,' said Adam.

'Well, I don't see how I can possibly be expected to feed you all! Laura's turned up with her four and Caris will be back in a moment wanting feeding and I haven't been able to get down to Doniford all week, you know, and I really think someone might have thought to bring just a loaf of bread or a bit of cheese with them,' she said. 'It's incredible, really, how little people think. There's Laura with a fridge at home the size of a room, all full of whatever it is her children *will* eat, and she takes it upon herself to have lunch here, where she says everything's past its sell-by date. She's been round all the cupboards, taking things out and throwing them away! Then she complains because there's nothing left!'

'Don't worry, Vivian,' said Lisa sourly. 'We won't be troubling you for anything to eat.'

'Oh, well,' said Vivian, 'I'm sure I can find something, it's just that you mustn't mind what it is. I was going to boil up these potatoes, that's all. I was sure there was a bit of ham in the larder but it seems to have gone. Perhaps the dogs took it.'

'Mine don't really eat ham,' said Lisa. 'Just a bit of pasta will be fine.'

'I don't know that we have pasta,' said Vivian. She said it to rhyme with 'faster'. 'That's all anybody eats now, isn't it? When I was little we used to call it worms.'

'That's disgusting,' said Janie.

'We dropped in on dad yesterday,' said Adam, in a significant voice. 'He's feeling a bit lonely.'

'Is he?' said Vivian. She looked around, as though expecting someone to step forward and explain why.

'He'd like to see you,' said Adam. 'I think he was expecting you a couple of days ago.'

There was a silence.

'Well,' said Vivian finally, 'to be completely honest, I've been having a few problems with the car.'

She shook her hair down over her face and then looked up at us innocently through her fringe.

'The car?'

'Yes. I don't really like to drive it.'

'Why not?'

'There's something wrong with the windscreen. Something's happened to the glass.'

'What do you mean?' said Adam. 'Has it broken?'

'Oh no, nothing like that. I think it's just got a bit old.'

'Old?'

'What are you talking about, Vivian?' said Lisa.

'It's you who aren't listening! I've told you, the glass has got too old to see through!'

With shaking hands Vivian flayed the skin from a potato and dropped it, scalped, back into the muddy pile from which

168

she had taken it. Brendon picked it out fastidiously with his fingers and put it with the others in a saucepan of water.

'Vivian,' said Adam, 'have you been to an optician lately?'

'I don't see what an optician's going to do about my car!' said Vivian, laughing rather wildly.

'It might not be the car. It might be your eyes.'

'There's never been anything wrong with my eyes. It's sitting up here in the dark all winter – they get unused to the sun. It isn't my fault, you know! When I go to Spain,' she said, to me, 'the problem simply disappears, even though one's in the brightest sun day in and day out. I barely have to wear my sunglasses!'

'It's p-probably stress,' said Brendon. He was wearing a short-sleeved shirt with multicoloured flying saucers on it. His face looked slightly lopsided, as though he had slept heavily on it. 'Have you ever tried St John's wort, Vivian? I can give you some if you like – I've got l-loads.'

'Look,' said Adam, 'I'll drive you down to the hospital this afternoon. It's really not such a big deal.'

'We get no light here from November to March, you know,' said Vivian, to me. 'We're north-facing, that's the problem. The sun goes all the way around the other side of the hill, where nobody actually lives! I can't think why they built Egypt here, can you? Perhaps they did it in the summer not knowing how it would get. Sometimes I wish I could just pick it up and turn it around the other way. There's a day in April when it comes back – one day a little triangle of sunlight appears on the floor, and the next day it's a little bigger, and the day after a little bigger and so on, and then before you know it it's starting to get smaller again,' she concluded morbidly.

'If we could go straight after lunch that would suit me,' said Adam. 'I've got some things I have to do this afternoon.'

'Sometimes I'll open a door or a cupboard and without expecting it I'll feel as though I'm falling into a void, a *well* of blackness,' said Vivian. 'I almost feel a sort of presence. Do you know,' she said suddenly, 'when that happens I can often hear someone speaking my name, quite clearly speaking it!'

'Vivian? Is it all right if we go straight after lunch?'

Vivian looked at him roguishly. I wondered if she was drunk again.

'I think I'd rather go tomorrow,' she said.

'But he's coming home on Monday!'

'Well, in that case,' said Vivian, 'I don't see what everyone's making such a fuss about.'

'Vivian,' said Lisa, smiling, 'surely you'd want to see Paul while he's in the hospital?'

'When I had my operation,' said Vivian, staring beadily at her, 'I was in hospital for five days. He wouldn't come and see me because he was worried about carrying foot and mouth on to Egypt.'

'Well,' said Adam, 'at the time that was understandable, when you think about it.'

'I was losing my womanhood!' cried Vivian. 'I was being mutilated, and all he cared about were his sheep!'

'Don't you think you should let bygones be bygones?' said Lisa.

'A lot of people did things then that they regret,' said Adam. 'Don Brice threatened the inspectors with a shotgun, for heaven's sake.'

'He never apologised!'

'You know what he's like,' said Adam. 'He doesn't like it when people are ill.'

'When I came back,' said Vivian unsteadily, her cheeks ablaze, 'he sent me to Coventry for forgetting to write the cheques before I left. I think that rather takes the cake, don't you? Don't you think that it does? He wouldn't let me go upstairs until I'd sat at the desk and signed them all! And he wouldn't speak to me – not a word!'

None of us said anything. Vivian looked around with a mixture of triumph and concern, as though she had unintentionally extinguished us into silence too.

'Well,' said Adam finally, 'I don't really know about that. All I know is that he repeatedly said that he wanted to see you. Doesn't that make a difference?'

'I know why he does,' snapped Vivian. 'He wants to know what I'm up to. Well, if he asks you can tell him – I've had enough! Tell him that and see what he says!'

'I'd rather you told him yourself,' said Adam.

'You've got to tell him yourself,' nodded Lisa. 'He's your husband, Vivian.'

'He isn't my husband, you know,' said Vivian darkly. 'Not in the eyes of the church he isn't. I was already married, you see. In the eyes of the church we're living in sin!'

'Janie,' said Lisa, alarmed, 'can you take Hamish and play outside?'

'I don't want to,' said Janie.

'I'm asking you to,' said Lisa.

'I'm frightened of that boy.'

'That's between you and dad,' said Adam.

There was the sound of footsteps out in the hall. A woman came into the room carrying a baby. Both of them were very large and fair-haired and wore light-coloured, clean but very crumpled clothing, so that in the gloom of the kitchen, in their detailed amplitude and luminosity they had the appearance of figures from a religious painting. The woman's face had a sort of wistful purity to it, in the trenchant setting of her thick-bodied, abundant middle age, that deepened this impression. The yellow light from the window, which some peculiarity of the Hanburys' kitchen dictated should remain in compact beams like those of a searchlight rather than diffuse itself around, fell squarely on her face and on the maze of creases in her clothes. Another fair-haired child, of about Hamish's age, came behind her and stood clutching her skirt with his fists. Rosettes of colour were appended to his fat cheeks.

'You're all here,' observed Laura, for it was she, recognisable to me only by the stubborn, little-girlish convexity of her forehead. 'Have you all come up for lunch?'

There was something in the way she asked this question which made the matter of how to reply to it more complicated than it ought to have been.

'Not really,' said Adam. 'We just dropped in.'

'Because mummy's running pretty low,' Laura continued, heaving the baby around on her hip. 'If you're all going to stay someone should really go down to Doniford and pick up some things. We've been over at the stream,' she added, with red in her face. 'Toby's been trying to spear a fish. Didn't there used to be trout in there?'

'They've netted it lower down,' said Adam. 'The people who bought the place at the bottom of the hill are starting a trout farm. Don't you remember,' he said to Brendon, 'that was what dad went so crazy about last year.'

'Spear it with what?' asked Lisa. She wore an expression of distaste.

'You just tie a penknife to the end of a stick,' said Laura, as though Lisa was likely to try it.

'He said he was going to put sh-sheep dip in the water,' said Brendon. 'But I don't think he ever did.'

'Do you want to run down or shall I?' said Laura.

'I was going to boil up these potatoes,' said Vivian.

'Laura,' said Lisa, drawing confidentially to Laura's side and speaking into her ear, 'you might want to check on Rufus. He's walking around with a crossbow. He says you gave it him.'

Laura looked straight ahead while Lisa addressed her ear, an expression of amusement on her face, as though she were hearing something entertaining on the telephone.

'Is he being really awful?' she said delightedly.

'It's just that he says you gave it him.'

'He got it for his birthday,' said Laura. 'He's quite a good shot, actually.'

'The thing is,' said Lisa discreetly, 'the other children won't go outside.'

'They've just got to stand up to him!' cried Laura. 'Tell

172

them to shout at him if he bothers them. Is he being really awful?' she asked again. 'Nobody at school invites him home any more, you know. They've been told not to invite him home. He's quite upset about it.'

'I think they're a bit frightened to go out,' said Lisa.

'What are they frightened of? Polly's out there, isn't she?'

'Polly's got an axe,' said Janie.

'Look, shall I just leave the children here and run down to the shops?' said Laura, looking around at us with purpose flaming in her pale blue eyes.

'What do you mean?' said Lisa.

'She's got an axe. I saw her.'

'Shall I?' said Laura. She inched towards the door. 'Look, I'll take the baby,' she added, as though brokering her own escape.

'There's no need to go if you don't want to,' said Adam. 'We don't want much. Vivian's going to boil the potatoes.'

'If you let her go she won't come back until tomorrow,' Vivian interjected from beneath her brows. 'I tell you, she won't – she'll phone from Doniford and say that something's come up and could we keep the children overnight.'

'That's charming!' shrieked Laura, laughing robustly and nevertheless keeping her hand on the door handle.

'It's true,' said Vivian quaveringly. 'You don't realise you'll have to do it all again,' she said, to me. 'It's all right for the men – they just claim a sort of immunity, don't they? They say they don't know how to do it because they didn't do it the first time and now it's too late for them to learn, and that sort of thing, don't they?'

'Laura, Janie says Polly's got hold of an axe,' said Lisa.

'I saw her,' said Janie.

'Well, you tell her it's naughty,' said Laura.

'I don't want to tell her,' said Janie.

'You're not frightened of Polly too, are you?' said Laura. 'You're frightened of everyone! Is she shy?' she said to Lisa.

I heard footsteps in the hall and the kitchen door slowly

opened with Laura's hand still holding the handle. Caris put her bushy head into the room. Her manner was ostentatiously cautious. I was arrested by the distinctive expression on her face: she looked excited and slightly devious and somewhat ashamed. It was an expression I had seen before only on the face of my wife. Slowly she digested the fact of the crowded kitchen and as I watched I saw subjectivity break as though in rays or waves over her physiognomy. Her obscure knowledge of who she was rose into her face and shone glaringly through the strange derangement of her features. With her same great deliberateness of manner she stayed like that for several seconds, her body out of the room and her head in it, regarding us all with an expression of wonderment.

'Not particularly,' said Lisa, who had looked at Caris and looked away again.

I wondered if Caris had gone in some way mad, for she did remain in utter self-consciousness at the door, moving her eyes from one to another of us with a little smile. Her head, unbodied, began to look slightly eerie. I noticed that no one spoke to her. It struck me that this might be reinforcing her madness – that her expression could be that of someone whom numerous people are feigning an inability to see. I thought I understood, though, why no one did speak to her: it was her air of great import, which seemed to presage an announcement that never came.

'Polly's completely harmless,' said Laura, who appeared not to have noticed that Caris's face, with its mystical expression, was suspended a mere ten or twelve inches from her own. 'You can't be frightened of Polly!'

'She's got an axe,' said Janie. 'I saw her running after that boy with it.'

'Oh, she's only playing. She wouldn't actually hurt him, you know. Oh look!' Laura laughed, pointing at Janie. 'She's terrified, the poor little thing!'

Caris finally made her announcement.

'Mum's here,' she said.

Vivian looked up.

'Here?' she said.

'She brought me up in the car. She's outside talking to Rufus. I thought I'd come and warn you.'

'What's she doing here?' said Vivian.

From outside I could hear the sound of the dogs barking.

'She's just come up to say hello,' said Caris. Her look was inscrutable.

'Well, no one invited her,' said Vivian. 'It's a bit much, just to turn up uninvited!'

'Vivian,' said Adam pacifically, 'come on. Mum's always up here with you and dad.'

'If she wants to see him she knows where to find him,' said Vivian. 'She can't just come turning up here uninvited!'

There was a commotion out in the hall and suddenly the door was thrown ajar against Laura and the dogs tumbled through, tearing around Caris's legs and into the kitchen. They skidded over the flagstone floor and hurled themselves with a deafening volley of barks at Vivian's chair. Vivian shrieked and got to her feet, knocking the chair to the floor. The dogs snapped their livid, fleshy muzzles at her over the upended legs and made contorted shapes around her with their scruffy bodies.

'Get down!' shouted Adam, lunging for their collars. He kicked one of the dogs and its skinny, unresisting legs skated over the floor.

A woman's voice drifted in from the hall.

'What on earth were Nell and Daisy doing locked up?' she said. 'I found them out in the stable – I couldn't believe my eyes!'

Adam held both dogs by their collars and they strained madly at his arms, barking, their clawed feet skating and scratching over the flagstones.

'What *are* you doing?' said Audrey, appearing in the doorway. 'Let them go, Adam! You look like that man at the gates of hell.'

'I can't,' puffed Adam. 'They keep going for Vivian.'

'They just went mad,' said Lisa.

'I don't like them!' wailed Janie.

'What do you mean, they keep going for her? They're just a pair of silly old girls. Aren't you? You're just a pair of silly old girls. You don't go for people. No, not like the hounds of hell. Not like the horrid hounds from hell.'

Audrey had advanced into the room and was caressing the dogs' slobbering muzzles as she spoke. They made high-pitched mewling sounds. She was wearing a close-fitting brown coat made of some kind of skin or pelt. Her slim, shapely legs were bare. On her feet she wore narrow, high-heeled boots of the same brown, hairy material as the coat. I became aware of her scent, which was moving in a body over the room. It was a heady smell composed of numerous elements – perfume, face powder, soap, leather, a smell of varnish – and their notes sounded on me randomly and repeatedly.

'Do you like my new coat?' she said girlishly, whirling round to face us all. 'I got it in London last week. It's pony. Don't you think it's divine? The boots were made to match. They cost the earth! But I had to have them, didn't I? The pony has to have her little hooves shod.'

'Was it really a pony?' said Janie to her mother. Her expression was perturbed.

'God, it's fantastic,' said Laura enthusiastically, stroking Audrey's arm.

'Was it really?' said Janie.

'It's absolutely lovely,' said Lisa. Her tone was uncharacteristically professorial. She looked slightly stiff beneath Janie's scrutiny.

'I'm going to put the dogs back out in the yard,' said Adam.

'I love clothes,' said Laura, 'but I never buy them any more. Look.' She lifted her shirt cheerfully to reveal the zip of her skirt peeled open to accommodate her white, fleshy middle. 'I can't do anything up.'

'There isn't another baby in there, is there?' pouted Audrey.

'Don't!' shrieked Laura.

'No more babies,' said Audrey, shaking her manicured finger.

'It's awful, isn't it?' said Laura delightedly.

'I met one of yours outside – he wanted to show me how to use his crossbow. It's rather fun, isn't it? I shot my bolt straight into a tree and imagined all sorts of people it might be. He was very gentlemanly when I showed him my new boots, and he climbed up and got it himself, gorgeous boy.'

'Roger would divorce me if I had any more,' said Laura.

'I made Paul get his tubes tied after Brendon,' said Audrey. 'He protested mightily. Oh, how the lord and master protested. He said it was the death of possibility. I said to him, darling, we've got three lumping great possibilities already. How much more possibility do you want? I said, if I have any more possibilities I'll have to start wearing support tights and girdles. That galvanised him, I'm telling you.'

It was difficult to get a sense of Audrey's face, submerged as it was beneath a meticulous mask of make-up. Two pencil lines described the surprised arc of her brows. Her eyelashes stood out in great curving black fronds which fanned up and down when she blinked. It was in her mouth, a red, wrinkled, oily delta of lipstick, that her age declared itself. Her eyes glittered erratically beneath the black fronds. She had retained, I saw, the tousled hairstyle of her earlier era, although today it looked slightly askew, as though it had been thrown at her head and nearly missed. I wondered whether she had had a facelift. The skin of her face had a boiled appearance, and there was about her generally an air of frantic uplift, of a bodily effort to ascend as though from some sinking substance in which her feet were mired. Caris was looking at her mother with her arms folded and the same strange, lilting smile on her face that she had worn earlier. Brendon remained at the kitchen table, but he had pushed back his chair and was holding his arms and legs slightly out to the sides, as though someone had just placed their hands on his chest and shoved him forcefully backwards. Adam still gripped the straining dogs by their collars.

'I'm just going to put them out,' he said again.

'You'll have to shut them back in the stable,' said Vivian, who remained as though for defence behind the upended chair. 'Right in, do you see, otherwise they get out through the gate.'

'What are they saying?' said Audrey, looking about her with gracious incredulity.

'I'm putting the dogs back in the stable.'

'Why on earth are you doing that?'

'They've got a bit wild with dad away.'

'Nonsense,' said Audrey. 'Come and see mummy, darlings. Don't listen to what those horrid people say about you.'

'They bark at Vivian.'

'They bark at *me*,' said Caris, still smiling.

Audrey looked around the room in distress. Her garlanded eyes met mine.

'Perhaps *you* can tell me what they're talking about,' she said sweetly. 'They're talking about locking up animals, aren't they?'

'If you're going out I'll go out with you,' said Laura to Adam, edging towards the door with the baby in her arms. 'I'm just going to run down to Doniford.'

'Do you know Paul?' said Audrey, to me. 'He's very fond of these old girls. I don't think he'd like them being locked up, do you?'

'They're only dogs,' said Vivian quaveringly. 'They're not children. It's not as though we're talking about locking up children.'

'*What* an extraordinary thing to say!' gasped Audrey comically. 'Are you suggesting something, Vivian darling, about my reputation as a mother? Because from what Caris tells me you've got some history of your own in that department!'

'I was just saying that they're only dogs,' Vivian said.

'I always think you can tell a lot about a person by the way they treat a dog,' said Audrey, to all of us. 'Particularly men. I like a man who gives a dog a good tousling. I can't stand it when you see a man sort of cross his legs. And the ones who claim to be allergic are the worst.'

'I'm the one that feeds them, you know,' said Vivian. 'I'm the one that looks after them.'

'Is this dogs or children, darling? I suppose you'd say it was both. The feeding hangs heavy in both cases. Still, locking them up is a little extreme. I don't think I went down that road, even in my worst moments.'

'They should have gone to kennels,' said Adam. He had an uncomfortable expression on his face, as though he were slowly being suffocated by his own body.

'I always thought that about all of you,' Audrey said. 'I remember there used to be a sign on the way down to Doniford that said "Cat Hotel". Every time I passed it I used to wonder whether they'd make an exception.'

'That isn't actually all that funny,' said Caris.

'It might not seem funny to you,' said Audrey. 'I think people don't really develop a sense of humour until they have children,' she added, to me. 'It's hard to take things quite so seriously once you've wiped a few bottoms. Mine seem to think that I don't know about their bottoms. Perhaps it'd be better if I didn't. There's a point at which one's information becomes obsolete – it's terribly bad for the brain. I often look at women my age and think that they're just slated for extinction, like the dinosaurs.'

'In a way, you did put them in kennels,' Vivian said, as though the idea were not unpleasing to her. 'The children. You did board them in a way.'

Audrey laughed. 'What a horrible thing to say, darling! And I suppose you were the kennel master. Of course,' she said, to me, 'everyone forgets the fact that they were with their father. He'd never have let them go in a million years.

But don't try telling that to anyone. If you're a woman people think you owe them an explanation. And if you ever find one that feels sorry for you it's even worse! They start telling you what you should be doing to get them back, and sending you the names of lawyers and asking whether you've rung them.'

'Janie,' said Lisa, in her 'discreet' voice, 'I asked you to take Hamish and play together outside.'

'All right,' said Janie. 'I'm not going out that way, though.'

'Go out the front,' said Lisa, 'where we can see you from the window.'

She came to where I stood and held out her hand for Hamish. He took it quite willingly. Together they went to the other door and a moment later I saw them through the window out on the lawn. Hamish was walking over the grass in a straight line, like a toy that had been wound up. Janie walked beside him in a crouched position that suggested vigilance.

'And had you?' said Caris.

'Had I what, darling?' said Audrey.

'Rung them.'

'What, rung a lawyer? Of course not! We never needed lawyers, did we, Vivian? We were all eminently reasonable. The only one who got lawyered was Vivian's poor old husband. We lawyered him all the way to the Isle of Wight, if I remember.'

'He threw a rock through the window,' said Vivian, looking around her abjectly, as though expecting to find it still lying at her feet.

'I'm not surprised he threw rocks, darling. He was terribly upset. Paul always said what a rotter he was, but then it suited him to say that. Men tend to take the path of least resistance, I find. He was actually rather sweet, wasn't he, Vivian? And he did love you desperately. They had these pet names for one another. He was Hippo and she was – what were you, Vivian?'

'Elephant,' said Vivian miserably.

'That's right!' said Audrey, delighted. 'Paul told me that Ivybridge was full of them, you know, little figurines of hippos and elephants. They collected them, the two of them! They were absolutely everywhere, apparently, all over the house. Whatever happened to them?'

'I threw them away,' said Vivian.

'You might have let him have them,' said Audrey reproachfully.

'He didn't want them.'

'Poor Hippo,' said Audrey. 'Poor submersible creature.'

'I don't understand,' said Caris, who was wearing her expression of wonderment again.

'We're talking about hippos and elephants,' said Audrey, with an adversarial glint in her fronded eye. 'You know what hippos and elephants are, don't you? They're big, sweet creatures that tolerate captivity. Some animals don't, you know. They get sad and lethargic and their fur goes all mangy.'

Caris shook her head from side to side as though she were trying to dislodge something. Again I saw in her face the strange effort of self-realisation.

'You make it sound so simple,' she said.

'Well, it was. Or is there something you don't understand? Perhaps I'm being insensitive. The thing is, I never had the luxury of sensitivity. I had to take things as I found them. That's the problem with children,' she said, to me. 'You go to the trouble of having them and then you find that all you've done is guarantee you'll come in second place for ever more. I gave you life, sweetie,' she said to Caris. 'Wasn't that enough?'

'It wasn't simple for *me*,' said Caris.

'That's so typical,' said Adam. 'Little Miss Self-Obsessed. If anyone found it hard it was Brendon. He was only six.'

'The same age as Janie,' nodded Lisa.

'It wasn't as bad for him as it was for me,' said Caris, with her lilting smile.

'Brendon used to bang his head,' said Vivian strangely.

181

'What do you mean, bang his head?' said Adam.

'He used to bang his head against the wall. It made the most horrible sound.'

Brendon looked around at everybody with an expression of astonishment.

'See?' said Adam triumphantly. 'It was worse for him.'

'I couldn't stop him,' said Vivian. 'He did it in his sleep, you see. I used to make him go to bed wearing a hat.'

Brendon laughed loudly.

'The things that went on!' marvelled Audrey, drawing her coat tighter around herself. 'It's a good thing I wasn't here to see it all. I don't think I could have borne it! You see, they used to be like puppies,' she added, to me. 'They tumbled around together like lion cubs. Then they started to develop human characteristics – that was where the problems began, with the human characteristics. Now they're like those countries that are always at war. They're dug in, if you see what I mean.'

'I'm not at *war*,' Caris said.

'When you were puppies I could resolve your disputes, darling. It was all about who had whose thing. I was rather good at that. Whoever could hang on to it could keep it as far as I was concerned. It was when the human characteristics came along that I got out of my depth. I remember I started to think about shoes. I used to lie there at night and think about the silliest, most impractical shoes I could imagine. It was the only way I kept my sanity while all of you were at each other's throats. The problem with shoes was that I could never wear them up here. I had to move to Doniford. I exchanged human characteristics for shoes,' she said, to me. 'It was the most enormous relief.'

'You make it sound as though you planned it,' said Caris, with a smile.

'There's no harm in a little planning,' said Audrey. 'A little planning goes a long way in human affairs. The people with characteristics don't see it like that, though. They don't like it when you've got characteristics of your own. Your father used to say that you were predators. They'll take it all, he said, if you let them. They'll rip your heart out and eat it if they have to.'

Adam, Caris and Brendon did not, it had to be admitted, look particularly capable of this gruesome feat. Adam still held the dogs awkwardly by their collars. Lisa stood next to him with the baby on her hip. I looked at the baby's rubescent, startled face, which shone blankly like a little sun in the gloomy room, and at her plump, soft body, possessed by incomprehension. Beside Lisa, Caris looked black and monumental and unkempt. Her arms were folded and her face looked stormy and disordered, as though it had been taken apart and wrongly reassembled. Brendon sat blanched and prostrate in his chair. The air was charged with their mother's force of will: next to her they seemed anomalous. Behind them Vivian haunted the cooker: she hovered, dark and frayed and threadlike. Audrey, compact, scented, her face blazing in its make-up, presented herself as an advertisement for the virtues of self-preservation.

'Audrey,' said Lisa, 'I'm sure Paul didn't actually mean that.'

'That's sweet of you,' said Audrey vaguely. 'But I think he probably did. Look at you all!' she burst out with a gay laugh. 'You look like a queue of dissatisfied customers! I think I'd better slip away, before I have to start apologising. You don't ever want to apologise,' she said, to me. 'That's how you give people the idea that you've done something wrong. Vivian darling, I just came up for that cheque. I think the postman must have pocketed it. It was due last week. It doesn't matter, if you can just write me another now.'

Vivian stood over the saucepan of potatoes, which had begun to boil. Clouds of steam enveloped her head. The lid rattled on top of the pan and the water spilled out in little hissing spurts.

'I don't think I can,' she said.

'Usually I don't like to bother you,' said Audrey. 'It's so tiresome when people bother you, isn't it? I think it must have got lost in the post. I've been lying in wait like a panther for the postman all week. When he comes I leap on him.'

'But I didn't post it,' said Vivian.

'And now I've had to come all the way up, and I had a thousand and one things I meant to do today – it was the last thing I wanted to do, to start coming up to Egypt! I always get embroiled when I come up here. Embroilment was not in the plan today. Today I was going to be all efficiency so that I could be carefree tomorrow.'

There was a silence in the kitchen. Audrey stood in an expectant pose, one hand slightly raised, as though to catch something she believed was about to be thrown to her, or as though she were holding a vessel from which she had just poured the last dregs of an important substance.

'Vivian,' she said meaningfully, 'you do see how annoying it is for me to have to come up?'

Vivian said nothing. The baby made a plaintive sound.

'In the middle of everything I had to start getting in the car and running around! Paul always said I wasn't to do that, you know,' Audrey said, to me. 'Don't wear yourself out, he said. Women always wear themselves out. By the time they get to fifty they're like a set of old tyres. They've lost their tread.'

The telephone rang in the hall and before Audrey had finished speaking Vivian had darted out of the room to answer it.

'Has she gone?' said Audrey smartly, looking around. 'I didn't know she could move so fast. It's because she's being evasive – she's moving fast to evade the issue.'

'She won't see dad,' Adam said. 'I've been trying to get her to go in but she won't. I don't understand what's going on. Dad said that none of you have been in. Only Uncle David.'

'I sent David as a sop,' said Audrey darkly. 'I suspected your father of shenanigans, but now I'm not so sure. I think Vivian may be acting alone.'

'Oh, for heaven's sake,' said Adam. 'I don't know what you're talking about, mum.'

'That was Laura,' said Vivian abstractedly, coming in again. 'I thought she was here but then the telephone rang and it was her. She's in Doniford. I don't know how she did it. She says she's got the baby but the three older ones are still here. I haven't seen them, have you? I don't know how she did it,' she said again. She looked around, as though thinking she might find her. 'I was sure she was here.'

'I was always good at that,' said Audrey. 'I used to leave you everywhere! Once I left Brendon in a shop. I completely forgot about him – he was there all afternoon. He hid like a little marsupial in a rack of clothes.'

'You've had enough, don't you think?' said Vivian, looking at Audrey through her fringe. 'Don't you think you've had enough?'

'Had enough of what, darling? I've certainly had enough of babies. That one's lovely but the very sight of her makes me want to run a mile.'

'She's really no trouble to you, Audrey,' said Lisa, who had gone slightly white. She clutched the baby to her chest and jiggled her up and down. 'I don't think you can accuse her of having been any trouble.'

'There has to be a limit,' said Vivian. 'It can't just go on and on. It can't be like a cow giving milk, on and on.'

'A cow?' said Audrey. She looked around at everyone in comic mystification.

'They call me a cow,' said Vivian flatly. 'I heard them in the supermarket. Someone said, where does she get all her money, and they said, don't you know, she's got a cash cow.'

'Who has?' said Audrey.

'You. Marjory said I'm your cash cow. I heard her say it. I was in the supermarket last week and I was bending down so they couldn't see me, because they were in the next aisle, you see, and I heard them.'

'Darling, it was probably nothing to *do* with you! They

were probably talking about *real* cows, you know, moo –'

'They said my name. They were in the next aisle, you see. It was as if they were standing right beside me. They said I was a cash cow.'

'Well,' said Audrey lightly, after a pause, 'people are very silly – you know that, Vivian, as well as I do. The fact is that we have our arrangement and what other people say about it isn't really the point, is it?'

'It's horrible,' said Vivian.

'Poor darling. Poor Vivian,' said Audrey, slightly impatiently.

'It means that every time you want money you come and milk me. You and Paul pull the udders and the money comes out!'

'I know what it means,' said Audrey, tapping her foot on the flagstones.

'That's what people say. It means that you exploit me.'

'Nobody exploits you!'

'If you keep milking me I'll run dry, you know. I'll have nothing left – all the money daddy gave me, and not a penny of it left for Laura and Jilly!'

'You got plenty for it,' said Audrey. Her voice was unkind. 'You got plenty for your damned money. I gave you my house. I gave you my children. I gave you my man. He was my man. Mine!' She struck her pony-haired chest unexpectedly with her small, pale fist. 'I left the field. I bowed out gracefully and for that you had to pay.'

'There was nothing to give, you know,' said Vivian, to me. 'All this talk of giving! She didn't give me the house – I bought it.'

'That isn't true,' said Caris.

'They cooked it up between them!' cried Vivian.

'Mum, that isn't true,' said Caris.

Audrey gave a little shrug and turned to the window with her arms folded.

'Vivian did help daddy out a little with the farm,' she said

'I never knew by how much. I think I can be forgiven for not wanting to know, can't I?'

'He got a valuation from that friend of his in town and he said that was what I had to pay – it was far more than it was worth! My husband told me that. He said, get your name on the deeds. Whatever you do, get your name on the deeds.'

Audrey snorted.

'What would Hippo know about the valuation?' she said. 'The submersible was usually submerged in gin by lunchtime.'

'It didn't last them long! They ran through it all!' said Vivian. 'All of it!'

'Honestly, Vivian,' said Audrey, 'you make it sound as though you were frog-marched into it. The fact is, darling, you went to bed with my husband.'

'He seduced me, you know,' said Vivian forlornly, to me.

'Nobody made you do it,' said Audrey. 'Nobody forced you.'

'He sent me a lamb. It was a little white lamb for the children. We all thought it was terribly sweet but after two months it was enormous. They used to give it all sorts of food, you see, and it got very big and aggressive until in the end it used to run at them and knock them over. It was like a bull – it wasn't like a sheep at all!'

Audrey laughed. 'That should have told you everything you needed to know, darling.'

'Jilly scratched her face until it bled,' Vivian said, to me. 'For a whole year she scratched her face. None of the women would speak to me. Then he said we should send them away to school because the house was too crowded. And I said, well, why don't we send them all away in that case, and he said, no, we can't do that, it would cost too much to send them all, so mine were sent and his stayed. So I was left looking after three children who weren't mine, do you see?'

'You didn't have to do it,' said Audrey.

'I suppose I wanted him to love me,' said Vivian. 'Sometimes you do things you oughtn't to, don't you? You can be quite outside yourself.'

'You're very sweet to talk about love,' said Audrey.

'Is it Vivian's name that's on the deeds?' said Adam.

'Of course it's not!' scoffed Audrey. 'Do you really think your father would do that, after everything we went through? That was definitely not part of the deal.'

'What deal?' said Caris.

'The arrangement, then. Everyone makes arrangements, darling.'

'Every month I pay her,' said Vivian. 'They won't talk to me until I do.'

'That's my alimony!' said Audrey. 'That's the least you owe me!'

'You always get alimony, Vivian,' said Lisa, 'in a case like this.'

'But it's rather a lot,' said Vivian. 'It's an awful lot, you know. It's a bit much, isn't it, when you think about it.'

'Have you got anything actually written down?' said Adam.

'Especially since I pay for the house separately and everything separately, do you see what I mean?'

'Why couldn't dad pay it?' said Caris. She seemed perplexed. 'He's got plenty of money. He's always had money.'

'He hasn't, actually,' said Adam, after a pause.

'Of course he has!' said Caris.

'He hasn't. I saw the accounts. He's been running the farm at a loss.'

'They haven't got a penny between them, you know – that's why they got their cash cow. They came and found me!' said Vivian, her hands gyrating at her sides. 'They hunted me down, both of them! Don't you think I don't know what you did!' she said, to Audrey. 'I know! Everybody knows!' She turned to me. 'They cooked it up between them!' she cried. 'Ask anyone – they'll tell you!'

She buried her fists in her black mop of hair and looked at us all wildly. A sort of electricity seemed to be coursing through her body: her eyes were alarmed and her face wore a strange grimace, and where her hands were clutching her hair it stood on end.

'Everybody just did what they wanted!' she said.

'Including you,' said Audrey. 'You did what you wanted. In fact, you had a high old time.'

'They call it living in sin, you know,' she said, to me. 'It's rather a good expression for it, don't you think?'

'Oh stop it!' said Caris. 'I won't listen to it any more! All this talk about sin – if you want sin, don't look for it here! Look for it outside in the world, because there's plenty of it, Vivian! There are places that are drowning in it! It's feelings that matter,' she concluded, clutching at her heart.

'She didn't want them, that was part of it,' said Vivian, to me. 'Her own children! That was the part that was really beyond belief.'

'I won't hear you!' cried Caris. 'I won't, I won't!'

She put her hands over her ears. Her expression was triumphant.

'Personally,' Adam said presently, in a statesmanlike tone, 'I respect mum for it. You can't put a price on Egypt, Vivian. Our family belongs here. It wasn't that she didn't want us. She did it *for* us. There's a bit of a difference, don't you think?'

Audrey was looking at her son with an interested expression, her finger resting on her chin.

'The thing is,' said Vivian, 'it was only because my husband told me. I wouldn't have known otherwise. I wouldn't have known to ask. But he said, whatever you do, stick to it. Stick to it or they'll have you lock, stock and barrel. It's awful in a way, when you think of how we treated him. He got nothing out of it himself, you know. He lives in a flat. Laura says it's awfully modest. I paid far too much for it, of course. They ran through it in a year!'

'Do stop it, darling,' said Audrey. 'You're sounding positively addled. What was I supposed to do? I had to get my house – I couldn't just go and camp in a field, could I? And that sort of property is terribly expensive in Doniford. Everyone wants it, you know.'

'He called me a bloody viper.'

'Who did?'

'A bloody viper. Don't you think that's vicious?' said Vivian, looking around at us. 'He said he'd never forgive me!'

'You had to do without Hippo's forgiveness,' said Audrey. 'We all did. Thank heavens for the Isle of Wight!'

'He said, I'm not giving Egypt to a bloody viper. I'm not giving my house to a bloody snake in the grass, that's what he said. And I said, well, I shan't come then, you can manage on your own. He was terribly rude, you know. But he signed. He had to sign – he had no choice, do you see? I felt rather pleased with myself. I wanted to ring my husband and tell him but of course I couldn't by then. He wouldn't speak to me.'

'Sign what?' said Adam.

'I don't think he ever *has* forgiven me, you know,' said Vivian miserably. 'At the time I thought I'd been rather clever, but now I wish I hadn't done it. I sometimes think he might have felt more for me if I hadn't. And you don't forget it, someone calling you a bloody viper, not when you have to see them every day. It wasn't as though I even wanted the farm! Ivybridge was much more sheltered, you know – one got the sun all year there. I wonder sometimes if my husband knew that was what would happen. He was the one who encouraged me, you know. He was the one who said I had to get it all in my name.'

There was silence in the kitchen. The Hanburys stared at one another, stared and stared, with faces that filled with calculation and then emptied and filled again. There seemed to be no air in the room, no suspending element – it was as though we stood in the lee of a gathering wave as it sucked everything back into itself. I felt the presence of a catastrophe, an emergency whose tumultuous moments we had entered as a boat might enter a field of rapids. A bitter smell assailed my nostrils. I realised that the room was filling with smoke.

'I think the potatoes are burning,' I said.

Just then there was a child's cry out on the lawn, a wail that went up and down and came closer like a siren, until it was in the hall, echoing horribly in the confinement of the house. There was the sound of something being knocked over and falling with a clatter to the floor. Janie burst into the kitchen. Her face was a wreck of tears.

'Rufus shot the little boy!' she shrieked. 'They're out in the garden! You have to come! He shot the little boy with his crossbow!'

I don't know what the others did. I ran out of the house and over the damp lawn, towards the ring of oaks where Caris and I had once kissed, and where I saw the fair heads of the children, clustered together like the bright little heads of flowers, weaving and moving as though in the ecstasy of their impermanence.

NINE

I returned to Bath and to Nimrod Street and found that the rubble from the fallen balcony, including the three large segments of broken limestone slab, remained strewn over the front steps.

The journey from Doniford had taken most of the day though it was only sixty miles or so. There was no one to drive Hamish and me to the railway station: Lisa, whose sensitivity to practical matters could normally have been relied on, was not at home; and Adam had bidden us a sincere but unavailing farewell over breakfast, before vanishing up the hill to Egypt in his car with an expression of grim preoccupation on his face. Alone in the warm, silent, airless house we packed our things. A sense of failure dogged me as I went through the rooms retrieving those items that belonged to us as though they were the detritus of some breakage or disaster, the evidence of a lack of love or merely care of which was conveniently cleansing the scene. I could not attribute this failure entirely either to myself or to the Hanburys. Instead I was possessed by an awareness of how little survived the business of human encounter. What would be left of Rebecca and myself, once the storm of our association had abated? What did we have to show for ourselves? Hamish watched me as I put my violin in its case and laid the purple cloth like a shroud over its carved face. He seemed to tremble with a precarious, pregnant stillness, like a drop of water hanging from the corroded lip of a tap. For a moment his insubstantiality enraged me. I felt that I could have dashed him, shaken him off and demanded instead to know where the life was that made its robust demands, that insisted on itself in the face of everything that reverted to inconsequence.

We closed the front door behind us and it locked with an automatic, impersonal click. For nearly an hour we stood in Doniford on the grey, shuttered Sunday high street waiting for a bus, which presently emerged from the empty streets and carried us through the deserted haunts of its route, through tracts of green hemmed by frayed, budding hedgerows, through indifferent villages that we patiently unearthed from their tangle of narrow, muddy, aimless lanes, as though we were circulating around an organism that otherwise would have lapsed into its own mysterious, unregulated version of existence. The driver pursued his destiny with cursory speed, flying past some stops and observing unfathomable pauses at others, during which he switched off the engine and read a newspaper folded on his lap while Hamish and I, his only passengers, sat side by side on our oversprung seat in a clear torrent of silence far louder than the crowded din of the train that subsequently bore us in long, smooth surges to Bath. At the station we took a taxi: passing through the city I was struck at first by its rich, historied appearance and its textured, flesh-toned buildings that seemed like living things after Adam's house. Everything was moving, almost undulating: the cluttered light, the noise of traffic and voices and garbled ribbons of music, the teeming pavements, the rows of shopfronts opening and closing their doors in numberless mechanical embraces, the scatter of pigeons and the clustered fall of water from fountains, the dark, stately motion of the river – it all churned and moved in a body, rising and falling inchoately like the sea. The taxi went at walking pace through the obstructed streets. People snagged and formed blockages around every shop window and restaurant and frequently spilled out into the road. There were so many people that on the pavement beside us the crowd ceased to move and instead seemed to swell, pushing inwards at its core so that people staggered or were crushed against each other, and I saw a look of uncertainty pass like a great shadow over their faces. A man was forced backwards off the kerb and stumbled as his shoe came off. I thought how hard it was, and yet how necessary, to love. Hamish's hand rested beside me on the seat and I picked it up and held it. It was so small and soft and limp that it almost seemed as if it might dissolve in my palm, but I hung on to it as though it were the last thread connecting me to the earth, until his fingers grew warm and flexed themselves and he returned the pressure of my grip. We stopped and started along the street until at last we reached London Road, unfurling east from the packed core of the city, its beauteous facades casually dirtied by passing traffic.

It was a grey, gelid afternoon. There was no breeze: the air in Nimrod Street was so still that it caused a physical sensation of numbness. The black twisted railings made little frozen, anguished forms amidst the broken stones. There was a quality of weightlessness to everything, of ceaseless intermission, that did not belong here but appeared to have followed me from The Meadows. It was clear to me, though I couldn't have said why, that it was easier to build a hundred houses in Doniford than it was to remove three pieces of broken masonry from Nimrod Street. The green, shiny leaves of the laurel hedge beside the front steps were still thickly coated in white dust. Inside, the house was full of grey light and its rooms had a creeping edge of staleness, as though no one had entered them while we'd been away. Everything had contracted a little with unfamiliarity, become flat and angular like a garment removed and hung in a closet.

Rebecca was sitting in the kitchen with a person who had her back to me. I did not immediately recognise this person. Two cups and a teapot stood on the table between them. The kitchen looked different: it was untidy, in a light, girlish way. Rebecca's things – scarves, items of jewellery, a pink hairbrush – were strewn over surfaces that now betrayed no relationship to the preparation or consumption of food. The atmosphere of repudiation that I had picked up on my way through the house was far stronger in here: it emanated powerfully from its source – Rebecca – where she sat a few feet away.

'You're back,' she said, nevertheless failing to rise from her chair.

Hamish ran towards her, his feet making loud slapping sounds on the floorboards. Rebecca smiled a great smile and held out her arms to him, still sedentary, as though some misfortune which she was too stalwart to mention had paralysed her legs in our absence.

'Look, Charlie's here,' she said to him as soon as she had got him in a clinch.

'Hey, Michael,' said Charlie, turning around in her chair and smiling brilliantly at me. A moment later she rose and kissed both my cheeks. I received a warm, confused impression of hair and teeth and rattling jewellery, borne pungently over me in a suede-smelling wave from her jacket.

'I didn't recognise you,' I said.

The last time I saw Charlie her hair had been blonde. Now it was black.

'Charlie's come to stay with us,' said Rebecca to Hamish.

'It's the hair,' said Charlie. She grasped a strand of it and held it out to one side. 'Becca says it looks like a wig.'

I saw that somehow, in the person of her friend, Rebecca had contrived to erect a barrier around herself that promised to withstand not just this moment of our return, but an indefinite number of days that projected impossibly outwards like a diving board over cold, unbroken waters. Feelings of disappointment, and of what appeared to be more fear than anger, knifed me soundlessly in the chest, in the back.

'There's nothing wrong with wigs,' Rebecca said. 'I actually like the superimposed effect. It makes you look like one of those Andy Warhol lithographs.'

I wondered why I had phoned Rebecca so frequently while I was away. It was, I now saw, a pointless, self-referential act by which I had succeeded only in illuminating myself as an object, as though I had taken the trouble to write letters to

195

myself and post them home from Doniford. She looked at me occasionally in uncertain flashes. She was wearing a strange dress that I had never seen before. It was pale pink, with little sleeves the shape of cowslips and a neckline that revealed most of her freckled clavicle. The wistful colour did not flatter her. On her long, calloused feet were a pair of strappy pink sandals with six-inch heels like daggers.

'How long are you staying?' I asked Charlie.

My voice sounded out of turn, like an instrument playing loud notes not indicated in the score.

'Oh, *listen* to him,' cried Charlie, with comical pathos. 'He's all disappointed, poor thing!'

'Did you miss me?' said Rebecca to Hamish. She buried her nose in his hair with an obscure look of satisfaction.

'He was hoping to have you to himself,' Charlie persisted, 'and now I've come along and spoiled it. I'd be touched Michael, if I wasn't frankly offended. People like me only get through life by being humoured, you know. We non-conformists depend on the charity of you family types.'

I thought of taking off my coat, but the atmosphere in the room discouraged it.

'How's Ali?' I said to Rebecca.

'Actually, she's really well,' Rebecca replied, having given the matter a few seconds of consideration that she gave the impression were overdue, as though she hadn't thought about her mother's health in weeks.

'Has there been any news?'

'What? Oh, that,' she said, waving her hand dismissively in the air. 'That's all fine.'

Her manner was disconcerting: I wondered whether she was exercising this uncharacteristic discretion as a result of Charlie's presence, but a moment later Charlie said, pitying ly:

'Poor Becca's been worried sick about Ali.'

'Thank God you were here,' Rebecca fervently responded, grasping her friend's hand across the table.

I said: 'I thought someone might have started clearing away the rubble at the front.'

If I had hoped to kindle a propitiatory spark by the route of disgruntlement I was disappointed. Rebecca and Charlie looked at me as if they didn't know what I was talking about.

'Yes, what *happened* out there?' exclaimed Charlie finally, opening her eyes very wide.

'The balcony fell off,' I said, because although it was improbable that Charlie hadn't deduced this fact, she seemed to require an answer.

'Thank God no one was on it,' she said.

I hadn't actually considered this possibility before. No one ever stood on the balcony. It was ornamental, and could be reached only by climbing out through the windows on the first floor.

'I *know*,' concurred Rebecca, who to my knowledge had, like me, never set foot on it.

I said: 'I came out of the front door one morning and it fell off. I was on the second step down to the street and it crashed down behind me. It missed me by a few inches.'

To my surprise, both women laughed.

'You're obviously *completely* traumatised!' shrieked Charlie. 'He's obviously *completely* traumatised,' she repeated, for Rebecca's benefit.

I had no concrete objection to Charlie, other than in her current function as a sort of wrapper or container for Rebecca, by which I could see that Rebecca intended to elude me for as long as she could. She and Rebecca had been friends at school in Bath, but for as long as I had known her Charlie had lived in London, so that it was a tenet of their association that it had never been geographically easy to sustain: they pursued it with a sort of hectic diplomacy, as though they were the representatives of two distant states endeavouring to maintain relations.

Three or four years ago I had attended Charlie's wedding, a cold, rain-sodden event I could only remember now in the light of the fact that Charlie had left her husband a year or so after it. Rebecca used to complain that her friendship with Charlie had become one-sided and perfunctory, as though it were the victim of ill-disposed market forces: these same forces reversed their direction when Charlie began to emerge from the carapace of marriage, sweeping Rebecca up in an ecstasy of renewed importance whose unforeseen consequence was that she now often accused me of disliking Charlie, or at least regarding her with suspicion. Rebecca's theory was that I suspected Charlie of a cultish determination to motivate her friends to leave their husbands as she had left hers; or, less stridently, that exposure to Charlie would inadvertently result in the contagion of divorce entering our midst. In fact, if my awareness of Charlie possessed a certain clarity, then it resulted from a strange association I felt with the idea not of her notoriety but of her shame. Her wedding was bombastic and strikingly conventional: when the music started I remember she and her husband waltzed around the mud-spattered marquee before the applauding crowd, he in a dinner jacket and she in a long white dress too modish and flattering, somehow, for sincerity or even passion. Every time I saw her I remembered with what determination she had engineered the public display of her mistake.

'It might have fallen on any of us,' I observed.

'That's what I said to mum and dad,' said Rebecca. 'I said, look, why all the fuss about the insurance? It's *good* that it's come down. Nothing can insure you against a balcony falling on your head. Thank God it happened, I say,' she concluded urgently.

Charlie laughed. 'You do put things in the funniest way, Becca. Mark says she reverses into her sentences,' she said, to me. Mark was Charlie's boyfriend.

'Mark's in Germany,' Rebecca informed me, darkly, as though I might find myself there too if I wasn't careful.

'For work,' Charlie added. 'Not on holiday.'

She appeared to find this distinction so significant that a

moment later she said: 'Does *anybody* go to Germany on holiday?'

'My parents go there every year on their way to the Salzburg festival,' I said.

'Do they?' she replied, contriving to seem enthusiastic. Her manner contributed to my mounting impression that I was being humoured.

'They like music,' I said.

'I didn't realise you came from such cultivated stock.'

'Oh, they're obsessed with it,' Rebecca said, as though cultivation were generally agreed to be a nuisance. 'They made him start violin lessons when he was about three. That's why his fingers are such funny shapes.'

'Let's see!' Charlie exclaimed.

I held out my hands in front of her with the fingers splayed.

'My God,' she said, 'they *are*. That one bends inwards.' She pointed at the smallest finger on my left hand. 'Look, Becca, it's almost at a right angle to the others.'

'I know,' said Rebecca absently.

'It's the equivalent of foot-binding!' Charlie exclaimed.

'Not quite,' I said.

'Actually,' Charlie resumed after a pause, as though to pacify me, 'Mark says Germany's lovely.'

Rebecca gave an astringent laugh.

'Of all the things I can think of to say about Germany, that's about the least convincing. "Auschwitz? Yes, it was lovely."'

'I think he was talking about the countryside,' said Charlie vaguely.

'Oh, the countryside,' said Rebecca. 'Where people said they never noticed anything.'

'In fact, he *did* mention a few strange things,' Charlie said. She gave the impression of continually arriving late in the conversation. It was unclear whether this was deliberate or not.

'Like what?'

'His German associates disapprove of his use of public swimming pools. Apparently it's become a sort of standing joke. One of them said to him that he hoped Mark washed properly afterwards and Mark asked him why and he said because the pools are used by black people. Don't you think that's horrible?'

Rebecca looked stricken. 'And what did he say?'

'I don't know,' Charlie said. 'I don't think he said anything.'

'I would have come home,' Rebecca declared. 'I wouldn't even have hesitated.'

'It's funny how little we know about each other, isn't it?' Charlie said, to me. 'Mark's collating a study for the EU about the way national populations spend their time.'

'I wouldn't even have hesitated,' Rebecca said again.

'Apparently the Germans do hardly any work. That's not what you'd think, is it? The French spend all their time grooming. I can't remember what the English do. Could it be cooking?'

'I never cook,' said Rebecca dramatically. 'Never.'

'Mark thinks it's interesting, anyway,' said Charlie, shrugging her shoulders.

'Well, he would, wouldn't he?' said Rebecca. 'He's a man. Any chance to be dispassionate – any chance to surrender your humanity in the face of a statistic!'

Charlie said to me, with a rueful expression: 'You can see we've been working ourselves up into a fever of female indignation in your absence.'

'You should have heard Michael when I was in labour!' exclaimed Rebecca, turning her sights on me. 'He'd look at his watch and tell me I couldn't be in pain because it wasn't time yet!'

Charlie laughed.

'Poor Michael,' she said, shaking her head and then laughing again.

'Why?' said Rebecca. 'Why "poor Michael"? Why does everybody feel sorry for him?'

I saw that she was actually angry: there was a brief thickening of her voice as she spoke which betrayed the fact.

Hamish was sitting on Rebecca's lap in an attitude of extreme limpness and pallor. He jolted this way and that each time her body discharged its surfeit of discontent.

'Everybody doesn't feel sorry for me,' I said.

'It's just that he's only just walked through the door,' Charlie added, in mitigation of the awkward way I had phrased my remark. 'He's only been here five minutes and people are accusing him of deformity, and strange cruelty to pregnant women.'

'I'm not *people*,' Rebecca said.

She folded her arms and looked down into them as though something were cradled there.

'Anyway,' Charlie continued, 'where have you two *been*?'

I sensed that she meant to recompense me for the bitter welcome I had received and perhaps for something else too, for other conversations by which I hadn't been wounded because I wasn't there to hear them.

'A friend of mine has a family farm in Somerset,' I said. 'Hamish and I went to help with the lambing.'

'What fun!' cried Charlie, by which cheery expostulation I deduced that Rebecca's revelations had been more gruesome than ever. 'Was this a he-friend or a she-friend?'

'A he,' I said, although I thought it was a strange, suggestive question to ask, particularly in Rebecca's presence. I caught a glimpse of something I had noticed in Charlie before, a certain blindness to the concept of virtue. Then it struck me that the tastelessness of the comment might be Rebecca's own.

'And how do you know each other, you and this sheep-farmer?'

'It's his father who owns the farm. My friend is a chartered surveyor.'

'Gosh,' Charlie said. She wore the expression of someone who has just opened a door and found something unexpectedly horrible behind it. 'A chartered surveyor from Somerset. He must be scintillating company. Or is he one of those people like in Tolstoy, who make a philosophical occasion of themselves?'

'I've met him,' Rebecca said, as though this indicated we were about to hear the last word on the subject. 'He's the sort of person who seems quite exciting at eighteen but then ends up middle-aged before he's thirty.'

Chagrined, I turned away from the table and began to look for something I could give Hamish to eat. I opened the fridge and was surprised to see it lavishly stocked. There were numerous luxurious packets of things, olives and expensive-looking cheeses and handmade pasta like little wrapped gifts in muted shades of green and cream.

'We're making Michael cross,' said Charlie behind me. 'Let's stop or he'll leave us sitting here on our own. We were discussing the chartered surveyor and his universal values. Is he superannuated, like Becca says?'

'He doesn't think he's young,' I said. I was speaking into the open fridge and so I allowed myself to say it a little spitefully.

'I sense we're being mocked,' Charlie said to Rebecca. 'Is he going to be a chartered surveyor for the rest of his life?'

'I don't think so. He always expected he'd take over the farm one day.'

'Imagine that. I can't think of anything nicer. Or worse, I'm not sure which.'

'Nor is he. He's considering going up north to work for his father-in-law.'

'Who's the father-in-law?'

I turned around with some of the things from the fridge in my hands and was surprised to see a look of protest, almost of affront, flit across Rebecca's face as she saw them, as though my taking of food were inappropriate, or as though I were taking what she wanted for herself.

'He sells jacuzzis,' I said. 'He's offered him a job.'

'My God,' said Charlie. 'I hope he's not going to do that, in any case.'

'He might. The farm's losing money. It turns out his step-mother has been financing it all along, out of her own pocket.'

'So it's all a sort of illusion.'

'Sort of.'

'For whose benefit?'

I took a saucepan out of the cupboard and lit the gas with a match from a box beside the cooker. Taking the match from its box I was aware again of Rebecca's strange gaze and its accusation of theft.

'God knows,' I said. 'If you'd been there you'd have thought it was the father. The stepmother thinks that he – procured her. He and his wife, to bail themselves out. She claims now that they set out to destroy her marriage in order to get their hands on her money.'

Charlie shrieked.

'What a scandal!' she cried. 'And is it true?'

I smiled at her tone.

'I don't know. It might be.'

'But what's she like, the stepmother?'

'She's slightly saturnine. She mopes around this great dark house. And Audrey is very vivacious.'

'Is that the mother? The minx!'

'They always seemed perfectly amicable. It was what I always liked about them. They seemed so uninhibited by their situation.'

'Well, now you know why,' said Charlie. 'The second one couldn't believe she'd got the man and the first one couldn't believe she'd got the money! Are you listening to this, Becca? What I want to know is how it all came out. Were you there?'

I nodded. 'Paul, my friend's father, was in hospital for a few days. It seemed to be precipitated by his absence. Adam said he'd gone through the farm accounts, and then Audrey came up demanding money and Vivian wouldn't give her any, and suddenly everyone was fighting about who'd done what to whom. Then one of the children shot his brother with a crossbow.'

'My God,' said Charlie in a reverent tone. 'Over the money?'

'No, no – a small child, one of Vivian's grandchildren. He'd been given a crossbow as a toy and there was an accident. The bolt went into his little brother's hand. A boy Hamish's age.'

At the sound of his name Hamish slid off his mother's lap and came to stand beside me at the cooker. His food bubbled in the pan. He rested his hand on the back of my leg; he leaned, as though against a tree or a solid section of wall.

'It all sounds barbaric!' exclaimed Charlie. 'What happened? Was he all right?'

'It was strange,' I said. 'His parents weren't there and nobody seemed to want to take him to hospital. There was some doctor they all knew, a family friend who lived in the next valley, and they spent ages trying to track him down and arguing over where he was and talking to ten different people about him on the telephone and then it turned out he'd retired years ago and didn't practise any more. Finally Adam's wife took him to the hospital in Taunton. I don't know what happened after that. She hadn't come back when we left.'

'What on earth were you two doing in this den of vipers? How did you come across them in the first place?'

I said: 'I knew Adam at university. We lived next door to each other.'

'I see. And –'

Charlie paused to remove her suede jacket. Beneath it she wore a black silk shirt which strained across her breasts as she moved, so that a string of gaps suddenly opened among the buttons down her front. A black lace garment was momentarily visible through them. The sight of it caused me to feel a confused sense of both suspicion and sympathy for her: for reasons I could not establish, her underwear reminded me of her humanity, of her native power both to wound and be wounded. Her hair snaked darkly over her shoulders as she turned and hung the jacket on the chair next to her. When she faced me again her countenance was flushed. I sensed that she had felt my notice of her and wasn't sure what it meant.

'– and at the weekends,' she continued, 'he used to take you back to the family pile.'

'The first time I went there it was his sister Caris's eighteenth birthday party,' I said. 'She'd never met me but she invited me anyway. The place is called Egypt Farm and on her invitation it said something like "Please come to Egypt". It really annoyed me, but when I got there it suddenly seemed romantic.'

'What about the sister?' Charlie said, with the suggestive tone that irritated me. 'Was she romantic too?'

'She was far too sophisticated for me,' I said. 'She was having a relationship with an artist who used to paint her naked.'

'Who was it?' Rebecca enquired, in a remote voice.

'I think he was called Jasper Elliot.'

Rebecca raised her eyebrows but said nothing.

'So you admired the sister from afar,' Charlie said, 'and at eighteen you thought it was exciting that two women could be married to the same man and still be civil to each other. And we know Adam was more interesting in those days because Becca says he was. What about the father? I sense the father is at the root of all this.'

A feeling of discomfort, almost of apprehension, stole over me. I felt a sensation of nakedness across my back, a coldness, as though someone were standing behind me. As much to relieve this feeling as anything else I turned to lift Hamish and set him on a chair at the table. My hands cleaved to his slender ribcage. I was almost disappointed to feel how small he was, for in that instant I had been visited by the perverse illusion that he could offer me some protection. Instead he seemed so small as to be barely human.

'He let me drive his car,' I said.

'I may be being obtuse,' said Charlie, 'but the symbolism of that is escaping me for the moment.'

'The first time he met me,' I explained. 'He threw me the

keys and asked me to go down to the town for more wine.'

I laid Hamish's plate in front of him. Tendrils of vapour curled upwards around the fixed peaks of his face. Rebecca was watching us with an expression of unidentifiable emotion.

'For the party?'

'My father never once let me drive his car,' I observed.

'Perhaps your father attached more value to things.'

'I don't know. He might have.'

'But the point was that he recognised you as a man and your father didn't. And there he was with his two wives and his gorgeous daughter and his parties and his big house. Did you feel flattered?'

'I felt relieved.'

'About what?'

'That things didn't have to be so hard.'

At this Charlie sat back with an expression of triumph.

'So he bought you too!' she exclaimed.

'Why would he bother to do that?' I said, though I didn't entirely disagree with her.

'Maybe he envied you your incorruptibility. What I want to know is why you fell for it. You're such a *puritan*, Michael,' she exclaimed. 'All this talk of aristocratic largesse and car keys – you don't even *have* a car! You pay yourself slave wages down at that slum you call an office. You're the least materialistic person I know and yet there you are getting all seduced and concupiscent over a sheep farmer! Perhaps this is your weakness,' she said, with a devilish glint in her eye. 'Perhaps this is your dark secret.'

'It wasn't like that,' I protested, laughing.

'Then what was it?'

I remembered that golden day of Caris's party, which remained untouched in my recollection in all its exquisite irretrievability.

'Something happened to me almost as soon as I got there,' I said. 'I had an – intimation.'

'Of what?' said Charlie.

'That my life was going to expand and expand and become beautiful.'

A silence followed this disclosure. The gaze of the two women grew so discomfiting that I added:

'It was a quality they had. The Hanburys.'

'And what was this magic quality?' said Charlie.

'They made it seem as though all you had to do was something other than what you thought you should do.'

Charlie nodded her head abstractedly, as though this proposition pleased her.

'I see,' she said presently. 'And that became your motto, did it? To live adjacent to your own conservative compulsions. That's not bad. Of course, I didn't know you before you experienced this divine revelation. Was it as transforming as that? Would you be sitting here now, for example, in this gorgeous, crumbling residence, with the gorgeous Rebecca, if these Hanburys hadn't got their claws into you?'

'I didn't say it was a revelation.'

'Oh yes. It was an *intimation*. You haven't answered my question.'

I wasn't sure I wanted to answer it. Rebecca had turned her head and was looking at me with a shadowy, inscrutable expression. I realised that I still had my coat on. It seemed for a moment as though I could leave, as though I had given them all the satisfaction it was in my power to give.

'It might have been the feeling that I didn't need to possess things to experience them,' I said. Charlie's face was blank. 'Think of it as a picture,' I added.

'A picture.'

'Of a house on top of a big hill overlooking the sea, with these people in it and a party going on.'

'Is this a point about art?'

'Sort of,' I said.

'And suddenly you decided to visit this charming little picture,' said Charlie. 'You took your life in your hands. Was this by any chance related to your near-death experience on the front step?'

'I thought I should see Adam,' I said. 'I suppose it was a social compulsion.'

'You forgot it was a picture.'

'I couldn't remember any more what it always made me remember.'

'So you went back,' said Charlie, 'and these models of bohemian living turned out to be a pack of money-grubbing reprobates. Egypt!' she snorted, shaking her head and laughing.

At this moment Rebecca spoke.

'It isn't anything to do with art,' she said. 'It's to do with cowardice.'

Her voice was so cold that it abraded me like a fierce, freezing wind where I stood. Had we been alone I believed in that instant I would have rushed to her in my petrifying nakedness and begged her for warmth and forgiveness; but then the moment passed, and I found myself subsiding once more into a familiar accommodation with our remoteness from one another. Charlie gave a surprised laugh.

'That's a bit harsh, Becca,' she said.

'It's true,' said Rebecca, obstinately but with a little less frigidity. 'Anyway, it's unnatural not to be possessive. Men are *supposed* to be possessive.'

'Are they?' said Charlie.

'It doesn't mean they're compromised,' Rebecca persisted. 'It takes courage to set the terms – look at dad, for heaven's sake! He's always out there, taking risks, making things happen, and for what? To make us *safe*.' She raised her hands aloft, to indicate the very roof under which we sat. 'You could call him domineering or macho or possessive, but the fact is that he lives life ten times more passionately than the rest of us!'

This way of speaking about her father was quite a new facet of Rebecca's personality. I sensed she deployed it as a tool, to make the work of exposing my own shortcomings less time-consuming. Yet I remembered that when I first met her, it was the very qualities she was now claiming to admire in Rick that used to cause her pain.

'Well,' said Charlie, 'I suppose we can't all be like daddy. It's Michael that I'm worried about. His whole philosophy of life is in ruins.'

'It doesn't matter,' I said.

'I always find that the less things matter the harder they are to live with. He looks like he's about to leave us, Becca. He's got his coat on. Tell us you'll stay, Michael.'

'He'd never leave,' said Rebecca sullenly, as though my steadfastness were one of the irritating constituents of marriage to which she had been forced to reconcile herself. 'Never. It isn't in his nature.'

'I wouldn't be so sure,' said Charlie. 'Tell us you'll stay,' she repeated.

Pulling out a chair next to Hamish I sat down at the table. He had finished his supper and he clambered on to my lap and laid his cheek against my chest. Earlier I had marvelled at his fragility but now he felt like a boulder pinning me to my seat. My heart was thudding uncomfortably. For a moment the sense of my own precariousness was intolerable. It inflamed me with feelings of violence: I wanted to smash and break, to turn the table on its side and send the teacups sliding to the floor, to demonstrate what was mine by destroying it. This feeling passed as quickly as it came. In its wake a terrible loveliness seemed to adhere to everything around me. The first stain of dusk tinted the room unexpectedly before my eyes. I looked at the two women sitting in their chairs. The chairs were antiques with wooden backs carved in the shape of hearts: they belonged to Rick and Ali, as did most of our furniture. They were beautiful, though not particularly valuable. Rebecca, in her draining pink, with her sandy-coloured hair gathered in a tangled knot on the top of her head, had her arms folded and her legs crossed. Her head was turned so that she could be seen in profile, eyes down-cast; a posture redolent of some inadequacy, some lack she perennially found in her experiences, so that she gave an impression that was familiar to me, of being in silent corre-spondence with the concept of a shortfall, of looking down into it, as though it were a hole bored into the ground next to her. Charlie made a dark shape, denser and more solid. She sat straight and kept her eyes ahead. I could see the edges of the heart-shaped chair backs around each of them, like pairs of wings; and it may have been this illusion that gave me the sense of a relationship to their femaleness that was tenuous and fleeting, almost unworldly, as though their robustness as human beings was attended by something fragile and flutter-ing, something of which they themselves were barely con-scious, something that every word and gesture crushed but that rose again and again, released into the air by each new pause like a delicate butterfly from a dense, fibrous confusion of greenery. I felt a desire both to help them and to be indis-tinguishable from them, to be incorporated into whatever mystery it was that gathered in a mist around them. It seemed a sort of tragedy to me, because within that desire was con-tained the trace of a memory, a streak of recognition that ran across it; not of any particular event but of a state that was less combative, less rooted in the body, a harmonious time that I supposed must have been childhood, though I wasn't sure which part of it.

'Charlie's thinking of moving back to Bath,' said Rebecca.

'Are you?' I said.

'She's got a job at the university.'

'I've got an interview,' amended Charlie. 'I haven't got a job.'

'You'll get it,' Rebecca replied, with a far-seeing tone.

'There are a lot of things I have to work out first,' said Charlie mysteriously.

'Mark doesn't want her to go,' said Rebecca. She said it to me, with an air of unspecific accusation.

'I don't really want to go either,' said Charlie. 'It's just that
think I should. I'm seeing it as an opportunity for spiritual
advancement.'

'People don't often come to Bath for that,' I said.

'Oh, I could be going anywhere. It just so happened that it
was here. The thing is, I've never been alone in my life and I'm
banking on it being good for me. You're right, though – I'd
hate to be too comfortable. It would spoil the penitent effect.'

'You won't be alone,' Rebecca said. 'You've got hundreds
of friends here.'

'You see?' said Charlie to me. 'That's the problem. When it
comes down to it I'm not prepared to suffer at all.'

'At least Mark will suffer,' I said.

Charlie gave a little melancholic smile.

'That wasn't really the idea. I'm beginning to see that my
plan is flawed.'

'It isn't your fault! You can't tailor your life to suit other
people. You have to go where the opportunities are,' declared
Rebecca, for whom opportunities had only ever dared to present themselves in one way, which was to her immediate convenience.

Charlie said: 'Do you remember when I was doing my doctorate?'

'I remember you were obsessed with a brown cloud,' said
Rebecca.

I said: 'What was your doctorate on?'

'Climate change. Signs and portents thereof. It was a little
idea I had, that we were recreating the concept of an apoca-
lypse in the form of anxieties about the environment. Then I
had to turn it into a much bigger idea, and in the process I
rather became the victim of these anxieties myself. I'd spend
all day in the library reading about glaciers melting and the
world getting hotter and hotter and the fact that half of it was
going to be under water in fifty years' time, and I would sit at
my desk and become distraught at the thought of this ruina-
tion, this doom, actually nauseous with terror – I felt I could

211

see the whole planet darkening and dying, and I was con sumed with this hatred of human beings and at the same time fear for them, pity for them. Then I'd walk home looking a everything, the sky and the people and the buildings and i would seem so sort of heedless and alien, you know, some one in a car getting angry with someone for pulling out, and people talking on their mobiles and the sky all grey and bor ing, and I would think, well, maybe we get what we deserve Then I'd go home and Sam and I would argue.' Sam was the name of Charlie's ex-husband. 'Quite often I'd find mysel distraught again before bedtime, except this time it would be about housework, or the fact that Sam said I'd spent too much money. There was no connection,' said Charlie, shaking her head. 'There was no connection anywhere.'

Through the window the sky was blue-grey. The indistinc green furze of the little garden stood rigid beyond the glass Rebecca looked perplexed.

'I don't think anyone could blame you because you could n't reconcile your marriage with global warming,' she said.

'It made me think for the first time that I needed to be bet ter than I was. Because otherwise there was nothing. It's dif ferent for you. You've had a child.'

Rebecca shrugged. 'So have one.'

Charlie laughed. 'I can't! Or not yet, anyway. Possibly no ever.'

'Anyway, having a child doesn't make you a better person, Rebecca declared presently.

'Doesn't it?' Charlie raised her eyebrows. 'I'd have though it gives you less time to be a bad one.'

'It doesn't have anything to do with it,' said Rebecca.

She looked as though she'd meant to say it matter-of-factly but I saw a tremor of awareness pass through her, as though at the unexpected magnitude of her realisation.

'It doesn't have anything to do with it,' she said again 'Anyway,' she continued, 'I thought everything with Mar was perfect.'

Her ironic intonation of the word "perfect" suggested a well-known abhorrence of the idea.

Charlie shook her long black hair self-consciously away from her face. 'It is, in a way. But to be honest that's a bit of an illusion too. If he ever found out what I'm really like it wouldn't be perfect any more.'

'God!' cried Rebecca, so unexpectedly that the rest of us started. 'That's so *bloody* typical!'

She thumped the table top with her hand and I felt Hamish jump on my lap.

'How do they do it?' she asked wonderingly, shaking her head. 'How *do* they do it?'

'It's just that he's so good,' Charlie said. 'And I'm so bad that I have to lie to make myself seem better. I've lied about everything! So now there's that on top of all the other things.' She put her head in her hands and laughed. 'Not that he ever asks me anything.'

'That's so typical,' said Rebecca again.

'No, I mean he never pries. Of course, he already knows about Sam and he doesn't like it, I can tell. He doesn't like the fact that I left. Poor Sam – I embellish his villainy mercilessly. You know, I'd really like to do something I could be proud of,' she said, looking fervently at Rebecca and me. 'I'd like to do something hard. Sometimes I even think that I should go back to Sam. That really *would* be hard. It would make the perfect cross.'

'You can't do that!'

'Why not? I'd only be keeping all those promises I made. Think how much Mark would admire me!'

'That's just silly,' Rebecca said petulantly.

'All I'm saying is that I have a distorted nature. I've never felt the right sort of pain. I've felt the pain of being wrong but I've never felt the pain of being right. I've never suffered out of forbearance.'

'Why should you suffer? What would be the point of that?'

Charlie laughed. 'I have the feeling that the health of the organism depends on it.'

'Is that what *he* says?'

'Oh, it's completely selfish! Otherwise what story do yo
have to tell about yourself? That all you've done is gorge o
emotion – that you've just lived in yourself? The problem i
that when I get close to it, virtue begins to seem like anothe
bizarre illusion.'

'What have you done that's so terrible?' Rebecca burst ou
'I mean, really, compared to – compared to the *Nazis*, wha
have you actually done wrong? I mean, you haven't *kille*
anybody, have you?'

The two women looked at each other.

'In a way, I have,' Charlie said.

'I don't accept that,' said Rebecca defiantly. 'Everybody ha
abortions. *I* nearly had one.'

I felt Charlie's eyes flicker questioningly over my face. T
my knowledge, Rebecca had only been pregnant once. I ha
noticed before her growing tendency to lay claim to an iden
tity more chequered than her own. Suddenly, it seemed, sh
couldn't bear the idea that she was more straight-laced tha
other people: it struck me that in her thirties she was experi
encing an explosion of adolescent feelings of rebelliousnes
Her clothes, her demeanour, her pretence of being "bad"
she had even, I noticed, taken up smoking, a heartbreakin
spectacle of ineptness that she determinedly staged two o
three times each day. Rebecca had often told me how obedi
ent and sensible she was as a child and teenager, a positio
she adopted in answer to her parents' refusal to behave in
'normal' way. She felt she had no entitlement to youth an
irresponsibility: Rick and Ali would not relinquish them.
remembered with what rational belligerence she had wante
a baby, as though this were the next foothold, the next step
ping stone in her faltering progress across the torrent of lif
She was on the verge, I saw, of flinging herself into this mae
strom; which was not, in fact, life but subjectivity, was th
treacherous expanse of everything pre-existing that she need
ed to make her way over before she could consider herse

safe. I felt pity for her, and guilt that I had not helped her more, but more than anything I felt fear.

'I was the third woman Sam got pregnant,' Charlie said, to me. 'He kept the identity bracelets the others were given when they went into hospital. He had them in a little box. When I came back from the clinic he showed them to me.'

Rebecca laughed. Charlie looked at her quizzically.

'I'm not joking,' she said severely. 'It's true. Do you remember that flat I lived in after I left Sam?'

Rebecca laughed again. 'Oh God, I do remember that flat.'

'The door wouldn't lock properly and the armchair looked like someone had died in it and on the wall beside the bed there was this funny shaped stain, and one day I was looking at it and I realised the shape was human, that it was the outline of a person who had sat on the bed leaning against the wall for so long that he'd left a sort of imprint there.'

'Please,' said Rebecca, putting her hands in front of her face.

'Anyway, I used to have these dreams when I was there and in the dreams I was always where I actually was, in that bed, in the dark, with the mark on the wall next to me. And then I'd wake up and I'd be there, in the same room. There was no difference between my dreams and reality, do you see what I mean? That was hell,' she said consideringly. 'I found it in that funny room.'

Out in the street, on the far side of the house, the sounds of several car doors closing came into the sedate room like a muffled volley of gunshots.

I said: 'I don't think you can say that you haven't suffered.'

'Oh, I'm just making you feel sorry for me,' said Charlie. 'It's all part of my routine. This is why no one's ever dared to hold me to account.'

'But what have you actually *done*?' Rebecca exclaimed. She looked prepared to be amused.

'At least you've resisted the temptation to be honest,' I said.

'I'm not sure I *can* resist it,' Charlie said.

'Is it *infidelity*?' interposed Rebecca, making quotation marks with her fingers around the word "infidelity".

I was arrested by her tone, as well as by the quotation marks.

'Why do people make such a fuss about "*infidelity*"?' she repeated. She examined her nails. I noticed her hand was shaking. 'Rick and Ali positively use it as a sex aid.'

'Do they have a – what's it called? An open marriage?' said Charlie, wide-eyed.

'They like to speculate about other people,' I said. 'It's not quite the same thing.'

'You don't know what you're talking about,' said Rebecca. Presently I realised that she was speaking to me.

'It's completely harmless,' I said.

'It's not an open marriage,' Rebecca said to Charlie, 'it's a bloody bazaar. It's an end of season sale. Don't tell me Rick's never come on to you.'

Charlie shook her head. 'Should I feel insulted?'

'Come to think of it, you're probably too old for him. He hasn't slept with one of my friends for years. He's got all Marco's girlfriends to distract him now.'

'Oh, for God's sake,' I said. I wanted to put Hamish down but he had locked his legs tenaciously around the backs of my knees. 'That is a complete misrepresentation of the facts.'

'Don't use that language against me!' shrieked Rebecca, gripping the edge of the table. 'I'm not asking for your judgement! I don't need you to authorise my conversation!'

'I'm only pointing out that saying things isn't the same as doing them.'

'Isn't it? Isn't it?' Rebecca cried. 'No, come to think of it, it's worse! At least there's some honesty in doing it – at least there's some fucking implication! They're so fucking frightened of it happening that they can't stop talking about it!'

'Becca,' said Charlie, reaching out to take Rebecca's hand.

'I don't understand your shame,' Rebecca said to her in a jagged voice. A tear sped down her cheek. 'I just can't understand it. I wish I'd done things I couldn't account for. I wish I had the guts. I'd tell everyone about it – I'd shout it from the fucking rooftops!'

She put her face in her hands. Her shoulders shook so that the little frilled sleeves of her dress trembled.

'I wish I had the guts to tell them all to go to hell,' she wept.

'Mummy,' said Hamish.

Rebecca sat and cried into her white hands.

'I wish I could send them all to hell!'

Charlie gave me a look of enquiry which Rebecca raised her tear-streaked face in time to notice.

'Oh, don't expect him to care!' she cried. 'We're all sinners in his book, you know! Don't expect him to lift a finger – he let me go a long time ago!'

'Mummy mummy,' said Hamish.

'He never stood up to them. You ask him, you see if he did! He never judged them on my account!'

'You wouldn't have wanted me to,' I said.

'I wanted you to fight for me!' she shrieked.

'I love you,' said Hamish.

Rebecca put her face in her hands again and the tears dripped through the grille of her fingers.

'I'm tired of being good,' she sobbed. 'I should have gone crazy – I should have gone completely crazy. I should have told them just to go to hell!'

'I love you, mummy,' said Hamish.

'I want to find out what will happen if I stop being good,' wept Rebecca wildly. 'I want to stop being good!'

Hamish got off my lap. Charlie was leaning across the table in the gloom with her hands outstretched, her prominent features casting little blocks of shadow over her face. My wife sat weeping in her chair. The pale silky material of her dress and her light-toned skin and hair gave her a formless, undulating appearance in the unlit room: she glimmered like some unearthly creature and water streamed from her eyes. She folded herself over so that her face rested on her knee and her

217

back shook as the long tremor of each sob passed strenuously through her. Hamish stepped around the table to where she sat and spread himself carefully over her. He laid his chest over her back and wrapped his arms around her quaking sides so that his feet were almost lifted off the ground. He pressed his cheek into the back of her neck. He covered her unresponsive body with as much of himself as he could, as though in preparation for the great indifference of the latitudes towards which he saw himself now embarking; like some creature, a barnacle, an anemone, that knows only how to adhere, to cling on for dear life.

TEN

I phoned Adam at The Meadows. He said:

'You'll never guess what's happened.'

'Tell me.'

'Vivian's done a bunk,' he said.

'What do you mean?'

'She's gone.' I heard him take a drink of something. 'Packed up her things and gone.'

'When did that happen?'

'Yesterday. I brought dad back from the hospital and she was nowhere to be found.'

'Do you know where she is?'

'We do now,' he said. 'She's in Spain. She called Jilly from the airport. Said she was going to those friends of hers, the ones with the ranch.'

'Oh well,' I said. 'I'm sure she'll come back.'

There was a pause. The ice in Adam's drink made pebbly sounds in the receiver.

'I don't think she can,' he said. 'Dad says he'll have her arrested if she sets foot on Egypt again.'

'That's a bit strong, isn't it?' I said.

'She killed the dogs,' Adam said.

'She didn't.'

'She did. She put rat poison in their feed. We found them locked in the stables. They were lying there in the straw as stiff as a pair of boards.'

I pictured their silent, rough-haired bodies clearly.

'We never realised she was such a – such a bitch,' Adam said in a thick voice. 'Now that she's gone, well – Caris says it's like a spell has been lifted, a curse almost. And she's right, the whole place feels different. It's like it used to be.'

'When?' I said.

'What?'

'Like it used to be when?'

Adam put his hand over the receiver. I heard him say, 'It'
Michael,' in muffled tones to someone else in the room.

'Anyway,' he resumed, 'the big news is that mum's movin;
back up. She's selling her place in Doniford and moving bacl
up to be with dad. Property in Doniford's gone through th
roof – she got a valuation today and it's enough to make you
eyes water. One thing's for certain, she and dad won't have t;
worry about money again. She's selling right at the top of th
market and she bought right at the bottom. They couldn'
have done it better if they'd planned it.'

I said: 'Vivian seemed to think they had.'

'Had what?'

'Planned it.'

'Oh, that nonsense,' Adam said roughly. 'Actually, whei
we were searching the house we found a letter. Before w
knew about the dogs, this was. We were a bit, you know, con
cerned at that point because Vivian seemed to have vanishe;
into thin air and her breakfast things were still on the tabl
and her car was in the drive. It all seemed a bit suspicious. I
almost looked like someone had offed her, until dad foun;
this letter she'd put on his desk. She'd gone and got a solicito
in Doniford to write it. At least she had the decency to d
that.'

'What did it say?'

'Oh, it was just a formal thing,' Adam said. 'You know, sta;
ing that she was transferring the deeds to the farm back to da;
and all that. As I say, at least she had the common decency. It'
a big relief actually. For a second there . . .' He tailed off. 'Da;
says it was his moment of weakness,' he continued. 'His on;
real moment of weakness in his life. Apparently she had him i;
an impossible situation. He let his heart rule his head – I sup
pose you'd say he forgot who he was. You should see hir
now, though. He's like a spring lamb. They're even talkin;

about getting more dogs. Mum's got some aristocratic German breed she's after, great big things. All white, of course. Dad says it'll look like we've got polar bears at Egypt. They're at it already, as you might have guessed. The old routine.'

There was a silence in which some receding object seemed to be contained: a pause like a vista of the sea through which a boat was making its way, dwindling and becoming indistinct while barely seeming to move at all.

'I really rang to ask about Toby,' I said.

'Who?'

'Laura's little boy. Toby.'

'Oh!' said Adam. 'Yes, yes, he's fine. Good as new. No harm done. Lisa did the right thing taking him in, it turned out.'

'Thank Lisa for me,' I said. 'Tell her I appreciate everything.'

'I will. Of course I will. I'll tell her when she gets back.'

'Has she gone somewhere?'

'What? Yes, she's gone back home. Up north, to her parents. She's taken the girls.'

I was startled to hear this: there was something troubling in the sound of it that caused me to guess at what it meant.

'She just wanted to, you know, go home for a bit. Get away from everything for a, ah, while. What's that?' he said, with his hand over the receiver again. 'No, I'll tell him. I said I'll *tell* him. Caris says hello,' he said garrulously, to me.

'Is she there?' I was surprised.

'She says you should think about shaving off your beard. Maybe that makes more sense to you than it does to me.' He laughed. 'God, she's dancing around like a big bloody gorilla! Shave it off, she's saying. Just shave it off! She's doing the hand motions and everything. God, you should see her!'

He laughed and laughed. I could hear her, a faint female echo shouting and laughing somewhere in the distances of the telephone.

*

I had a letter of my own. I found it on our bed one evening, resting lightly in an envelope on the cloud of the covers.

Downstairs Charlie and Hamish were cooking something. The rich smells came up into the white room. Charlie was staying for a week, maybe more. She picked her way over the rubble on the front steps as she came and went. She was on the shortlist for the teaching job at the university. She was sleeping in the room above ours and at night I could hear the creaking sounds she made as she moved around in bed. If she got the job I supposed she would move down here permanently, and though I doubted she would want to stay with us for ever I thought she could. I recognised in her presence something that spoke to my own weakness for transitoriness and dispossession. I thought that if only people lived the life that was in front of them everything would be all right. I didn't think Rebecca could ever know how much it galled me to have become someone she thought she needed to get away from. The letter was written in pen, in large urgent scrawls and curlicues that left the paper pock-marked with indentations. It said:

Darling M,
  The time has come for me to take my leave. You think that you don't know it but you do.

I sat down on the bed and half-expected a wreath of its familiar scent to rise and lay itself over my shoulders, but all I could smell were the fumes from downstairs. I heard Charlie shrieking, 'Quick, quick!' and then raucous laughter.

Do you remember that lovely funny building near your old flat? The one that sat there and sat there with pigeons nesting in the roof and squatters moving in and out, and how we always talked about buying it and turning it into an art gallery or something – and then one day we saw a notice on the door that said 'Change of Use', and we realised someone else was doing what we'd said we would do and we felt sad, as if something had been stolen from us.

That was before Hamish was born, and whenever I think about that building and wonder whether our life could have been different, I know that it couldn't, because you can never be anything other than what you are.

You'll laugh when you hear I've gone home, for now at least – but maybe you'll be glad too. I'm sure you of all people would agree that I need to acknowledge the man who is my father, and to face my mother as a rival. A RIVAL!! Niven says that nurture for Ali is a threat to her femininity and I know he's right. When I thought she was going to die, I realised how absent she was from my life as a nurturer. I needed HER to comfort ME! But she was the child too, she was the poor thing. I think she can only be happy with me when she's giving me things, because then she can feel she's got more. And the one thing she really has is HIM!! She plays the role of the child as a way of competing with me for his attention. As for HIM! I think it may take me my whole life to understand him – the way his charisma has afflicted me with the sense of my own betrayal. Michael, there was a time when I thought you could save me by possessing me, but now I know that can never be. Now I only want freedom. I want the freedom to be what you could never accept that I was.

I used to feel that you'd failed me, Michael, but now I think I can see you as the victim you really are. I think you have a very misconceived idea of morality. You seem to think that there's a world of bad things and a world of good things whereas the truth is that there are only feelings. There is only emotion, and emotion is what you're not good at, Michael. I think you have a lot of work to do on yourself. I don't see your repression, your coldness, as being your fault. I think it has a LOT to do with your family and your fear of disapproval, your fear of really LIVING and your need to be close to dangerous people, to people who are dirty and vibrant and alive and who really FEEL. The problem is that you criminalise those people by trying to control them. That's really your tragedy, Michael, as I see it.

As for Hamish – I know you will say that he should stay with you. I can give you that, Michael: I've decided to. Rick and Ali

think I'll change my mind but I won't. I think you need Hamish;
he's a sort of mascot for you, isn't he? I'll say one thing for you,
Michael, you're a bloody good father. They thought you might
want to find a house of your own, and I said I didn't think you
would. But you know I'll be your most frequent visitor – I'll be like
your bad fairy godmother, appearing when you least expect it. I'll
come and sit at your kitchen table and take off my silly shoes and
tell you all about everything that's going on in my mad life. I like
the thought of you both there in Nimrod Street. All safe and
sound, like in a fairy tale.

  Rebecca

I lay back on the softness of the bed and looked at the ceiling.
Then I went downstairs to find Hamish.

los Romanes
lake Vinuella.
Villa Milla Grossa.